Dear Iva,
Best wish
Janet

GOLDEN ICON

Janet Pywell

The Golden Icon

Copyright © 2013 Janet Pywell. All rights reserved.

The right of Janet Pywell to be identified as the author of this work has been asserted by her in accordance with the Copyright, Designs and Patents Act 1988. A CIP catalogue record for this book is available from the British Library.

ISBN: 978-0-9926686-1-7

Cover design by Estuary English

Cover photography copyright © 2017 Shutterstock Images

Published by Richmond Heights Publishing

For Mum and Dad
With all my love

Thanks to Veronica for her generous support and understanding. Over the years she has been an amazing friend and business partner. She has been with me on this journey and countless other adventures - may there be many, many more...

A debut book is never written without the support of family and friends both at home and abroad. Writing can be a solitary experience and just the smallest encouragement goes a long, long way, so thank you - for your faith in me. Sometimes the first toddler step is the most important, so thanks to Fontaine McClurg, who started me off.

My thanks also go to numerous people who gave me their valuable time and in particular to Soprano, Kay Lynch and Mezzo-Soprano Jennifer Borghi who shared with me details of their operatic experiences. Any errors or mistakes are purely down to me and my enthusiastic exuberance.

Grateful thanks for feedback from Tutors and fellow students at Queen's who read early drafts and pointed me in the right direction, and editors and fellow writers who helped shape early editions: Lorraine Iatrides, Mike McGlade, Martin Cromie, Sheila McWade, Sheila Llewllyn, and Craig Gibson. Finally, many thanks to Irish author Joe McCoubrey who has given me his time, advice and generosity of spirit to help produce my debut novel.

For more information visit:
www.janetpywell.com
blog: janetpywellauthor.wordpress.com

CHAPTER ONE

Art, in its mysterious way,
blends the contrasting beauties together...
Recondita Armonia, Tosca

Swarms of summer tourists admiring cheap clothes, fresh vegetables, colourful fruits and ripe cheeses fill the market place. I hurry past them, up stone steps and along the harbour wall where fishing boats bob gently on the lake. A man with two small children is standing on the slipway, feeding bread to ducks and overhead a gull squarks.

At the church of Santa Anna di Comaso, I twist the iron handle and tug open the door. A faint tang of incense hangs in the air and dust motes dance in the light streaming in through the stained glass windows. The cool interior is refreshing after the midday heat of the July sun and I pull my shawl across my shoulders. My footsteps click down the centre aisle in rhythm with the mantra revolving in my head. I am Tosca. I will be Tosca. I am Tosca.

I place wild flowers at the Madonna's marble feet, cross myself and close my eyes.

'Josephine?'

I turn quickly.

'Ciao, Padre Paolo,' I smile.

He is wearing trainers and brown cotton trousers. There is a nick in his cheek where he cut his face shaving.

'Glorietta told me the audition is on Monday.' His brown eyes are placed close together. His nose is small and his mouth wide and generous.

'Glorietta Bareldo?'

'Yes, she was practicing here yesterday.'

'But the idea to rehearse in the church had been mine…..'

The door bangs closed and we turn at the sound of quick footsteps. Cesare Serratore is striding toward us; his long, dark curls trail over his angular shoulders like a lion's mane. He is taller than my six foot frame and skinny. He is the most renowned operatic voice coach in Italy.

We hug and air kiss.

'You practised here with Glorietta?' I ask in greeting.

He knows she is my rival.

'It's one of my favourite Puccini operas.' Padre Pablo stands between us. 'It will be difficult for the theatre to choose between two talented sopranos. Just this morning Cardinal Rosso was on the telephone asking if it would be possible to get tickets. He read in the Corriere Della Sera that it will be televised.' His voice has a melodious note to it as if he is singing the Mass in Latin.

Cesare replies, 'It will be the first production in the new Teatro Il Domo and it is not only the Italian people who are excited, it is creating a stir around the whole world.' He delves into his bag and rustles music scores. 'They say that the President may even be there on the opening night.'

I am staring at him but he ignores my gaze as deftly as he has avoided my question.

My mobile rings from the depths of my handbag.

'Not more flowers.' Padre Paolo shakes his head. 'The tourists bring them in here all the time and it makes the church look a mess. I think I may have to lock the church. I caught a boy stealing candles last week and Cardinal Rosso is concerned about the amount of artefacts being stolen. He is worried about the paintings.' He raises his eyes to the ceiling in mock prayer to protect his church.

I look at the unknown number.

'They are like the purple ones that grow in the hills behind your apartment, no Josephine?' Cesare's eyes twinkle and his mouth twitches in a smile.

'Hello?' I say into the phone.

Padre Paolo gathers my hydrangeas, walks up the steps to the altar and through the door of the vestry. The wild flowers are crushed in his hands.

'Josie?' I recognise the soft Irish accent. Only my ex-husband ever called me by that name. The last time I had spoken to him, six years ago, I had been at the height of my international career.

'It's Seán. Can you hear me alright, Josie?'

Why is he phoning me?

'Josie, are you there?'

I press the phone closer to my ear and turn away. 'Yes, Seán. I can hear you.'

'Josie, I've got some very sad news. The Da died this morning.'

'Oh, no.' I sink slowly onto the nearest pew. The wood is cool against the back of my thighs and I lean forward resting my elbows on my knees.

'Are you there?'

There is a deep groove in the wood and I trace its outline. My stomach is knotted.

'Yes.'

'He loved you, Josie...' he pauses.

'I'm sorry about Michael,' I say. 'He was a lovely man.'

'He was Josie. He was the best.'

'Thanks for letting me know. I'll say my prayers for him. I'll be in touch, Seán.' I want to hang up. I need to practice with Cesare. I want to think about Michael.

'No, Josie, no, don't go. I want you to sing at his funeral. It was his wish Josie, one of his last ones. It was all he talked about at the end. He listened to your CD's every day, Josie. You meant a lot to him. He loved you more than he loved me. I want you here.'

'Seán, I'm rehearsing. This is the first time I've been called for an audition in four years,' I whisper. 'You know what happened to my career. It's Tosca. And it's in the new Teatro Il Domo.'

'That's okay. Sing Tosca at the funeral. The Da loved it. He always said you were the best Tosca. The only Tosca. Sing whatever you want. I don't care. I just want you here.'

Seán hadn't changed. He had always wanted me to do everything for him with no concern for my needs. He wanted me to do things on impulse but that's not in my character. I have to think things through but this didn't need thinking about.

'It's impossible.'

'The funeral's on Friday.'

'I can't.'

'Look, I'm going to tell you something,' Seán says into

my ear, 'I found your letter–'

'I'm about to begin a lesson–'

'You know the letter. It's the letter you wrote to Michael when you were married to me.'

'Letter?'

'The Da kept it. I found it in his house. He kept it beside his bed with your CD's. You must have really excited him speaking like that–'

'I don't know what–'

'Well, let me remind you. I've got five pages of your lovely handwriting here telling him just how much you love him, and how he excites you, and what turns you on, but it's not just that, is it Josie? You were still married to me at the time.'

I gasp. My mind is whirling. I remember writing only one letter to Michael after I went to sing in the Liceu in Barcelona. I can't believe he has kept it all these years. I place my forehead in my hand.

'Wasn't I the stupid one,' he continues. 'Here's me thinking I'd married a shy girl from Kansas, and when I read your letter, it turns out you're more like a porn star than an opera singer. For all these years, I thought that the Da just wanted to help you, and that he financed your career because you were married to me,' he laughs bitterly. 'And I thought he was just being a kind old man when he sent you a birthday card each year.'

I trace the unfamiliar pattern of the groove in the pew and it reminds me of the indented lifeline etched on my own palm.

'Seán, it was thirty years ago–'

'The funeral is in Monkstown. It's in the church we got married. Two o'clock.' Just for a minute I am confused

5

thinking he's talking about his second wedding to Barbara, but he is speaking about our wedding. 'Be there!'

'Seán…'

'Josie, I'm not asking. I'm telling. I know about your sordid little secret. I have proof. I have your pathetic little letter. The press'll be very interested in what I have to say. They will love it. And all your fans will be interested to read about your seedy, sexy fetishes. You remember Karl Blakey don't you?'

'K-Karl?' I stammer. The mention of his name sends a shiver through me. Karl had been the journalist who revealed my cocaine addiction and had printed the story that reverberated throughout the opera world and damaged my reputation and brought my career crashing to the ground.

'I-I thought Karl was in London.'

'I asked him to come to Dublin. I wanted to track you down. He knew where you were. He knows there's more that you're hiding, and now I have this letter well - he will be very interested.'

I rub my temple. The shock that Karl Blakey knows where I am has sent my head spinning. My throat is dry.

Seán's voice is a low growl. 'I want you singing here on Friday. It's what the Da wanted. It wouldn't look good now, you getting the part of Tosca, and then the press finding this letter, would it? Imagine all that bad publicity for the new theatre. The investors and backers wouldn't like that, would they?'

'You can't do this Seán. It would destroy me. I've worked so hard to make this comeback. It would ruin me forever–'

'See you in church.'

'Seán…' I plead, but he rings off.

I close my eyes and Cesare reminds me he is waiting with a gentle cough.

When I stand my knees are shaking.

'Strict instructions from Padre Paolo.' Cesare waves his arm. 'No Tosca and certainly no Don Giovanni. Only sacred music is allowed.' Curls flop over his face and he brushes them from his eyes. He looks so unassuming it is hard to believe he is the most sought after opera coach in Italy.

'Bene, I think we will start with Bellini's *Casta diva*.' He sits at the piano.

It takes me a while to regain my composure. I struggle with the first few notes. My tone seems deeper than usual. I hope I do not have a summer chill, so easy to catch with the heat of the sun, the storms over the lake, and the air conditioning.

I focus on my invisible audience that stare back from the pews. I breathe deeply and glance around at the familiar paintings. My eyes rest on my favourite, one with a grey and gold embossed frame. Jesus has been pulled from the cross and is lying on the ground bleeding. The disciples are gathered at his feet and the Madonna's imploring eyes are cast toward the heavens.

I try not to think of Michael but when my eyes close I imagine him dead. I brush my eye with the tip of my finger. He was the only man I ever truly loved.

I sing through a few arias and I focus on the drama and the emotion. I concentrate hard, blocking out my past life, thinking only of Tosca.

When I begin the first notes of *Ave Maria*, I turn to the illuminated statue and sing to the Virgin. I am lost in my rendition but as I focus on her I am reminded of Glorietta's china blue, doll like eyes, and I stumble over my words.

'Josephine, what is wrong? You are distracted today?' Cesare's face creases into a frown. 'Perhaps this is too much pressure for you?'

'Pressure?'

'It's been a long time since you sang—'

'I can still do it.' My voice is too loud. I see our role reversal reflected in his eyes. His success. My failure. 'The role is mine. I am Tosca.'

'I know,' he replies. 'But I worry for you. I feel…'

'I don't want your sympathy. I want the lead part. I will be Tosca again.'

'Well then, you must practice. This is your last opportunity Josephine. It will not happen again.'

I tear my gaze from Cesare's pitying eyes. Scattered on the floor at the Madonna's feet are dried petals from the confiscated purple hydrangea.

'I must light a candle,' I whisper, 'for Michael.'

'Bene,' he sighs. 'Let's begin again. This time no distractions.'

Raffaelle is incensed.

'You're going to Dublin?' His bushy black moustache frames his O-shaped mouth. 'Are you completely insane?'

We are in the bedroom of my apartment, I am packing a bag and trying to block out his anger.

'For the past few months all I've heard is Tosca this, and Tosca that.' He paces between the bed and the large window with views of Lake Como waving his arms. 'You

8

have hardly eaten or slept with worry, and now you are leaving, just like that?' He snaps his fingers.

His hair is greying at the temples and his face is etched with fine laughter lines around his dark eyes.

We have been lovers since I arrived here, three years ago, when I agreed to sit for a portrait, but at this moment he is like a stranger and he is shouting at me.

'You have worked hard. You have practised and you have rehearsed. You tell me that this is your final opportunity but now you are giving it all away. You are sacrificing everything for your ex-husband? Are you still in love with him?'

I shake my head. 'That doesn't even dignify an answer.'

'Then tell me, why?' He grabs my wrist, pulling my hand from my folded clothing. His artist fingers are paint-stained and there is an odour of stale tobacco from his breath.

I stare into his blazing brown eyes but I know I can't tell him. I cannot tell him the truth. It is my secret and mine alone. My burden. My responsibility. My shame. I think of the letter I wrote as a twenty-two year old woman in love with her sixty year old father-in-law. How could I have been so naive?

He interprets my silence as stubbornness.

'You are impossible,' he hisses. 'And, to think, I thought you had changed. I thought you were a warm and kind woman, and not the cold hearted and egoistical diva the press wrote about. How wrong I was.'

I say nothing as he storms from the bedroom banging the door, and I am still standing motionless as the front door slams downstairs. That is when frustration rises in me and tears begin trickling down my cheeks.

9

I telephone Cesare from the airport. His voice is terse and accusatory.

'You are going to Ireland? Are you mad? The audition is on Monday. Apart from the germs on the plane that are so bad for your throat, this is the most ridiculous idea. It's your last audition. I have promised Nico Vastrano and Dino Scrugli that you have changed and that you won't let them down, and if you are not here on Monday your career will be over before it starts. Are you crazy? I don't understand you—'

'I'm sorry. I must sing at Michael's funeral.'

'It's absolute madness.' I imagine him shaking his long curls like an angry mane, his eyes blazing. 'With your history with Andrei, you cannot afford to take this risk. He agreed to your audition because I promised him your voice was on form again. I pleaded with them. I told them you are not the diva you once were but now you run off to Ireland a few days before the audition. Glorietta will—'

'I'll be back after the funeral. It's only for twenty-four hours. We can...'

'You are throwing away your last chance. You will not—'

'I have no choice, Cesare. I must go.'

'The world is full of choices, Josephine. This one is yours and yours alone. You will only have yourself to blame.'

I cannot tell him that my secret would ruin us all. I cannot share with him my past mistakes, and I cannot begin to explain my fear, and the damage it would do if the truth came out. The lives it would affect. Instead, I turn off my phone and board the plane to go to the last place I ever wanted to return.

I concentrate on blocking out the memories of the past that are surging and swirling inside my head, gathering speed like the jet engine's motors as we hurl down the runway, and the feeling of utter despair that begins infiltrating the core of my soul.

CHAPTER TWO

I lived for art, I lived for love,
I never did harm to a living soul!
Vissi d'arte, Tosca

My flight from Milan arrives at midday. I ask the taxi
driver to take me to Monkstown.

'It's unusually hot,' he lisps, 'for July.'

I place my travel bag on the seat beside me. I have
brought cotton trousers and a blouse to change into for
the journey home. 'I never remember it being this hot,' I
say. I open the window and warm air from the Irish Sea
rushes in.

We are leaving the airport and joining the motorway.
'Do you know Dublin?' he asks.

'It's years since I was last here.'

'There's a tunnel now which makes the journey quicker
or do you want me to drive you through the city?' His blue
eyes look at me in the rear view mirror.

'Through the city.'

He speaks quickly as the car glides through traffic and I
have to concentrate on his unfamiliar accent. Have I been

on the Dart to Howth? Did I know the Luas goes to the O2? Did I ever guess the docklands would be transformed?

We wait at traffic lights near O'Connell Street then cross the bridge and I have my first glance of the River Liffey.

'All the young ones are emigrating.' He rests his tattooed arm out of the window. 'I can't say I blame them. There's no jobs, businesses have gone bust, shops have closed, restaurants are empty. The Celtic tiger is dead.'

Outside a pub, a few guys sit bare chested on wooden benches their skin turning pink in the sunshine. They are drinking pints of Guinness, and elegant girls in skimpy tops, sip chilled white wine poured from bottles wedged in ice buckets. I see busy streets, expensive cars and hundreds of tourists.

'It is different to the Dublin I left.'

'When was that?'

'Thirty years ago.'

'Sure it is.' Our eyes meet in the mirror.

I was a fresh faced, twenty-two year old from Kansas; young and excited to be in Ireland and to sing La Bohème in The Gaiety Theatre. The opening night was cold, snow had turned to slush and the February night was filled with tiny stars in a black sky.

Seán McGreevy had invited his parents to the theatre for their wedding anniversary Through friends they had been invited backstage and he had smiled at me like I was the only person in the room. Michael, his father, gushed praise but when I asked Seán if he had enjoyed the performance he replied, 'I'm a bit tired. I tried to sleep but your singing kept me awake so I only managed a quick nap.'

I laughed and allowed him to buy me a drink.

We began to meet after each performance and between rehearsals. Time was precious. It created an urgency with everything we did, shopping in Grafton Street, walking through St. Stephen's Green or drinking cocktails in the Shelbourne Hotel. Seán was starting his own construction business. He was trying to get a loan from the bank to finance a small housing development in the suburbs. He was enthusiastic, optimistic, and it was exciting to be in Ireland where there were new opportunities. It was all so different to Kansas.

When the show finished, it was time for the Opera to move on; England, Germany, Holland and finally France. I thought I would forget Seán but I didn't.

When the tour finished in Paris eight weeks later, Seán insisted I return to Ireland for a holiday, and we were married six months later.

Seán's mother, Shona, died the following month after a short illness and so Michael began to spend most of his time with us. He financed Seán's business and over the coming months he witnessed my slowly diminishing confidence. He saw how I missed singing, and the opera and the stage. He encouraged me to perform in local productions but four months later there was an opportunity for me to audition for the role of Michaela in Carmen at La Scala.

'You must go,' he had insisted. 'This will be your lucky break. You are destined to become a star. You will be the next Maria Callas.'

Michael paid for my flight. He told me to follow my dream. After all, he reasoned with Seán, it would only be for a month or so. He valued my voice and gave me the support that my husband never seemed to think I needed.

'This is Merrion Square.' The taxi driver interrupts my recollections. 'We're going toward Ballsbridge.'

'And Blackrock?' I ask, thinking of where I spent my married life.

'We'll take the coast road to Booterstown. Blackrock town is on the left after the park.' He points with his finger and lisps, 'It's straight on into Monkstown.'

It has changed or I don't remember any of it.

We arrive at the church. I pay the driver and tip him well. On the pavement I stand looking around to get my bearings. There's the Protestant church on the corner in the fork of the road, an off-license, a newsagent and a few restaurants. It looks more prosperous than I remember.

I carry my bag and pull my shawl over my pearl-grey dress. I touch the sapphire necklace reassuringly at the base of my throat, walk up the steps and I am reminded of the time I last walked over its threshold on my wedding day. I pause and close my eyes.

I see my mother's face lined with worry. She always said that she didn't gain a son-in-law but lost her daughter to an Irishman. I was twenty-two. My wedding dress had tapered out like a mermaid's tail and I wore a simple white lace veil. My blond hair was thicker and longer and it tumbled around my shoulders in a simple and unadorned fashion that had taken hours of preparation.

'Are you all right?'

I open my eyes. Beside me is a small, rotund man with a bald head.

'Yes, thank you,' I smile. 'I was just thinking…'

'Ah! You're not from around here then. I wasn't sure if

you were visiting the church or er... here for the er…'

'The funeral.'

'Ah, you're from America. The East coast?'

'Kansas.' I hope he doesn't start talking about America. Even though I still have an accent, I hardly know the country. I've lived so long in Europe.

There are small, broken veins across the top of his nose and along his cheeks.

'I'm here to sing for Michael...Michael McGreevy,' I say.

'Ah yes, you must be Josie Lafelle.' He offers me his hand to shake.

'Josephine Lavelle,' I correct him.

'Father Doyle.' His handshake is limp and he grips only the tips of my fingers. 'I'll introduce you to our organist when he arrives. Gregory is quite punctual, not to worry.' He barks a laugh and takes my elbow guiding me inside. 'I believe you'd like to practice before, um, before the family arrive?'

The church is cool and I shiver.

'Have you been here before?'

'Once,' I reply. 'Many years ago.'

He rubs his nose and waits but I don't elaborate.

'Michael's body was peacefully at home with the family last night,' he says. 'Now, I'll just go and get ready myself and see where Gregory has got to.' He hurries off on short legs and I wonder if there's a back entrance to the local pub.

The church is smaller and the curved gothic walls are whiter than I remember. I pause at the marble statue of the Sacred Heart of Jesus, and my footsteps echo as I visit the Stations of the Cross. I stop beside the altar in front of the statue of the Madonna and light a candle, and I am reminded of the Madonna in the church Santa Anna di Comaso, of my rehearsal, the day I spoke to Seán. I remember Cesare's anger and disappointment and I think of Tosca. It's my last chance.

I am Tosca.

But Cesare is right. Raffaelle is right. It is madness to be here. Who would ever understand?

I turn at the sound of footsteps.

'Sorry to interrupt your silent prayers. This is our organist Gregory Might.' Father Doyle has changed into his vestments. Beside him, the contrast couldn't have been greater, Gregory Might is under thirty, tall and good-looking.

I stand in the gallery at the back of the church. Behind me is the wooden organ and sunlight floods in through a round stained glass window above my head. Thankfully Seán hasn't insisted that I stand near the coffin. It would be too emotional for me to see the faces of the family and friends, and besides the acoustics are better up here. The sound travels up toward the ceiling over the heads of the congregation and echoes softly around the church.

As the pall bearers bring the mahogany coffin down the aisle I sing, *Vissi d'arte*. I remember Michael. I hear his laughter and see the smile in his eyes. I can feel his love, kindness and understanding but I know that to survive the emotion of his funeral, I must block out my feelings as I have for thirty years. They must remain locked and hidden away. I know that the truth would be harder to bear than the grief that sustains me today.

I am filled with mixed emotions and I am blessed that I am a soprano. My voice is heavy and rich in colour but I must be careful. I am here to add music to a sad ceremony not to perform. I must pull back from a stage performance. It is the beauty of tone that will add respectful meaning to Michael's funeral.

At the sound of my voice some people turn their heads toward the gallery. It is not my usual audience but I am delighted to sing again in public and my lungs swell with each note. I am filled with pride, with hope and with something much deeper and so precious to me, that few would understand. It is my destiny to sing and to give pleasure.

I hope this will not affect my audition on Monday.

It's a Catholic Service and I am led into each hymn in the liturgy by Gregory who is a talented and considerate musician. Then Seán rises. His foot is in plaster cast and he hobbles to stand beside the coffin at the golden lectern. He has put on weight and now has grey hair. He coughs and clears his throat.

'Michael McGreevy is - was - my father, and I am proud to be his son. He was a kind man, a loving man and above all a warm and generous human being,' he begins. 'At the end of World War Two he was a medic in the British Army, saving lives on the Front, in France with the Allies....' He talks about Michael's bravery during the war and the risks he took to save fellow soldiers. 'He was a doctor and fellow at the Royal College of Surgeons and he was a man to be respected and admired...' He speaks of his dedication to his patients in Ireland, and friends and family. It's a touching tribute and I am lost in the past. This could have been my family. They were my family.

'For those of you who remember our beloved mother, Shona, our father will be buried alongside her in

Glasnevin.'

I barely remember Shona. She had died so soon after our wedding I hardly knew her. The grief of her death cast a shadow over our happiness, an omen for the future, a headstone to our grave marriage.

Seán's voice is low though strong, and he smiles. 'The best thing about a wake is that it is a celebration of life and, it is better than going to a birthday party, you get invited to a few drinks and a meal if you're lucky, you don't have to bring a present and you don't have to send a thank you card afterwards.'

There is a ripple of laughter in the congregation and he invites them to join his family and his brother William, for refreshments at his home, at four o'clock. I check my watch. My flight is at eight o'clock to Milan. I will have time to collect the letter and I will be home just after midnight.

The procession leaves the church. The family follow the casket, and I focus on the stained glass window above the altar, but when I sing Gounod's *Ave Maria* a single tear slides down my cheek. I hold my hand to the sapphire necklace, a gift from Michael thirty years ago.

Seán is limping. In one hand he holds a crutch and with the other he hangs onto Barbara's arm. Behind them two teenage children walk with their heads bowed. Seán looks up and his eyes stay focused on me until he passes underneath the gallery.

In the congregation, amid the many faces of strangers, a man turns and nods at me, as if I am his best friend.

It is Karl Blakey.

I do not go to Glasnevin. I have no desire to see where Michael will lay with his wife for all eternity. Instead, I stand on the church steps in the shadows, avoiding friends and family, and Karl Blakey who has fortunately disappeared. I am watching the funeral cortege when a ginger haired boy with freckles approaches me and holds out his hand.

'I've got something for you,' he says, 'from Seán.'

My heart flips. It's the letter. Now I don't have to go to his home. I can go straight to the airport. I smile gratefully.

'Thank you.'

But it isn't a letter. It's a folded piece of paper with Seán's handwriting.

If you want the letter, meet me at four o'clock at home, Seán.

My hopes fade. The thought of speaking with Seán face to face fills me with dread. I know how manipulative he can be. I cannot trust him.

I find a coffee shop, eat a sandwich and kill time.

Seán's house is wedged between two imposing prestigious Victorian houses which makes his look inferior and cheap. It is near the sea but his views are obstructed by a large hedge that borders a gravel drive. I am ushered in to the busy house, through the front door, by a man who looks vaguely like Seán and seems familiar.

'You remember my brother William?' Seán says, slapping his brother's back.

'Of course.' I hold out my hand.

'Josephine, how delightful—' William leans forward and kisses me on the cheek. There is an ugly scar across his forehead that I remember was the result of a fire at the family home when the boys were young.

'And this is a family friend David Mallory. He works for the Irish Consul and he's based in Milan.'

I raise an eyebrow at the sandy-haired man. He wears a black suit and mourning tie.

'I believe you left Germany and you live on Lake Como now.' David Mallory shakes my hand.

'Seán told you?'

'As if Seán could keep a secret.' His eyes are like grey clouds.

Seán laughs and I smell alcohol on his breath. 'Take no notice, take no notice of him at all. Of course I can keep a secret, can't I, Josie?'

'You sang magnificently in the church. I was always a fan of yours,' David Mallory says.

'The Da always played your music too,' William adds. 'He played it at full volume, non-stop. His favourite was Tosca and that piece you sang today.'

'*Vissa d'arte,*' I say. 'It is very special.'

How many times had I sung that for Michael?

We all smile. Then Seán's hand is in the middle of my back propelling me down a corridor. 'Excuse us gentlemen, I've a few things to discuss with Josie but I may get her to sing for us before she leaves.'

'That would be lovely.' William's eyes widen in delight.

I am about to protest but Seán's grip on my arm is strong and he pushes me through a timber door and into an oak panelled room that reminds me of a formal lawyer's office. Shelves of hardback reference books are along one wall. There is a large desk with an austere lamp, two framed photographs of Barbara and the children, a swivel chair and in front of the fireplace two deep seated leather armchairs.

On the wall is a familiar painting and I lean closer to inspect it.

'The Fighting Temeraire,' he says nodding at the artwork. 'On its way to its final resting place to be broken up. Turner painted the original in 1839 but this unfortunately, is only a copy. The original is in the National Gallery in London.'

'A copy?' I sit in a chair beside the unlit hearth. 'Or a forgery?'

'Same difference.'

'Is it?'

'Unless you try and sell it,' he laughs.

I imagine him in this house in winter, lashing rain outside, a roaring fire, and a loyal dog at his feet. But today it is hot. The room is oppressive and I want to fling open the patio glass doors. My chest is tight, my throat is dry.

'How long ago is it since I last saw you?' He uncorks a bottle of wine.

'When I was performing Violetta in Verdi's La Traviata.'

He has receding grey hair and his pink cheeks are ingrained with deep lines. His movements are quick and his eyes stray constantly to the window as if looking for something or someone.

'That must have been the pinnacle of your career. You were travelling all over the world.'

'It was one opera after the next; Puccini's Turandot in Barcelona, Verdi's Luisa Miller in Paris, Strauss's Ariadne in New York.'

'Weren't you promoting a new album?'

'Yes, and an operatic documentary on BBC television.'

He pours a large measure of red wine into a crystal goblet.

'I bumped into you in Covent Garden,' he says, 'and, I remember you wouldn't sleep with me.' He hobbles over leaning on the back of the chair for support.

'You were drunk and we were divorced.'

'Ah, yes, so we were although I'm surprised that would have mattered.'

I ignore his jibe and take the glass he offers me.

'And then you messed up. You started taking the naughty stuff.'

'I was under a lot of pressure.'

He wobbles and grabs the desk. 'Feckin' leg,' he complains.

'How did you do it?' I ask, keen to change the subject.

'Stupid accident. Two days ago. Tripped in the street. Nearly got hit by a car.' He tugs his tie loose and unbuttons his shirt. 'But you look good Josie, you've got better looking. Those weren't flattering pictures of you in the papers a few years ago...' He sits opposite me and takes a large gulp of wine. 'I've tried coke myself but I like to be in control.'

I stare out of the window.

'You looked like an angel up there singing in the church today. The Da would have loved it.' His eyes are tired and bloodshot. 'You've still a fair talent Josie. You're on great form. Must be the Italian air or is it an Italian lover? You were always a woman with a man in tow, and always a few more waiting in the wings. A pretty woman like you shouldn't be on your own. You need stability,' he yawns. 'Did you never want to get married again? Did you never want children, Josie?'

I cross my legs.

A few guests have drifted into the garden to smoke. They have removed their jackets and their laughter comes in through the closed window. Inside the air is stale and heavy.

'Of course,' I reply. 'It's just life and the way things happen. Wrong man at the right time, right man at the wrong time.' It was a glib response and one that I had perfected over the years. My heart is beating quickly, I have a feeling he is leading up to something, and I am nervous.

'You don't know what you're missing. Children give you so much happiness but they are a drain on your resources. They cost a fortune but then again,' he laughs. 'Then again, you know all about losing a fortune, don't you?'

I don't reply.

'You lost it all? Nothing left?'

'Only fresh air and healthy living.'

'And one last audition for Tosca. The Da always said you were born to play the part. He said you were Tosca. The Da loved you. Then again, you know that too. But we'll come to that later. Do you remember the Ma? Do you remember Shona? She died soon after we were married.' He begins to reminisce as if I am not in the room, one memory after another about how we met, our wedding, Shona's illness, Michael and our life together in Dublin.

'We had it all Josie. Why did you…'

'We didn't have it all! You wanted a trophy wife on your arm to entertain your clients. You married me for kudos and credibility. You drank heavily and you weren't even kind–' My body tenses and I regulate my breathing. I must be careful.

He leans forward and lowers his voice. 'The Da helped you. He got your career on track. He was there for you, but you didn't have to screw him.'

I feel my face flush.

'The thing is, I've got terrible problems, Josie.' His tone changes and he leans back.

'You're married to someone else. You should speak to Barbara.'

'Barbara,' he chuckles. 'She would kill me if she knew half the truth.'

'I don't want to know. I have agreed to my part of the bargain. I sang at the funeral, now I want the letter and I want to go home.'

'What's the rush? You'll never see me again so hear me out. You're the only person in the world I can speak to Josie. You see, you're the only person I trust.'

'I doubt that–'

He holds up his hand to silence me. 'They all want something. They're scavengers. You see, I'm bankrupt.' He reaches over and replenishes his wine glass. A few drops spill onto the carpet. 'I'm going to lose everything. All this.' He waves his arms. 'The house, the garden, the business, Barbara and the kids…'

'Barbara and the kids?'

'They won't want to stay with me if I haven't got money. Don't get me wrong I'll be pleased to see the back of Barbara. She's a money grabbing bitch. She's not like you Josie. Although you cheated on me you always had a good heart. Even when we separated you had the guts to look me in the eye, and as soon as we could get divorced in Ireland, you did it Josie. You did it, so that I could marry the bitch and make my children my heirs, but what's it all for? She'll turn the kids against me and poison them with her lies but I don't want to lose them. Children are precious.'

'Barbara is your wife.'

'She's ruthless. She hasn't shed a single tear. She never got on with the Da.'

I think of my own tears, I look away and swallow hard.

He speaks in short staccato sentences. 'I had it good for so long. I couldn't build the houses fast enough. Cash in hand. Houses, apartments, rent or buy. You wouldn't believe it, Josie. People were prosperous, happy and positive. Businesses were booming. Then it just stopped. I had loans like everyone else. I had to pay them back. Interest rates went up.' The glass topples and wine spills onto his trousers. 'Shite!' He flicks the stain with his hand and licks his fingers.

'Did Michael know?'

He pulls his lower lip between his thumb and forefinger. 'Well, that's the thing.' Our eyes lock. 'He always said everything would be all right when he died. There's a family heirloom.'

I raise my eyebrows. 'So, problem solved,' I say.

'Well, no, there is a problem, this.' He smacks the plaster on his leg. 'I can't go and get it.'

'So? How long will it be until it's taken off?'

'Four weeks but I haven't got that long. The banks are foreclosing on me on Monday.'

'That's the day of my audition.' I want to open the window and feel fresh air on my face. It's like my lungs are being squeezed by an iron fist.

'I need you to go and get the heirloom. It's in Germany. It's being looked after by a friend of the Da's.'

I have no intention of doing anything else for Seán. 'Why didn't Michael give it to you beforehand if he knew you had financial problems?'

He shrugs. 'I don't know, but I do know, it will pay off all my debts.'

I stare back at him.

'You've got to help me, Josie.'

'Me? No! I'm not going to Germany. Get William to go or one of your family–'

'I haven't told William about it. I can't trust Barbara or the kids and there's no-one else.'

'No employee? What about that man I met outside? The Irish Consul?'

'David?' he laughs. 'I couldn't trust David with a thing like this.'

'Why can't Michael's friend in Germany bring it here?'

'He's older than the Da. He's ninety. I don't trust anyone else. They would steal it from me.'

'Steal? What is it?'

'I think it's a very valuable painting. When I went through the Da's things there were some documents in his desk and I phoned the man who's looking after it–'

'Even if you do have the painting by Monday you can hardly sell it that quickly to pay off your debts,' I argue.

'Reggie is the bank manager and if I have some collateral, like the painting, well that'll give me some time and I can get the bank behind me and on my side while I get it valued.'

'And how do you know it belongs to you?'

'Because I do! Look, Josie, all I want you to do is to fly

to Munich. There's a flight at seven o'clock. I've booked you back to Dublin on the first flight in the morning and you can be on the four twenty, flight tomorrow afternoon, to Milan. I've got the address and everything.'

'No, Seán. I came over here to sing at Michael's funeral and to get the letter. You promised me–'

'Ah, now there's a point. I didn't exactly promise you–'

'I'm not going.' I place my untouched wine glass on the table and stand up. 'Give me the letter.' I hold out my hand.

Over his shoulder I see several guests in the garden drinking and smoking, and I recognise Barbara's tanned suit. She is sipping champagne and I wonder, if he is bankrupt, then who is paying for it all.

'Josie, come on. This is the last thing I'll ever ask you to do for me. I promise.' As he stands he grabs my arm. His breath is hot and sweet on my face. He stumbles, grabs my waist and pushes his body against me and his lips brush mine. I turn my head quickly shoving him away. Barbara is staring at us through the window her face is set like cold marble.

He regains his balance and rests his hip against the desk. His eyes are like cement, hard and dull. 'I didn't want to have to do this.'

He pulls an envelope from his pocket and I recognise my handwriting from thirty years ago. 'My dearest darling Michael,' he begins reading.

'No!' I shout.

I glance at the window. Barbara is gone.

He continues, 'How I miss you. How I dream of your loving touch and your warm lips. Every moment I am separated from you feels like–'

I lunge for the letter but his hand shoots out and he grabs my throat. 'Try it, and you'll never sing Tosca again,' he hisses. 'The press love a good story. Remember Karl Blakey? The reporter who stalked you and wrote about your drug habit, and the bust up you had with your German voice coach? Wait until he knows you've got the part of Tosca. When is your big comeback, this summer? Is your audition on Monday?'

I pull from his grip. My eyes are welling with tears. My throat throbs. I swallow and rub my skin. I can't let Cesare or Raffaelle know about this letter. Glorietta would be thrilled at my downfall, but Nico, Dino or Andrei would never cast me in the role of Tosca. It would ruin the reputation of the new Theatre Il Domo, and I would be finished, forever.

'I'll give it to Karl.' He waves his hand in the air. 'It will be front page news on Monday all around the world. Imagine the headline *The Fading-Diva's Come-back*, and they will all read just how much you like cock.'

I slap his face. 'You haven't changed. You're still the same old slimeball.'

I am lost. When I run from the house my eyes are blinded by my anger, fear and frustration. I hurry down one leafy lane and into another deserted road, each mansion more remote with high gates, expensive cars, and secluded gardens. I am cursing myself. My stupidity. My head aches and I am thirsty. Eventually my pace slows and I take stock of my situation but I can't think. I must get the letter. As soon as I heard Seán read the first few words I remembered how graphic I had been in my writing.

Thirty years later and I can still recall my love for Michael and the letter, that meant so much to me then, now seems crass and cheap.

Now Michael is dead.

I wipe my tears, grip my travel bag and cross the road.

A car cruises alongside me and I am tempted to hail it, and ask for directions but where will I go?

The shiny blue Ford, pulls ahead of me and the window comes down. I lean inside to ask the way.

'Long time, no see.' I recognise the familiar voice. It nudges unpleasant memories to the forefront of my mind and I move quickly away.

'Pretending you don't know me? Wouldn't blame you,' he calls.

I am disoriented but before I can run Karl Blakey is out of the car and standing in front of me. He's fatter than he was when I last saw him four years ago. His cheeks are blown out like a gerbil, his green eyes are pink rimmed and small.

'You look good, Josephine. Getting back on your feet?'

'I have nothing to say to you.' I walk away.

He follows me. 'Seán said you were uptight. He tells me you're making a comeback and there's a story for me. Tosca is it? You were born to play that role. No-one sings it like you.'

My throat is dry. 'I'm not interested in your false compliments. You've done your worst. There's nothing else you can write about me in your seedy magazines.'

'That's not what Seán says. Besides I've got a name for myself now, thanks to you. Whatever I write goes to the biggest newspapers all over the world. I believe Glorietta Bareldo is the new soprano. She's taking your place. They say she's a young Monserrat Caballe. Wasn't she married to the famous artist Raffaelle Peverelli until you appeared in Lake Como?'

'They weren't married.'

'Sex and drugs. They always sell a magazine. You should know that by now. Anyway, enough of us, Seán asked me to give you this.' He holds out a package.

Thinking it maybe the letter I glance inside but it's a boarding card to Munich.

'It's only ten minutes if you walk that way, you can get the Aircoach to the airport. We all have to make money in the recession. A little story goes a long way. It snowballs as you know.'

'You are an odious little prick,' I say, and I hear his laughter echoing in my wake as I head in the direction he is pointing; toward the bus stop on the sea front.

In the airport I phone Seán.

'I'll go,' I say, 'but I want the ginger haired boy who gave me the note at the church, to meet my flight tomorrow morning with the letter, and I will give him the painting. I never want to see you, or have anything to do with you, ever again. Do you understand me?'

'Yes, I promise. Josie I swear.' I hear the elation in his voice and I hang up.

If the painting that I am supposed to collect isn't framed, I will roll it up and it should fit in my travel bag that I will carry onboard. At least I won't miss the audition on Monday. I change into my summer trousers and blouse and when I go through passport control I notice I have a missed call from Cesare, so I dial his number.

'Ciao, Josephine,' he says. I imagine him sitting at his
piano with glorious views of the Lake, and the curtains
blowing in the early evening breeze.

'Ciao, Cesare,' I reply. 'I must cancel my rehearsal
tomorrow morning.' And I explain that I must fly to
Germany on a family errand.

'But Josephine, we are supposed to practice. You will
have no time. Your phrasing needs work, you need more
time to sing in the role.'

'I can rehearse on Sunday with you.'

'You should rest your voice, besides Glorietta…'

'Glorietta? What has this to do with her?'

'You know that I sometimes coach her too. She is
powerful now.'

'So am I. Tosca is in my blood. You know the role is
mine.' My voice is getting louder and it isn't because he is
in Italy that I am shouting. A few people turn to stare.
'Cesare, you know how much this means to me. I - am -
Tosca.'

'If this means so much to you, then you would not have
gone to Ireland, would you? If you are not serious about
this, then what do you expect? I cannot be at your beck
and call. I have many opera singers who want me to be
their mentor and who don't let me down and fly off, pouff,
around Europe, at a moment's notice.'

'It was a friend's funeral.'

'I know, but this is Tosca, in the new prestigious Teatro
Il Domo. This is your big comeback. Carlotta has been on
the phone. She wants to be your agent and she has lined
up press interviews but Nico Vastano is not going to put
up with your diva-like attitude in his theatre. You cannot
upset him.'

32

'I'm sorry Cesare, but I have to go to Germany.'

'You said after leaving Germany the last time, you would never return.'

'I know. Cesare, please, please be patient with me.'

'Bene, call me when you are home and we will see. Ciao Josephine.'

It takes a few minutes to walk to the boarding gate. Several people are looking at me and I realise tears are pouring down my cheeks. I touch the sapphire necklace with my fingers. Michael's life is over. Everything else now is too late. Nothing matters. Only Tosca. I must get the role for him. I must sing it for him. For us.

But I need reassurance. I need support. I have to speak to Raffaelle. I dial his number and imagine it ringing in his villa. When he picks up I hear music.

'Caro,' I say softly. 'I miss you.'

'Josephine? Is that you?'

'Sì, I miss you,' I repeat.

'Sì? I am pleased to hear that.'

'Were you sleeping?'

I think I hear voices in the background.

'I am painting.'

'Oh?' I want to ask if he is alone but I don't. 'I have to change my flight. I will be home tomorrow evening now.'

'What about Tosca? I thought you were coming home tonight and you were rehearsing with Cesare tomorrow?'

'I promised Seán I would collect something in Germany for him.'

'Germany? You are going to Germany? That's crazy! And Tosca? You've told me for the past two weeks you can't do anything apart from rehearse. All I listen to is

Tosca, Tosca and Tosca, and now Seán asks you to do something for him and you drop everything. I understand you want to sing at the funeral but going to Germany - it's ridiculous.'

'I know, I don't want to go. You know how badly they treated me there.'

'Then why are you going?'

'Because…'

'It is your life Josephine. You must do as you want but don't come crying to me when Glorietta is given Tosca. Don't cry on my shoulder when your ex-husband is ruining your life. Why are you giving up everything for him? Even Glorietta and Cesare don't understand you–'

'What do you mean? Have you discussed it with them?'

'Not exactly,' he pauses. 'Glorietta invited us all for lunch.'

'And you went?'

'Of course, you cannot expect me not to. We are still friends. We were together for over ten years.'

'I think she still loves you,' I whisper.

'Rubbish! Don't get jealous Josephine it is not becoming. Besides I am not a young schoolboy.'

I want to reply that he behaves like one when Glorietta is around but I don't.

'What did they say?' My voice sounds pathetically humble and I curse myself for my tone.

'They said that they didn't understand why you went running off. It doesn't make sense. No-one understands you. They all know how important this comeback is for you. Yet you are throwing away this opportunity. You need to practice. Glorietta is singing at her best now.'

'How do you know she is singing so well?'

He hesitates and I wonder if I have lost the connection.

'There were a few people there and she sang.'

'A few people at the lunch?' My mind is whirling. 'Who?'

'Nico Vastano and Dino Scrugli.'

I am handing over my boarding pass to the ground crew and my legs give way. I hear Raffaelle calling my name as the phone falls from my hand. A girl in a green uniform stares at me as I recover the phone and I take the stub of the boarding pass from her. Walking along the airless corridor I am imagining Glorietta's villa in Bellagio overlooking the Lake, and a select group of admirers clinking Prosecco glasses at the terrace table. They would insist she sang, and she would resist, and then frightened they would not ask again, she would give in gracefully.

'I bet she sang *Vissi d'arte*,' I say.

'Yes.'

'Did you know Nico and Dino are on the audition panel on Monday?'

'I know, amore mia.'

'And you went to her villa and she sang for them. For all of you.'

'I didn't know she would sing.'

I check the numbers and find my seat on the plane. 'She did. That was the whole point of inviting you there or did you think it was because she was trying out her cooking skills?'

The man across the aisle stares at me.

'No.'

'She is manipulative.'

'No!'

'She invited you and you gave her your support.'

'It wasn't like that.'

'You are my partner now.'

'Sì amore.'

'You endorsed her in my absence. How could you?'

'I didn't think– I'm sorry.'

'Me too.' I hang up the phone. My head is throbbing. I lean back and close my eyes conscious of my neighbour's staring eyes. The words from *Vissi d'arte* revolve in my head, round and round and round. *I lived for art. I lived for love. I lived for art. I lived for love.*

And the only face I see belongs to Michael, when we were lovers.

CHAPTER THREE

And I die in desperation!
And I never before loved life so much,
Loved life so much!
E lucevan le stelle, Tosca

A German lady sitting beside me on the plane tells me that the train service into Munich city centre is excellent. In my previous life I was ferried by a range of sleek cars, chauffeurs and secretaries, and I have never worried about transport.

As I leave the rail carriage a surge of hot air surrounds me. The Hauptbahnhoff is busy and noisy. There are a multitude of exits and after consulting the instructions Seán put in the envelope, I find the main road and the Meridian Hotel, opposite the station entrance.

I take a few minutes to stop and look around and inhale the city air. I stayed here many times, in my past life as an opera singer, and I know it's a short walk along the Bayerstrasse to the Merienplatz. I remember the old part of the city, the restaurants, the cafes, the beer cellars and the shops. I have strolled through the English Garden, enjoyed coffee in the sunshine in the Karlsplatz and wandered through the farmer's market buying fresh food and luxuries from the delicatessen. Although my last few months in Germany were difficult, I have many happy memories, and I take a deep breath. It seems like a good omen and my spirits are lifted.

Checking the paper in my hand, I turn away from the city centre and follow a maze of grey streets. Although it is now dark, I know it isn't the most attractive part of town. Shop fronts have seen better days, cafes are run down and the few bars that are open, seem subdued and seedy.

I walk for almost ten minutes, stopping at the traffic lights, checking the names of the streets, and looking constantly over my shoulder. Since I talked to Karl Blakey I have felt a shiver of fear inside me, tugging at my nerves and pulling at my conscience. Painful memories, lost opportunities, words regretted, destructible actions, all add to my feeling of revulsion and disgust. No-one could imagine my utter shame.

Who was I? Who am I?

Tosca.

The grey apartment block has chipped brickwork, paint peeling from grubby window frames and a steel gated door. I press the buzzer and wait.

I glance into the neighbouring bicycle repair shop. Although it is late it is still open. A single bulb dangles from a high ceiling. The floor is stained with oil puddles, and strewn with mismatched saddles, wheels, inner tubes and bolts, screws and nuts. A bald, well-muscled man in a soiled vest stands wiping his greasy fingers on a dirty rag. He is watching me.

A trickle of perspiration slides down my spine. I look over my shoulder; a couple holding hands cross the street, and a young boy with a rucksack at a bus stop chews gum with his mouth open. No sign of Karl Blakey. Would Seán have sent Karl to follow me? I stab the buzzer again. It is past ten o'clock. Perhaps the old man is asleep? After my third attempt a muffled voice grunts in German.

'Herr Dieter Guzman?' I shout into the intercom.

'Come up. Third floor,' he says. 'There's no lift.'

The stairs reek of cheap disinfectant which irritates my throat. I don't touch the handrail and on the second floor I stop. I take a bottle of water from my bag, cough, wipe my mouth and hope there is no damage done to my trachea. I replace the water in my bag, walk up the one remaining flight of stairs and the lights go out. Suddenly I am plunged into blackness. I search for the glow of a red light on the wall. I think I hear footsteps. My heart is racing. I press the button on the wall and the corridor is suddenly illuminated. There is no-one. Only two brown doors facing me. My heart continues beating rapidly. My palms are perspiring.

3B.

I ring the bell and wait.

There is shuffling and the door clicks open.

'Herr Guzman?' I ask.

An old man stands behind a Zimmer frame. His mouth is too big for his face and he has patches of white stubble on his chin. He nods his head to one side inviting me into the dark corridor of his home, and a few strands of dirty hair dangle over his shoulder.

'Go through to the room at the end.' His voice is rough and, when he slams the door behind me, I believe I am imprisoned.

The living room is ill-lit. The walls are lined with

shelves and bookcases covered with an inch of dust. Scattered on the threadbare carpet are untidy piles of used paperbacks all shapes and sizes, and thumbed magazines; cars, antiques, sculptures, paintings, and naked women.

I sneeze. I pull a tissue from my pocket and cover my nose.

His shuffling footsteps and laboured breath comes from behind me. 'Don't bring your germs in here,' he says.

The once blue sofa is faded grey and patterned with dubious stains. An armchair is stuffed with an assortment of ill-matched cushions with pictures of cart horses and cats. A dining table is covered with debris; plates, cutlery, and glasses. Tin cans and wrappers have been thrown toward an overflowing bin in the corner of the room.

At the window, wooden plastic blinds are half drawn against the night sky. They are covered in dust, cobwebs and red spider's nests.

'Seán telephoned you,' I say. 'He told me you were expecting me. I've come to collect the painting.'

'Sit down.' He struggles into an armchair. His lean frame is fragile.

'You look familiar.' His rheumy brown eyes undress me.

I square my shoulders and stare back down at him. 'Do you have the painting? I'm in a hurry,' I speak in German.

He scratches his chest in a slow easy manner and I look away. I gaze out of the soiled window and see lights in another similar block across the street, and another beside that; all housing built after the last world war.

'You speak good German,' he says. 'But you're foreign, American?' His shirt is buttoned wrong revealing white hairs on his stomach. His English is good.

I cover my nose with the tissue and nod.

'Who are you?' he says.

'Josephine Lavelle.'

'Nein, nein nein!' He waves his arm impatiently. 'He wouldn't just send anyone.'

'Seán asked me to come. He's Michael's eldest son.'

'The property-man, the one that phoned me. Ja, but who are you? Why you? Sit. Sit!' He waves his hand.

I perch on the edge of the sofa conscious of the discoloured patches and damp stains on the floor at my feet. 'I'm a friend of the family.'

He coughs and continues to stare at me, and in that instance I realise, this man is probably the same age as Michael. Until now I have only thought of Michael as a fit and handsome sixty year old, the man whom I loved, not as an ill old man. I blink attempting to remove the image I have of Michael with this man's frail body. How were they ever friends?

'It was Michael's funeral today,' I venture. 'There were lots of people there. He will be missed. He was a gentleman.'

Guzman snorts. 'We are all going to die. I'm surprised he lasted this long.'

Rebuffed I reply, 'I'm in a hurry, Herr Guzman. Do you have the painting?'

'I am not in a hurry. I have nowhere to go and besides it's not often I have a pretty face to look at.' He smiles with yellow rotting teeth, and taps thin fingers on the arm of his chair, and I begin to wonder if I have been sent on a false mission.

I take out the bottle of water. My throat is parched and I am developing a headache. Under normal circumstances

I would get up and leave but the thought of Karl Blakey digging into my past, and the explicit letter I wrote thirty years ago, leaves me with no option.

'May I open a window?'

He nods, so I tug the window and a stream of warm air rushes into the room causing me to cough. I am tired and my patience is ebbing. My head is also throbbing.

'I really need the painting, Mr Guzman.'

'Call me Dieter.'

'Dieter. The painting - please?'

'Michael was no gentleman. He was a scoundrel and a thief.' His eyes glaze over and he stares past me. 'All four of us were bad, but we were only boys and we've paid the price.

'He killed Terry. Seven years after the war was over. He shot him dead and he took his share of the treasure.' Dieter leans forward. 'But he wasn't going to kill me.'

'Michael?'

'We thought we would outlive him. We waited. What's the point of having a fortune if you can't spend it? He was a coward just like he was in the war. We all were.'

'D–Did Michael kill someone?'

'Maximilian.'

'Michael killed Maximilian? In the war?'

'Nein! Nein!' Dieter heaves himself to his feet and shuffles to a wooden cabinet. He opens a drawer, pulls out a creased photograph, and shambles over to sit with me on the sofa. Automatically I shift my knees away from him. His bony finger stabs the black and white snapshot of four men.

'That's me,' he says, pointing at a skinny boy in uniform.

He is tall, thin faced with a sharp nose.

'You were in the British army, but you're…'

'Yes, I am a German. A Jew. But my mother was English.'

'That's Terry. He worked with the red cross.' He points to a boy with short dark hair.

Then he points to a smiling face squinting at the sunlight.

I say, 'Michael?'

He nods. 'He was a medic.' Dieter's breath is putrid and I lean away.

There is a fourth boy crouched below the others. He is small and wiry by comparison and has a mop of curly hair hanging over his forehead. 'That is Maximilian Strong,' he says.

I am holding the picture of the four young men, tilting it toward the lamp light to see their expressions.

'Have you heard of the Monuments Men?' He coughs phlegm and wipes his hands on a dirty tissue from his pocket.

'Yes, I think so. Weren't they a team of art experts who were assigned to the allied forces. Didn't they protect and record damage done to churches and monasteries in Italy during the war?'

'Not just Italy and not just buildings. The MFAA - Monuments, Fine Arts and Archives section also located missing movable works of art; all the stolen Nazi treasures from France, Holland and Belgium. The priceless paintings, sculptures, silverware, gilt-edged books and manuscripts, everything that was stolen from churches, museums or private collections and from the wealthy Jews.

'Hitler had plans to build a Führermuseum in his home

town of Linz in Austria and he put Goering in charge of collating all the artwork in Europe for his collection, but Goering was also a collector and he stored most of the stolen art at his estate in Carinhall, his hunting-lodge outside Berlin.' He scratches his chest. 'Goering supervised the removal of these artefacts. Many were stored in salt mines like the one in Austria in Altaussee because the temperatures in the mines kept the paintings relatively undamaged. But then, in the last months of the war, everything changed. When the Nazis started retreating they were determined to destroy the art and everything else, rather than let it be found by the British, Americans or the Russians.

'Hitler's Nero Decree listed facilities and sites for destruction. There were orders to destroy bridges and major sites of importance that I can't remember now, but when Hitler sent orders that the mines were to be blown up with the artwork inside, some of Hitler's Generals weren't in agreement with him, so they began dumping consignments in lakes, or hiding them in repositories hidden in the countryside.

'The Monuments Men had no real authority. They only had the help of officers and enlisted men but they managed to save and categorise a large amount of art and much of it, after the war, was eventually repatriated to the rightful owners.

'They found hoards of treasures in rural areas, in schools, cafes and houses where they had been stored for safekeeping, but hundreds of people were involved in the plundering; art experts, guards, packers, it was impossible to control. There were art dealers in Berlin and Switzerland trading in looted artwork. Some went missing, some were destroyed, some simply disappeared.'

He turns to look at me.

'We found a cartload of treasure. It was the day after the big discovery in Siegen. I remember it was the second of April. The experts were so excited they had found works by Rembrandt, Gauguin, Renoir and Rubens that they didn't take much notice of four uniformed men including two medics. I had the advantage of speaking German which gave me more authority and credibility with the locals and so it was easy. It was stored in crates. We confiscated it and found a secure lockup then we swore each other to secrecy.' Dieter rises to his feet. He holds on to the back of furniture and shuffles to another room that I hadn't noticed before.

It has gone eleven o'clock. I am exhausted. I yawn. It doesn't seem possible that I left my home only this morning and flew to Dublin. The funeral seems weeks ago. My neck aches and my head hurts. I pick up the photograph and study the faces of the four young soldiers. Terry the boy with freckles was killed. Michael is dead, Dieter is old and ill, and I am wondering about the wiry boy with the mop of hair across his forehead when Dieter returns carrying a tray.

'Tea?' His mouth hangs open in concentration and, with a determined thrust, he slides the tray onto a small table. Milk spills on the floor and a drop of tea sloshes from the spout of the flowery teapot over the bone china mugs.

'I told you my mother was English,' Dieter smiles.

'Is the painting…'

He ignores me, pours tea, licks his lips and blows into the mug. 'We were boys. We didn't know each other that well. We had only been deployed for six weeks but it turned out we were all opportunists. We all had that in common. We couldn't believe our luck; silver-gilt busts; altarpieces, decorations, sculptures and a couple of paintings.'

'You stole them.'

'They had been stolen from the Jews,' he replies sternly.

'But they didn't belong to you.'

'So?' He blows and sips. 'A few days later all the packers, movers, trucks and an armed guard from the infantry division were sent to another repository near Merkers where they found paintings by Rubens, Goya and Cranach. They even found gold bars and foreign currency including stamping plates to print Reichmarks.' He chuckles and wipes his eyes. 'They were so busy with the big hoards they forgot about the smaller stashes.

'After the war historians, art scholars, conservationists, curators from all the countries claimed their rights to the missing pieces; legally, morally and emotionally. It's complicated. They were all going to fight over them. So we kept them.'

'It was wrong.' I am horrified but he seems proud of his heist.

'We divided up the goods. We had no idea how much any of the pieces were worth. After the war, I settled back in Germany. I never married. I had girlfriends but I could never trust anyone with the truth. We didn't even trust each other. Not after Terry got shot.'

'Michael killed Terry?' I wipe perspiration from my lip.

'Nein, nein, Michael didn't kill Terry. Maximilian killed Terry.'

'Thank goodness. Michael was a doctor. He saved lives.

He was the only man I ever trusted.' I am surprised at my outburst and at my honesty. I am tired.

'Maximilian became an underworld antiquity dealer. A middle man: an importer, exporter, art specialist - you name it, he did it. He asked us to sell our stuff to him and Terry was the first to sell.' He stretches his legs. 'One day Terry phoned me. He told me Maximilian was fiddling him on each deal and he said he was going to confront him. A week later he was dead.'

'So you don't know for sure it was Maximilian?'

'Soon after Terry died, Maximilian went to Michael but Michael refused to sell. He had no way of getting all his possessions back to Ireland so I kept some of them safe for him here in Germany. A week later his house in Dublin went on fire. One son was very badly burned; his head and face, he was in intensive care for months. Michael was beside himself with grief and fear. His wife and other son managed to escape with less severe burns but Michael was scared. He knew what Maximilian was capable of,' he pauses.

I think of William's scarred forehead and remember Seán telling me of a fire in their home as children. William had spent weeks in intensive care and in the burns unit. They had been fortunate to save his life.

Dieter continues speaking, 'So, Michael decides to give Maximilian an ancient manuscript, and a ruby encrusted necklace, and tells him it is all he has left. Ja, Michael is happy, until Maximilian says that if he is lying he will come back and kill his eldest son, Seán. You see, that is when we both started hoping to outlive Maximilian because once he is dead, we can continue to sell our pieces but with him alive, we can't. It means that we have these precious things but we can't sell them. For if we do Maximilian will know we are lying and he will kill us.'

'So, Michael never sold anything else?'

'Yes, of course he did,' he smiles. 'Michael was very shrewd. He was a wily old devil. He waited for the fuss to die down and then his patience paid off. Europe was changing. The Berlin wall came down, the Russians had the Glasnost, and once again we were living in a different Europe. Private collectors began to spring up all over the place; Russian oligarchs and the nouveau riche. Europeans were filled with celebrity snobbery. There were rich Albanians and suddenly all the ordinary people wanted paintings, statues, busts, or they bought jewellery and precious stones. Everything was purchasable for a price.

'Michael leaked his goods little by little and over the years he managed to sell or dispose of everything, all except one item.'

I sit up a little straighter. My back is aching and my headache is turning to a migraine.

'Last year Maximilian's nephew Ian visited Michael. He's a nasty piece of work. His main trade is importing Eastern European girls into brothels in the West but after a stint in jail he is now his uncle's flunky. Perhaps Maximilian wants to provide a better future for his nephew or Ian wants to involve his father in his seedy business, I don't know, but I do know that Ian is ruthless and dangerous. He is a killer like his uncle. He tells Michael that he knows he has the ultimate treasure, and that Maximilian will stop at nothing to get it. He has nothing to lose. Like me, he is old and he is going to die soon.'

I am wondering if Michael financed the early part of my career with money from these stolen items. It is illegal and morally wrong. How could Michael have been involved in this?

'I'm not taking a stolen painting back to Ireland.' I say, standing up pulling my cotton trousers. Perspiration has made them stick to my legs and I wipe my damp palms on my blouse.

'Let me show you something.' Without waiting for an answer Dieter grabs my elbow and when I resist he squeezes my skin. I am shocked by his sudden energy and strength as he pulls me toward the front door until I realise the apartment is L-shaped. I had assumed that where we sat in the living room and the small kitchen was the entirety of the flat but it isn't. At the front door we turn right into the longer part of the L-shape corridor and the air is cooler. Our path is illuminated automatically by small overhead lights that I guess are made active by body sensors as we pass.

Dieter produces a key, unlocks a door and subdued lighting fills a room. The windows are blacked out. There is one single chair placed in the centre of an immaculate pine floor.

The paintings are originals; some are in gilt frames and others have simple frames. They are all numbered and catalogued with a square card on the wall. I release an involuntary cry of surprise and Dieter gives a hoot of pleasure. He hobbles to the chair and sits like a King on his throne.

I walk slowly. My sandals click against the floor. I pause beside each one reading their names gazing at their beauty. I don't know how long it takes me. There is a

Degas, a Manet, a Cézanne, two Van Gogh paintings, and several sketches by Leonardo da Vinci.

'I am pleased you are speechless,' Dieter says, and I wonder how many hours he spends simply enjoying their beauty. I return my attention to a display in a small pine cabinet. There is a crown with a tiara entwined with serpents and thorns; a marble-bust like Michelangelo's *David*; and a heavily embossed gilt-edged book.

What takes my breath away, hanging on the wall above the glass cabinet, is a familiar Vermeer painting with three musicians: a young girl sitting at a harpsichord, a man playing a lute and a woman singing. I am familiar with the painting. It was stolen from a museum in Boston.

'It's called *The Concert*,' he says unnecessarily.

'This cannot be the original,' I say. 'I–It was stolen, and it's worth a fortune.'

'It came from the Isabella Stewart Gardner Museum,' he nods, 'and yes, the original is probably worth over two million dollars. I only got a fraction of the price for it when I sold it to a friend in London.'

'But…'

'I had to finance the security of my home. I need to be protected,' he says simply. Then he speaks more slowly, discussing the sketches by Leonardo da Vinci, the necklace worn by Cleopatra, and jewellery once belonging to a pharaoh in Egypt, but I barely absorb his words. I am lost in the art and their beauty. I am also shocked that an old man could be the guardian of this precious hoard.

'Is this your share of the treasure?' I ask.

'Nein, nein. We probably only took six or eight pieces each but I have collected more over the years, and unlike Maximilian, I have been more discreet. He collects art to sell on for a profit or to subsidise a drug deal, but I am one of the few who collect art for its pure rare artistic appreciation and value.'

'My goodness. They are all beautiful,' I say truthfully.

He coughs a laugh.

'Is Seán's painting here?'

'Seán's?' His voice is sharp.

'Michael's painting?'

He stands shakily, leans against the wall and pushes a canvas to one side. It is Cézanne's *The Boy in the Red Vest*. 'This one is not valuable, it's just a very good copy done by a friend of mine in Spain.'

He opens a safe.

I panic. How will I get a painting through customs? What if he gives me a copy? Is everything a forgery here? What if he gives me a worthless fake?

Dieter thrusts a package the size of a shoe box at me. I am surprised by its weight and use both hands to hold it to my chest. He sinks back into his chair, relieved of the burden, breathing heavily.

'What's this?' I ask.

'This is the treasure Maximilian wants.'

'This isn't a painting.'

'Who said it was a painting?'

I remember Seán sitting beside the unlit fire holding a wine glass. He is drunk. 'He called it an heirloom; a family heirloom.'

'Open it!'

I place the box on the floor and remove the lid. Inside is a piece of worn and dirty linen held together by frayed string. I tug the knot and prise the cloth apart. The face of the golden Madonna is serene. She is looking at her infant son who is standing between the folds of her robe. Her right palm is open and her left hand holds the hand of the baby boy. His eyes too, are downcast, as if he is already aware of his destiny. The detail is magnificent; her pleated gown, her head scarf, his fingers and curls, are sculptured with such infinite detail it is hard to believe they are not real.

'It is beautiful,' I say.

'The Golden Icon. It is the most precious of them all.' Dieter leans forward and extends his hand and I pass it to him. 'Solid gold; almost six kilos. This is the gem of all gems. Only a few people know that it survived the war. It was modelled on Michelangelo's, *Madonna of Bruges*, do you know it?'

'Vaguely.'

He hands me back the Madonna and wipes his mouth, and says. 'Underneath is the stamp of the Vatican. With a magnifying glass you will see the date, eighteen twenty-nine,' he says, like a teacher to his pupil.

'It belongs to the Vatican?' I turn the icon with both hands. The figures are crafted onto a solid gold plinth. I cannot decipher the seal or the engraved signature.

'Not if you are Irish.'

I raise an eyebrow. 'What has this to do with Ireland?'

'Patience Josephine, patience.' It is the first time he has said my name and it sounds strange coming from his lips. He dabs the saliva at the corners of his mouth.

'The Vatican was concerned about the situation in Ireland. They wanted the support of the Irish Catholics and they intended to fund an Irish Rebellion after the Catholic Relief Act of 1829. They felt sure that if they sent money to fund a revolution against the British, the rebel Irish would win and the Vatican would have more support in Europe.

'They didn't want to send sacks of gold and they didn't have the resources or inclination to send an army, so instead they had this Golden Icon made with the Pope's seal of approval.'

'So, how did the statue end up here in Germany?'

'Rumour says that the Priest who was entrusted to deliver the Golden Icon was robbed and killed in Ireland before he managed to deliver it.

'Grave robbers took the Golden Icon to Cardinal McCade who lived with his son, a doctor at the Royal College of Surgeons and his brother's orphaned daughter in Dublin. The orphan girl had a friend who died of Typhus. It was a time of body snatchers, and the church versus science, and when the body was stolen for dissection the girl stole the Golden Icon and fled from her Uncle.'

'Where did she go?'

'She smuggled it to France. She later died of typhus in a convent in Holland. For many years the Golden Icon stayed in the convent protected by the Dutch Cellite sisters. During the war the convent was turned into a makeshift hospital and the Golden Icon was smuggled out, hidden from the Nazis and sent to the East, near Cleves. The local people had promised to keep it safe with other hidden artwork, and by coincidence we found out about it. During the confusion of the latter days of the war it didn't take us long to commander it.'

'You stole it,' I argue.

Dieter shrugs. 'That's a matter of opinion. Then we drew straws and picked the items we would keep. Michael had first choice.'

'But you don't display the Golden Icon in here?'

'Nein, nein.' He waves his hand. 'You must be careful. Seán must be careful.'

'Why?'

'Anyone who has attempted to use it for their own gain has suffered or died quickly.'

'And Michael knew this?'

'Ja, he knew, he knew. That's why he didn't want to sell it. Now you must take it.' Dieter grips the arm of the chair and rises.

'No! I am not taking it. Seán can collect it when his leg is out of plaster.'

'Plaster?'

'Yes, he had an accident.'

'Accident? What sort of accident?'

'He was almost knocked down by a car.'

'When?'

'Just after Michael died. Two maybe three days ago.'

Dieter groans. 'That was no accident. They are after the Golden Icon. Come, quickly! You must take it and leave now.' He takes the box and wraps the soiled linen around the icon. 'Come, come, hurry. It was a warning. You must take it to Seán immediately.' He pulls me from the room and pushes me along the illuminated corridor to the front door. 'Get your bag,' he orders, nodding toward the living room. 'Quickly.'

I grab my bag and the photograph of the four men in uniform falls to the floor.

'Hurry,' shouts Dieter.

I run back to the front door, the bag in my hand.

'Take this,' he says, thrusting the shoe box at me.

'No.'

'You must.' His breath is fetid on my face. 'You must take it to Seán. Maximilian will kill you. Ian is a murderer. They will stop at nothing.' His skeletal fingers grab my wrist. 'How did Michael die?'

'Seán never – his heart?'

'They killed him,' he says. 'Take this and go! Get it to Seán and return to your opera.'

'Opera?'

It is not until afterwards that I realise he uses my surprise and these valuable few seconds to open my travel bag.

'Opera? You know?'

'Ja, of course I know who you are. I recognised you immediately. Were you not world famous? Are you not Tosca?' He begins to hum *Vissi d'arte*, and suddenly his hand is fondling and squeezing my nipple.

I shove him against the wall, grab my bag and run down the three flights of stairs. I throw open the door but standing in front of me is a man whose eyes are dull and cold. He is the man from the bicycle shop.

I scream.

I am running toward the Hauptbahnhoff looking over my shoulder every few paces. Shadows greet me at every turn. Headlights blind me. Noises assail my senses. It's as if I am running blind. Convinced I am followed. I take a side street. A man jogs toward me. He has piercing blue eyes like Glorietta's. I lean closer to the wall and scrape my arm on the brick. Glorietta couldn't run like me. She is twice my weight and half my height. He passes me and I begin to laugh. I cough. Tears are streaming down my cheeks. I have a pain in my chest so I stop. I am panting heavily and when I look over my shoulder, a girl wearing headphones crosses the road, and a man on a bicycle passes by me. It is almost midnight. Where are they all going? A motorbike roars past and a bus pulls up to an empty stop.

My body is shaking and my arms ache. I am standing beside a window and when I peer inside, faces drinking beer stare back at me. I walk slowly taking deep breaths forcing my diaphragm lower to control my panic. I turn frequently to look over my shoulder. My lips are dry and perspiration clings to my blouse.

I am relieved when I reach the main road and the street lamps are brighter. At the entrance to the Meridian Hotel I pause and dart quickly inside. The concierge is busy. He doesn't look up. I follow the signs to the Ladies toilet where I tidy my hair and add make up with shaking fingers.

Although it is late I decide I will call Seán. In the bar I choose a table away from other guests and take out my mobile. I have several missed calls from an unknown number and two calls from Raffaelle. When the waiter comes to my table I pull my bag between my legs and order a gin and tonic with plenty of ice.

Seán has put me in danger. I have the Golden Icon but I will leave it in the airport left luggage locker. He can collect it when his leg is healed. I am not travelling with a stolen solid gold icon of the Madonna and child made by the Vatican belonging to the Irish, certainly not to Dublin.

I dial his number.

'Seán?'

'Who is this?' It's a woman's voice.

'Is Seán there, please?'

'Is that you, Josephine?'

'Is Seán there?'

'It's Barbara,' she says.

'I need to speak to Seán? It's urgent.'

'He's dead.' I hear her sobbing. 'He's dead.' There is scuffling, confusion, muffled voices then a man's voice.

'Josephine, this is William, Seán's brother.'

I think of William's scarred forehead and the fire.

'Can you hear me?'

The waiter bends balancing my drink on a tray and places a glass on the coaster. He pours tonic over the gin, bows, smiles and walks away. Bubbles gather on the sliced lemon, glistening like tiny diamonds.

'Josephine?'

I drink quickly, gathering my thoughts and calming my voice before replying.

'What happened?'

'It was a burglary. A man came to the house. A mourner. He shot Seán. We can't believe it.' William is struggling to regain his composure. 'On the night of the Da's funeral.'

I am in someone else's body leading someone else's life. I should be at home sipping Prosecco on my terrace. I should be preparing for Tosca. I should be rehearsing with Cesare. I must sing. I am an opera singer.

'Why?'

'The Gardaí are here investigating. You know Seán had financial problems? They are in his office going through all his documents.'

I think of my letter and I curse him aloud.

'What was that? I can't hear you?' William is shouting but I hear him perfectly. 'He stole the painting hanging in the study, the Turner.'

I end the call. I circle the bag with my feet tucking it under the table. I signal to the waiter for another drink and I take out the black and white photograph from my pocket and stare at the faces of the young men; all thieves, crooks or murderers.

CHAPTER FOUR

All the earth doth worship thee:
the Father everlasting
Te Deum, Tosca

The new Teatro Il Domo rises from the depths of the lake like a glorious shining orb radiating and reflecting the colours of the rainbow across the water. The recycled glass dome, not unlike the dome of St Paul's Cathedral in London, is especially designed to withstand the outside glare and heat from the sun. Inside, the theatre is constructed to offer acoustics with a quality unmatched by any other opera venue in the world.

In television reports and press releases, Theatre Director, Niccolo Vastano has emphasised that staging and productions will be minimalist, thereby relying on the talent of the actors, musicians and orchestras. Dino Scrugli's production of Tosca will be the first performance to verify this, and conductor Andrei Ferretti also testifies to the importance of these principles and standards. They are all at the top of their game and I want to be with them.

From my vantage point at the railing, there is a flurry of

early morning activity along the quay and the wooden floating pontoon. I absorb each detail. White vans delivering goods; trucks with machinery and laden with electrical equipment, cables, lights and furniture. The theatre has a main auditorium, a studio for rehearsals and auditions, a restaurant and a panoramic revolving bar that provides a three hundred and sixty-five degree view of the surrounding land. The pure aesthetic pleasure of the building is cooed over by the foreigners beside me clicking cameras and mobile phones.

Lake Como has the shape of an inverted Y. The round glass dome looks north toward the Alps where, in the winter, the mountains are covered in snow. As we sail past on the ferry we pass the reception where there are bronze statues that I find hard to identify, standing against the window.

Built by Antonio Giordiano, a pupil of Frank Gehry, he finished the commission to world acclaim and it is as revered by the opera world, as the Guggenheim museums are to the art world. Its originality and uniqueness stands like a beacon of beauty on one of Europe's most beautiful lakes against a backdrop of the Italian Alps.

I stand and marvel at its allure. This engineering feat and cost of completing this project is ambitious when most of Europe and America is suffering a recession. It has been built with money from sponsors, industrialists and investors, and rumour has it, with money from Eastern Europe.

On Monday morning my audition takes place there.

It is almost twenty-seven hours since I left Comaso. I left at six in the morning yesterday for my flight to Dublin, now it is nine o'clock on Saturday morning. I have been travelling all night. My head is fuzzy and disoriented with fatigue. My body is shaking with tiredness. I did not sleep on the train from Munich to Zurich, or on the train from Zurich to Como. Instead, I watched the dark countryside race past, the carriage flying through the night passing flat fields, hotels on busy motorways, churches lit like yellow beacons, and mountain villages illuminated with white lights. The same six words were reverberating rhythmically in my head: *Seán is dead. Michael is dead. Seán is dead. Michael is dead.*

The sun rises over the jagged Alps casting a warm pink glow across Lake Como and I am relieved to be on the ferry heading home. I lean against the wooden bench. It is hard against my back. I cover my mouth and yawn. My eyes water. They are red and sore with sadness. I sit watching the Teatro Il Domo fade out of sight and concentrate on the pattern left in the wake of the water. I have to block my mind from its overdrive.

I inhale large gulps of the Tivano wind that blows in the early morning from the Valtellina in the north-east, which is usually a sign of good weather, and I cast my face up toward the sun. As the boat turns north the red and white canopy provides me with shade, but as on the train, each time I close my eyes I see Seán's tired face. He had thought I would collect his family heirloom, a painting and return it to him, solve all his financial problems and he would live happily with his family.

I had only focused on getting to Dublin and retrieving my letter. Now I was numb. The shock of the events in Munich and the murder of Seán is overwhelming. I am concerned about the letter. What if the police find it? Or Barbara reads it? Or William - Michael was his father too.

A Japanese man gestures to his wife to smile and she poses, twisting her body at right angles toward the mobile phone he holds above his head. They wear colourful, comfortable clothes and have eager eyes and enthusiastic smiles. Over her shoulder I see the image he is snapping, and I admire the beauty of the village behind her. Like most of the villages on the lake, they are a multitude of subdued colours; terracotta, burnish yellow, shades of red, blue and okra, and they overlook a small harbour or church.

Bells for Mass chime across the water and when a German calls to his wife I instinctively tighten my grip on my bag between my feet.

The Golden Icon was the secret of four men; Michael, Maximilian, Dieter and Terry. Two are dead, and now Seán is dead. I am the keeper of their secret.

I drink water from a bottle. My throat is tight. How will I sing at my audition on Monday? I call Cesare, there is no answer, so I leave a message on his phone to tell him I am home.

The Japanese man redirects his wife. He snaps a shot and she looks over his shoulder at the finished result, nodding and smiling; a happy couple.

I look around at the other passengers and I focus on the man sitting on the opposite bench. He has gerbil cheeks and is the same build as Karl Blakey. I feel a welling of contempt for this stranger whom I have never met. Tiredness makes me want to shout at him, or push him overboard but when his wife returns with two hot cappuccinos, he smiles graciously, and I am ashamed.

The Comaso pontoon draws close. I am gladdened by the sight of deep red geraniums hanging in baskets at the

Alberge Luigi, and at the ticket office and hanging outside the lake-view cafe. The old stone village stretches up to the woods, its narrow roads are like tentacles in the hillside, and on the far side of the wooded ravine I watch the orange cable car bump over green pylons and descend to the village.

The ferry slows.

In front of the Santa Anna di Comaso church, rented boats in the harbour are lined up ready for hire; colourful fishing boats bob up and down; cars and scooters whine as they negotiate the lakeside road, and church bells toll across the sleepy village.

I sigh. I am home.

I lift my bag, conscious of the burden I carry.

The crew lower the plank to the pontoon and stand aside to let passengers disembark, before going up the lake, to the more well-known villages of Lenno or Bellagio.

I move with more agility than I feel. Sunglasses hide my red and tired eyes, but I stumble and one of the crew reaches for my arm.

'Grazie,' I say, but my voice is tired and he doesn't hear me.

I walk with the passengers waiting to embark with my head bowed. I don't want to be recognised. My footsteps resound on the cobbled pavement. I avoid the fountain square where Luigi and Maria are opening their restaurant, pass the ticket office, and the cafe where tourists sit eating breakfast. The fresh aroma of dark, rich coffee causes my stomach to rumble, and Madonna sings from the radio, *I was born this way.* A waitress leans over the table, fresh orange juice balanced on her tray and an ink tattoo of a butterfly rises up her arm.

In the harbour boats are tossed on the waves caused by the departing ferry, I dodge the cars, and a bus groans up the hillside. I skip across the road and open a half-hidden gate tucked beside a large laurel tree.

The okra-coloured villa has green metal shutters that are half closed. Its walls are adorned with rampant pink and purple bougainvillea and pots of azaleas stand like sentries on the steps to the back door.

The latch gate clicks closed and I secure it before walking up the grassy pathway. The hammock is hooked up and sways in the shade between two pine trees as if rocking an invisible body. The old stone well, covered with a plank of wood, is cluttered with a multitude of ceramic pots: red and pink geraniums, rhododendrons, camellias and magnolias. All are untrimmed and untidy, as is, the sweet smelling wild jasmine trailing up and over the door.

Branches of a gnarled wisteria provide a sheltered alcove for a bistro table and two chairs. On its surface are the remnants of burnt candles, the remains of the night before; two brandy glasses and an overflowing ashtray.

I ring the bell and wait.

Raffaelle smells faintly of tobacco and brandy.

'Amore mia,' he says. He takes me in his arms and in that instance all doubts are swept from my mind. His strength reassures me, his fingers make my skin tingle and I am alive again. My fear recedes and my sadness ebbs. My tears fall. He murmurs soothing words but they are not important. It is the tone of his soft deep voice and his lips that kiss my wet cheeks that make me feel I have lived a nightmare. He takes his time, he caresses and undresses me in the shuttered sleepiness of his bedroom and I succumb to a need that overwhelms me. A need to feel alive and a need to feel loved.

It is gone midday when I wake alone in the bed. I check my watch. I have slept for two hours.

I pull on a cotton robe and wander bare foot into the garden. The two brandy glasses have been removed and there is no trace of the ashtray.

'I thought you had given up smoking?' I call out. I sit in the shade at the rickety table and watch Raffaelle moving around the kitchen through the open windows.

'I have.'

'And brandy?'

'No, never brandy,' he laughs. 'Relax, amore. I am bringing coffee and fresh bread from the bakery.' He waves a ciabatta through the window and I am flattered he is going to so much trouble.

'I thought you would be in your studio painting.'

'Not this morning.' I wait hoping he will say it is because I am back and he missed me but all I hear is the hum of traffic; motorbikes and convertible cars and the occasional squeal of breaks or tooting of a horn. It reassures me of a normal life. I know that most drivers are from Milan seeking refuge from the scorching heat of the city, coming in search of beauty, the mountains, or motor cyclists seeking the challenging thrill as they lean into hairpin bends.

From a field above the villa a donkey brays and across the valley a dog barks. I am home.

Raffaelle wears boxer shorts and a blue T-shirt. He reaches for my hand and kisses my fingers. 'Good morning, amore,' he says. 'You had better tell me what has happened. You were very tired and upset when you

65

arrived home this morning. I wasn't expecting you. I thought you were going to Germany?' He pours coffee and slices bread.

I admire the feast on the table; fresh oranges, grapes, bread and honey and as we eat I begin to tell him what happened. I start with Michael's funeral and then Seán begging me to go to Germany to save him from bankruptcy.

'Seán said he can't trust his brother, his employees or the children. There was no-one else.'

'Not even his wife?' Raffaelle wipes crumbs from his moustache with a napkin.

'No, not even Barbara. He insisted I am the only one he can trust. He is desperate,' I correct myself, 'he *was* desperate.'

I do not mention my letter written to Michael thirty years ago. I do not tell him I was blackmailed. I do not mention Karl Blakey. Not that he would know Karl Blakey; Karl belongs to my past in Germany before I arrived in Comaso, before I met Raffaelle, and before I began to work and rebuild my career with Cesare Serratore.

His dark eyes watch me carefully and he tugs on his moustache.

I continue speaking and emphasise my unwillingness to go. 'You hardly think I would have gone to Munich if I didn't have to. You know how important Tosca is to me. Seán said they were foreclosing on his business on Monday and he believed that if he had the family heirloom it would pay off all his debts.'

The coffee is rich and thick and I sip it slowly. My voice is soft. My throat, that I should be resting, is tight with emotion. I describe Dieter and the filth and squalor of his home and the surprise of the treasures in his fetid apartment.

I stumble over my words explaining about the four young British soldiers in the black and white photograph. 'There was Dieter, Michael, Terry who died, and Maximilian who shot him.' I tick them off my fingers and when I look up Raffaelle is studying me with the scrutiny of an artist, and of a disbeliever.

I could go to the bedroom and get the photograph from my bag but I don't, and when I reach the part of the story of the hidden room with the treasures, his brown eyes widen.

'Did you recognise any of them? Who were the artists? Were they in a good condition? Framed?'

'Some, I don't know. I can't remember, Degas? Vermeer? There was one I think, it was a Cézanne, and a boy with a vest.' I take a grape and crush it in my mouth savouring the juice as it trickles down my throat.

'*Boy in a Red Waistcoat*? It was stolen a few years ago in Zurich.'

'He told me it was a forgery, done by someone in Spain.' I am trying to recall the details of Dieter's apartment. 'There was a Vermeer, *The Concert*. He said, he sold the original - it was a copy, and a few sketches by Leonardo da Vinci.'

'Sold the original?' his voice is incredulous. 'What sort of sketches?'

'For heaven's sake Raffaelle, how should I know? I am not an artist.'

'I know, but you should recognise…'

'No! I don't.'

'Okay, don't shout at me.'

'I'm not shouting,' I sigh. 'There were so many of them.'

'How many?'

I cast my hands wide. 'Six or seven?'

'And paintings?'

'Maybe fifteen.'

'Fifteen?' he whistles.

'Twenty-five?' I say.

He throws his arms into the air.

'There were other things too; a marble bust, a tiara with snakes and rubies, and a gilt-edged book.'

'I can't believe you don't remember more details.'

'Dieter spoke a lot about art and treasures but I couldn't take it all in,' I say. 'I was frightened and at the end when he touched me, ugh! It was disgusting. It's been a shock Raffaelle. So much has happened. Then with the burglary and Seán shot dead. I just can't believe it has all happened.'

Raffaelle pats my hand. 'You must rest. Try not to think too much about all this. Concentrate on Tosca. I know how much it means to you.' He stands and clears the table and I am left in the garden sitting under the gnarled wisteria branches lost in my thoughts. Perhaps I should show him the photograph and the Golden Icon. I trace the outline of the table with my finger and think of the overflowing ashtray and two brandy glasses.

Raffaelle is clinking mugs and scraping plates.

'Who was here with you last night?' I call out.

'Here?'

'Yes.'

'Er...'

'Drinking brandy with you?'

'Oh that. You saw the glasses? Er–, Angelo popped in.'

Angelo is the Mayor of the village. He has been friends with Raffaelle since they were children. Their families had grown up together until Raffaelle's wife left him fifteen years ago. Angelo is a diplomat. He is popular and supportive of all the town's fetes and fiestas and I have shared several dinners in their home. His wife is friendly and completely supportive of her husband but her complete submission to his needs makes me feel uncomfortable. She neglects herself. It is as though she exists only to serve him and I think of her as a *Stepford Wife*. I remember on my last visit to their home, a few months ago, Angelo had had a health scare and was worried about his heart. He said he wasn't drinking alcohol anymore.

Raffaelle reappears in the garden with a chilled bottle of Prosecco and two glasses. It starts as a small chuckle but gradually his laughter turns louder and deeper, his eyes fill up and he can barely speak, then he sits back in his chair and his chest heaves with suppressed laughter. 'But cara,' he says, 'this is a wonderful story you have made up. Are you sure you are not overdoing everything? You have been rehearsing very hard the past few weeks for your audition. You have driven yourself relentlessly. You have been stressed and hardly slept. The pressure is enormous. You are exhausted, no?'

'Made up? You don't believe me?'

He stretches his arms above his head. He is a man at peace with himself, comfortable and relaxed and I resent him. I am angry with his complacency and lack of understanding.

'It is not that I don't believe you, cara.' His arms settle behind his head. 'It's just that you do not need to make up stories for my benefit.'

'You think I have made this all up?'

He shrugs. 'Maybe you stayed on and you and Seán had a little something for old time's sake, but you have an important audition on Monday. Are you forgetting how important this role is for you? For your career?'

'Tosca is important but for heaven's sake Raffaelle so much has happened in the past two days. Seán is dead. He was murdered.'

'I know, I know. I am sorry about that.' He stands up, gathering crumbs between his thick fingers which he flicks onto a blue plate before carrying it like a waiter into the kitchen.

I sit alone. I could prove my story. The evidence lies on the floor in his bedroom still in my bag but I don't move.

'You think I haven't taken you seriously.' Raffaelle returns. 'I am sorry. Perhaps you want to tell me more? Is there anything else?'

I shrug. I am angry with him. I know that I have done the right thing in not telling him about my love for Michael and my letter. I would never have his understanding let alone his support.

'Come on, cara,' he cajoles. 'Don't look so miserable.'

'Dieter went to the safe and I thought he might give me a fake painting but he doesn't. He gave me a box, like a shoe box, and when I unwrapped it, there was the most beautiful Golden Icon. He tells me it was made by the Vatican to fund an Irish rebellion against the British, as they wanted the Catholics to support them.'

Raffaelle smiles.

I stop.

His smirk disappears and I continue.

'He told me that anyone who tries to possess it or use it for their own needs dies or is killed quickly.'

'Ah, so it wasn't a painting you had to collect but a priceless statue that had originally belonged to Michael.'

'It was stolen at the end of the war.' I couldn't bring myself to say Michael had stolen it and that Michael was a thief. 'Europe was in a mess and a team of men that he called the Monuments Men were sent from England and America with the invading troops to preserve and record damage to the cultural sites.'

'Yes, the Monuments Men. I believe they began in Italy, in Sicily…'

'They went all over Europe. They tracked art stolen from France sent from Paris by train, and toward the end of the war they discovered a big repository in Germany. That was at the beginning of April, in nineteen forty-five. Their attention was so taken with this discovery that these four boys, who were in the British Army, had the opportunity to steal this treasure.'

'Where did they steal it from?'

'Dieter said it had been hidden by the locals.'

'How convenient.'

'What do you mean?'

'It sounds as if there was a war to be won and these men had time to go off treasure hunting.'

'I am repeating what Dieter told me. Why are you so sceptical? Michael and Terry were medics. I suppose the other two were drivers. I don't know. I didn't ask. I just listened.

'When I told him that Seán's leg was in plaster Dieter

said it was no accident. He knew who I was, and he stuffed the Golden Icon into my bag and grabbed my breast.'

'Ah, the old dog fondled you?' He nods at my breast. 'He has taste.'

I ignore him. I tell him how I ran to the hotel and phoned Seán. 'Barbara answered Seán's mobile. She could barely speak. The next thing I know I hear William's voice telling me Seán had been shot. It was the evening of Michael's funeral,' my voice chokes.

Raffaelle takes my hand in his and brings my fingers to his lips. 'You still love him, cara,' he says.

'Who?'

'Seán.'

'No! I don't.' I snatch my hand away. 'But I am worried Raffaelle. He was killed in a burglary. The murderer took a fake Turner that was hanging in the study. Dieter told me Maximilian is after the Golden Icon. Once he knew Michael had it and that he was trying to sell it, to pay off Seán's debts, their fate was sealed.'

'I hardly imagine an old man breaking into Seán's home.'

'He has a nephew.' My voice sounds lame. 'Called Ian, who imports girls from Eastern Europe to be prostitutes. He told me that Maximilian threatened Michael once before when Seán and William were small, and that he set their house alight. William has a terrible scar across his forehead that he got in the fire.'

'So?'

'So it means Dieter isn't lying.' I lean across the table. 'Can't you understand? He's telling the truth. Don't you see? It means that Maximilian will kill to get the Golden

Icon.'

'So, amore, tell me.' Raffaelle leans forward and looks deep into my eyes. His hidden laughter is taunting me. 'Where is the Golden Icon now?'

I hesitate.

A blackbird hops onto a gnarled wisteria branch and the murmur of radio voices comes from the kitchen. 'I left it in a locker in the train station in Munich,' I lie.

'You did what?' His words come out in a rush and he leans back in his chair.

'I need you to believe me,' I say truthfully. I want Raffaelle to take me seriously before I show him the evidence.

He sighs.

'Please Raffaelle, this is important. I need you to believe what I am saying.'

My mobile phone rings from inside the villa.

There is the hoot of a horn beyond the garden gate, a squeal of brakes and a cry of angry voices.

'Of course, I believe you.'

'Good.' I release my breath. I stand up and go inside the villa to get the Golden Icon. I am relieved Raffaelle believes me. It is important that he trusts what I have told him but when I am in the bedroom my mobile rings again and so I answer it.

'Josephine? I got your message. Are you home?' says Cesare.

'Ciao, I got home a few hours ago. I am with Raffaelle.'

'It is your big day on Monday,' he says. 'You will be singing before a panel of the most important people in Italy. At our last rehearsal you were distracted and you were taking sneaky breaths,' he pauses.

'I did vocalise…'

'This is about opera. It is not just music. You need the emotion. You need to feel the sensation, and for every note - you must have intonation.'

'I know. I…'

'Josephine, there is no time left. On Monday you audition. I will see you there promptly at eleven. It has taken me a long time to persuade these men that you have changed and that you are not the diva you once were. I have told them you are serious. I have told them you are dedicated to your art again. Please don't be late and please - please don't let me down.'

'I won't. I'll be there.'

'No talking. Go home. Leave Raffaelle. You need to be alone. You need to focus. Go to your own apartment and rest your voice.'

'Thank you, Cesare.'

'Don't thank me, you haven't got the part yet.'

I take my heavy bag into the garden where Raffaelle is sipping Prosecco.

'That was Cesare,' I say.

'He is very frustrated with you. Go home. Get some rest. I am going to paint. There is a piece that I want to finish. I have been painting late into the night and I am tired too.'

My bag weighs heavy in my hand. Now is not the moment to reveal the Golden Icon or to take the creased photograph from my pocket. I must do as Cesare says and focus. I will need all my energy for my audition. I must rest. I will be Tosca. I will do it for Michael. I will sing for him again.

Raffaelle walks me to the gate. 'I am thinking that I

may exhibit my work. There is a new gallery opening in Milan and they want to come and see my new collection. They have heard about my work and are very encouraging.'

'Are you still mixing your techniques, using the principle of old Masters with surrealism and modern technology; painting Ipods and Ipads in the hands of copies of Vermeer and Caravaggio?'

He laughs. 'You remember?'

'Of course. I like the idea.'

'Even though I can copy old masters easily, I like to use my art to stimulate the mind not to gratify the eye, but sometimes I think my career would have been more successful if I was a forger of old masters instead of trying to do something original each time.'

'You would miss the creativity.' I place my hand on his cheek.

'You don't think forgers are creative?'

'They wouldn't be as talented as you.'

He smiles at me. He is almost fifty-five. His tanned face is deeply lined. 'It would seem that we are both reviving our career after a few dormant years. Let's hope we are successful.' As he kisses me I see a half open packet of cigarettes hanging out of his shirt pocket.

On Sunday morning, I shower and throw clothes into the washing machine. Once my apartment is organised, I tuck the Golden Icon out of sight beside the foot pedals of my piano, and focus.

I am Tosca.

I run through my exercises, breathing techniques and

concentrate on my vocalisation. I do not hurry, instead I empty my head of the past days and create energy and spirit into my being. I am born to sing. This is my life. My role. I am Tosca.

But when my confidence wavers and I think of my mistakes; my past and my secret. I am nervous. So, I block my thoughts, my emotions and feelings. It was always second nature to me, and although it should be easy, I struggle because of the recent events and the emotions they have stirred in me.

It is almost five in the afternoon when I sit on the terrace and stare at the lake below. Several speedboats, a small fishing boat and two jet-skis cross on the water leaving a wash in their wake. The sky is cloudless, the air warm and a comforting aroma of garlic wafts up from the apartment below. I hear my neighbour's hushed voices and I am comforted by their presence.

I live in an old villa at the back of the village. It is divided into four apartments with high ceilings and wide windows. My duplex apartment is upstairs. The other one beside me is rarely occupied. The owners, Alfredo and Luisa are a young couple, busy with their business and they only venture from Rome once a year, usually in September. There are two apartments on the ground floor.

My terrace is spacious and large enough for a wooden table and six chairs, two sun-beds with thick, soft mattresses and an assortment of flowers: sweet jasmine, bougainvillaea and geraniums. Below the railing I have a view of the cobbled street that leads down to the bakery, the small supermarket, and to the main square with the fountain.

Opposite me is a palazzo with a trimmed lawn and

palm trees that have an air of authority over the working garden below. A tangled hosepipe lays draped over each terraced segment, where tomatoes supported by bamboo canes ripen on vines and rows of lettuces, pink radishes and cucumbers.

Above, are several apartment blocks, a car park and a pathway that leads to the woods and to my favourite place, the Chiesa della Madonna dei miracoli - the Church of the Madonna of Miracles.

I often watch the tourists in the early morning heading down to the village and returning with fresh bread or croissants from the bakery. The pathway is steep, sometimes at a forty-five degree angle but steps by the wall make the walk easier.

I prop my bare feet on a chair and place the score for Tosca on my lap. My annotations in pencil are in the margin, and I recall the various venues I performed it in, but the past few days are whirling though my mind.

I berate myself for having written to Michael but I was young and in love. My marriage to Seán had been a sham and it was Michael who had loved me more deeply than anyone, before or since. What we had was special. I must block out what happened. I must focus.

But it is Dieter's voice that I hear constantly and cannot keep out of my mind.

Maximilian will kill to get it.

Seán is dead, Michael is dead.

No-one knows that I have the Golden Icon, only Dieter.

What do I do with it? It was made by the Vatican, given to the Irish and stolen by British soldiers. Why did Michael steal it? I cannot believe that he would have done such a thing. How well did I really know him?

Who does it belong to now?

I must make amends for what Michael did. I don't want him to be a thief. I must do the right thing.

What is the right thing to do?

I consider my options. In theory it belonged to Michael who wanted it to go to Seán, now they are both dead so it makes sense that it should go to Barbara so that she can pay off Seán's debts and continue living in their home. It will inadvertently go to his children and his heirs. Should I tell Barbara? Would that be the right thing to do? But then, didn't Seán say she was a bitch?

I tap the score with my pencil. I write in the margin: *Barbara.*

If it is stolen, which I know it was, then this is a police matter.

Maybe I should give it to the police. But the Chief of Police is Santiago Bareldo. He is Glorietta Bareldo's brother and he lives in Comaso.

Santiago has always been polite to me but there have been undercurrents in his behaviour that make me uncomfortable. Glorietta is my opera rival but she was also Raffaelle's partner for ten years, and since they separated Santiago and Raffaelle have not remained friends. I am under no illusion to think that Santiago would help me or do me any favours. I must be careful with him. He has not become a police inspector for nothing. He has a reputation for being alert and shrewd.

I write in the margin: *Santiago*

On the other hand, I reason, if it was stolen during the War then there must be a legal government department who investigate these things like a modern day Monuments Men department.

I write: *MM*

I tap my pencil. If it was made by the Vatican then maybe it belongs to them, but would that be the Church or to the State?

I write underneath: *The Vatican,* and underneath that, *Italian government.*

I fetch my laptop and Google the Golden Icon.

There are no photographs and information is scant. I find a couple of articles that tells me it went missing during the war from the St. Gertrude's convent in 1944, presumably taken by the Nazis for Hitler's private museum collection and never recovered. That is different to what Dieter told me. He told me that it had been smuggled to Cleves and it had been hidden by the local people to stop it from falling into the hands of the Nazi's.

There is an article tucked away on an Irish website saying there are no photographs of the Golden Icon, and it is only a myth and a rumour, and that it does not exist but I cannot find the author's name.

I Google the price of gold. A one kilogram gold bullion bar cost approximately thirty-four thousand euro, but the Golden Icon would be worth considerably more. I estimate it to weigh about six kilos. But I know it is priceless.

Flicking through more websites and reading more accounts in historical archives I discover an account written by an Irish historian, Seamus Donnelly from Galway. He wrote to the Irish Government in nineteen twenty-nine to insist they demanded the return of the Golden Icon from the nuns. That was ten years before World War Two started. On further investigation, I read that the nuns and the Dutch government ignored the correspondence from Ireland and Seamus Donnelly died in nineteen thirty-one.

I fear I have come to a dead end until I trawl a Dutch newspaper and find an article in nineteen thirty-nine, stating Cardinal Giuseppe, on behalf of the Cellite Sisters, denied the Golden Icon was in the convent.

In the margin, I add *Irish government* to my list. Then *Dutch government* with a question mark.

Clara Fey, was born eighteen fifteen and died eighteen ninety-four, she started the Cellite Sisters with a few friends but it tells me nothing about the Golden Icon. I remember Dieter's story that a young orphan girl stole the Golden Icon from her Cardinal Uncle, and escaped from Ireland. And, I believe, that if this convent also acted as a hospital, it may be where the young girl died of Typhus. I don't know her name and I make a note to find out more, perhaps in historical archives or there may be an official record in the convent.

A few hours later I am still sitting on my terrace with the same question revolving in my head, round and round like a twirling baton; it goes up in the air and is tossed around and my logic fails me. I am getting nowhere.

Who does it belong to? I tap my pencil.

Michael, I think, why did you get into this mess? Was it for money? Are you really a thief? Are you just as greedy as your son and I never realised?

I look at my watch.

There may be one man who can help me.

I dress quickly, pick up my travel bag, lock the downstairs wooden communal door behind me and step into the street. The back steps lead down a narrow stone passageway directly to the quay, so I can avoid the fountain square where the locals and tourists gather in the early evening for a chilled glass of Prosecco.

Traffic is backed up on the main bend, and horns are hooting furiously. I dodge the cars and motorbikes, all heading south back to Milan. I hurry past the moored fishing boats, stepping over nets laid out in the sun and head toward the church.

Evening mass has ended and the congregation are making their way outside. The older widowed women still dress in black, young children rush into the sunlight, and couples nod and smile to neighbours.

The Mayor Angelo, shakes my hand, and when he turns away I ask his wife. 'How is Angelo feeling? Is he still off the alcohol?'

'Yes, and he's feeling much better for it,' she replies. Their children are running around and she calls them to her.

Santé from the farmacia grabs my elbow. 'Good luck for tomorrow,' she whispers.

Ingrid, wife of Dimitri, the village butcher smiles across the pews and waves. I raise my hand mouthing I will see her next week.

Paulino the young beauty therapist admonishes me. 'You forgot your appointment with me last Friday,' she complains. 'It was one of my busiest days.'

'I'm sorry, Paulino. I promise it won't happen again.'

'It's not like you,' she replies, then she is gone, sucked up in the crowd leaving church.

The aisle is empty. At the altar I pause to look at the Madonna, I bless myself and turn at the sound of a door opening.

'Padre Paolo?'

'Josephine.' He kisses me on both cheeks. He is dressed in his robes. 'How lovely to see you.'

'I need to speak to you, Padre.' My voice is tired and husky.

'Should you not be at home resting for tomorrow?'

'I'm flattered you remember my audition.'

His brown eyes narrow in concern and he smiles generously. 'Come, let's sit here. You look tired.' He takes me gently by the elbow and leads me to a pew a few rows from the front. 'Is this comfortable or would you prefer the confessional?'

'No. That won't be necessary. Here is fine.' I clear my throat.

We sit for a few minutes silently. Patience is his virtue for it gives me time to think before I speak and I try to form my words carefully. 'Padre, have you ever heard of a Golden Icon?'

He blinks his eyelashes that are long and fair, then he stares into the distance. Not at the stained glass window behind the altar or at the Madonna in front of us but at the wooden lectern from where he speaks to the congregation.

'In what respect?'

'A Golden Icon that was made by the Vatican back in the eighteen hundreds to finance an Irish Rebellion against the English.'

'Is it important?'

'I wondered if there was some way I could find out?'

'It would perhaps be in the Vatican archives.'

'It would?'

'Of course. I believe all finances and treasures are recorded and itemised.'

'Oh, would it be that simple to find out?'

'Perhaps…'

'Padre I have an audition tomorrow and then, after that there will be rehearsals. It will only be three weeks until the opening night at the beginning of August, so I do not have much time.'

'Ah yes.'

I raise an eyebrow.

'Yes, you must focus on that,' he says. 'It is very important for you. You seem so much better now Josephine, than you were when you first arrived in Comaso. It seems a long time ago now, when did you come here?'

'Three years ago, and I am Padre, much better thanks to you, and to the church. You have been very supportive and given me the spiritual guidance I needed.'

'It was difficult when you first came here. They were dark days for you. The church is always here for you. So too, am I.'

'Thank you, Padre. Perhaps the church could help me now. Perhaps you might find the time in your busy schedule to make some enquiries for me?'

'I will do all I can to help you.'

'That would be wonderful, Padre, grazzi. You are very kind.'

'I do have a good friend. I could ask Padre Stefano. He is in the Vatican and the assistant to Cardinal…'

'That would be excellent.'

'Can you give me more information?' He sits with his hands folded in his lap. 'Do you have a description?' His eyes are soft and enquiring.

The marble Madonna is gazing down at me with curious eyes. Reaching down, I unzip the travel bag at my feet, remove the box and place it on my lap. The lid is torn and I hand it to Padre Paolo.

He weighs it in his hands, as I did. The linen cloth is tied loosely with the frayed string as it was in Munich, and when it falls away to reveal the Golden Icon, his expression doesn't change. He stares for a considerable time at the Madonna and at the young Jesus leaning on her legs. Then he holds the statue up toward the light and turns it in the palm of his hand. His eyes narrow as he studies the seal. A shaft of fading sunlight shines through the stained glass.

'Where did you get this?' His voice echoes between the strobes of moving rays.

'It belongs to a friend. He wants to know about its origins.'

'There are museums, curators and professionals. Why bring it to me?'

'Because you are a man of the cloth, Padre, I can trust you.'

In the silence of the church and the reflected awe of the statue I turn suddenly at the sound of quick heavy footsteps. Striding down the centre aisle toward us is the chief of police, Inspector Santiago Bareldo.

I grab the Golden Icon, wrap it irreverently, and thrust it into the box and into my bag, just as Santiago draws level with us. His face is long and narrow, his shoulders hunched. He has the same blue dolls eyes like his sister, Glorietta. He is her older brother.

My hands are shaking.

When I look up Santiago is staring at me.

'Dona Lavelle,' he says respectfully. 'I am surprised you are here. Should you not be resting?' His greeting is accompanied by a small bow. He is well aware of my rivalry with his sister both for the role of Tosca and for Raffaelle's affections.

'I am leaving now.' The bag is heavy on my arm as I negotiate my way from the pew into the aisle. 'Can I trust you, Padre?' I pause deliberately, 'to help me? Can I leave this matter in your confidence?'

'You have my complete trust. It is my pleasure Signora to be of assistance,' he replies.

Santiago looks from me, to him, and then to my bag. His eyes are watchful and I am not fooled by his half amused smile and his nonchalant stance.

Padre Paolo holds out a hand and when I offer him mine he raises it to his lips. Then he turns to Santiago. 'I suppose you are here to discuss the events of the procession next week, Inspector?'

I say farewell to them both and feel the heat of their eyes on my back but when I am half way to the door, Santiago's voice rings out.

'Good luck with your audition tomorrow, Dona Lavelle.'

'Thank you.' I continue walking. I do not turn around.

Outside on the church step I gaze across the lake. Dieter knew my name. He knew I was an opera singer. Padre Paolo is the second person to know I have the Golden Icon. It is a risk but one that I had to take. I won't have much time once the police go through Seán's documents and find out that he paid for my flight ticket to Munich. They will also find my letter.

Assuming that it was Maximilian, or his nephew who killed Seán I wonder how long it will take them to realise the Turner painting is a fake. What will they do next? Visit Dieter?

As I stand gazing at the scenic beauty before me, an awful realisation dawns, Karl Blakey knew I was going to Munich. He must wonder why.

CHAPTER FIVE

The noble army of Marytrs: praise thee.
The holy Church throughout all the world:
doth acknowledge thee;
Te Deum, Tosca

I am early for my audition. I am wearing a turquoise print dress, a gold necklace and pearl earrings. My hair is swept up in a chignon and I have added makeup to the shadows under my eyes.

Today is the day. I am excited, tense, nervous and my body is rushing with adrenaline.

In the majestic reception of the Teatro Il Domo, the life-size bronze statues that I saw from the ferry, along the edge of the glass foyer, are of operatic and music legends; Maria Callas, Plácido Domingo, José Carreras, Montserrat Caballé, Alfredo Kraus, Anne Sofie von Otter; there must be over fifty in total and although I was once amongst the best, I am not with them now.

Cesare is standing between a replica of Rudolf Moralt, and a young looking Keith Lockhart. When he sees me, he smiles, and pushes hair from his eyes. He walks quickly and I am reminded of a graceful gazelle with a long

87

mane; his arms are outstretched, his eyebrows knotted together over dark eyes.

'Josephine.' He takes me by the shoulders and kisses both cheeks. 'Thank goodness.'

'What's wrong?' I ask.

'The auditions are in the rehearsal studio.'

I raise an eyebrow. 'What is troubling you?'

He links his arm through mine but says nothing.

'Who is here?' I ask.

'Niccolo Vastano the theatre director; Dino Scrugli the producer, and Andrei Ferretti has just arrived.'

We walk as we talk. It is noisy, work men are making finishing touches to the building, carrying boxes, furniture, tool bags; singing, whistling and laughing. The opening night is one month away. Tosca opens on the third of August.

'Andrei has to be here.' My laugh sounds hollow. 'He is the conductor.'

'Yes, but he arrived with Glorietta.'

'I did not realise they were such good friends,' I say, feeling a surge of concern.

'They were invited to Glorietta's villa for lunch last week.' He looks sheepishly at me.

'I know, and she sang on her terrace for them,' I say. 'Raffaelle was there. She has tried to manipulate them all. Let's hope she hasn't succeeded.'

Cesare looks at me sideways and I squeeze his arm. The encouragement is as much for him as it is for me. Glorietta is determined to outshine me. In the past few years, since my decline, she has taken more pivotal roles and has become more revered for her performances. Her vivacious character makes her popular and she is sought after by theatres, directors, conductors and producers.

I do not tell Cesare that her photograph was on the front pages of every major magazine at the airport kiosks in Germany and Ireland, instead I block everything from my mind and focus.

I am Tosca. The role is mine. I will sing again for Michael.

We reach the door to the studio and I take a deep breath. I control my breathing, pushing my stomach down, and I lift my chest, my chin and square my shoulders.

Cesare stands aside to let me enter the room before him. 'Courage Josephine,' he whispers. 'Imagine in a few weeks when it is the opening night. Focus on that. Concentrate on your comeback.'

Inside the room a few people turn to stare at us.

'This audition process is demeaning,' I say to him, 'until four years ago they would have courted me like a patient young lover, persuading me to star in their productions, now I'm like a novice forced to sing in an audition pretending it is a matter of procedure.'

'Josephine?' A familiar voice greets me.

'Massimo, how delightful to see you,' I say happily.

Massimo Mallamo's hair is dyed. Once blond he is now reddish grey like a squirrel. We hug and kiss. My affection for him is genuine. We have shared many operas and many successes.

'How many times have we sung together?' he asks.

'I've lost count. Many, many times. The Paris Opera, the MET when I was the leading soprano in New York, and I think the last time was in Buenos Aires in the Teatro Colon.

'Yes, you are right, wasn't it Puccini's Turandot?' We stand smiling at each other and his hand remains on my waist as he greets Cesare and they shake hands.

'I also have to audition,' he whispers and shakes his head. 'This great tenor auditioning for the role of Mario Cavaradossi.'

'It has gone to Nico's head,' I reply. 'He's on a power drive.'

'Shush!' Cesare warns me.

Massimo laughs. 'It's good to see you Josephine. It's been too long.'

'I agree.' I am wondering if he will mention the unmentionable; my career demise and my breakdown on stage, and then as if reading my thoughts, he asks.

'Are you fully recovered?'

'What a lovely way to put it,' I smile. 'Yes, thank you. I am better. How is Mirium? And the children?'

'Good. Mirium grows plumper every day and the children are now adults. Stefano married last year.'

'Don't tell me you are a grandfather all ready?'

'Soon, very soon, in another few months.'

We both laugh.

'You look well,' he says.

His sincerity fills me with gratitude and I place my hand on his arm. 'Thank you.'

'The Italian air must suit you better than the German air?'

'I like the German air,' I reply. 'It was Guntar I had to get rid of. He became very controlling and demanding.'

'I hear he is like that with Angelina now.'

'His new protégé?'

'They say she will not last long with him.'

'He became insecure and bitter, and very jealous.'

'You went through a great deal. The press were very unfair to you. There was one particular reporter who stalked you—'

'Karl Blakey.'

'That's him. He was particularly brutal.'

'Yes, he's a weasel. I called the police and he never forgot that. He's a vengeful man.'

A door opens to the studio and I have a quick glimpse of a stage and then I hear the unmistakable voice of Glorietta singing, *Una voce poco fa*, Rosina's aria from the Barber of Seville.

She is note perfect.

When my name is called Massimo hugs me. 'You are still Tosca,' he whispers. 'No-one sings like you. Just remember that.'

'Thank you.'

As we enter the rehearsal studio Glorietta is stepping down from the stage. She is as dark as I am fair. Her blue eyes twinkle mischievously. I am pleased to say she is a heavier build than me, her hips are broad and her bust is large. Even though I am ten years her senior I am in better shape, and so I draw back my shoulders and stand taller.

Although we are rivals to the core. We remain civil and polite. She walks gracefully swinging her hips provocatively, and as she passes me, she whispers something but I don't hear her words. Instead I focus on the stage, the grand piano to the right and the audition panel who occupy the middle of the third row of seats.

Niccolo Vastano the theatre director has a trimmed beard. Dino Scrugli the producer is still small and fat, and

Andrei Ferretti the conductor has long and grey hair and he wears black, square glasses.

They all ignore me.

Cesare takes his place.

I remove copies of sheet music for the arias from my leather case. *Casta Diva* from Norma and *Vissi d'arte* from Tosca, and pass the music scores to Cesare.

Determined to take my time and control the audition, I walk slowly, gaining confidence as I stride to my place, at the centre of the stage. I like the familiarity that flows through me, my confidence soars and my heart races. I am where I belong. This is me. I am Tosca.

I have been singing in these roles with various orchestras and with different arrangements around the world. My vocal score is leather bound and marked with pencil. It was a present from Guntar, given to me when we first met, when I was awarded my scholarship in Frankfurt. It was a scholarship that Michael had arranged for me, one that Michael had paid for, and thinking of him, my concentration wavers.

'Still acting the diva,' Andrei Ferretti calls out.

I look up from my music score and smile back. 'It's hard to change *all* one's habits.' My voice rings out clear and confident and I smile.

'Have you changed at all?' asks Nico.

'But of course,' I reply. 'Only my voice is the same.'

Dino laughs.

'And if you decide you didn't like our production, or the wig we wanted you to wear, would you storm out?' Nico continues.

I look over at Cesare. He shakes his head and I turn back to the audition panel.

Golden Icon

'That only happened on one occasion and it wasn't a wig. They wanted me to wear a ridiculous mini skirt.'

'It was a modern production,' Nico replies.

'I didn't feel it was suitable for the role of Carmen.'

'And if you don't think our production is suitable?' Nico asks.

'I'm sure I will.'

'You also broke your contract.'

'My agent negotiated a way out with a clause in the contract.'

'He bribed the lawyers.' Nico folds his arms.

My mouth is dry. I pause and take a deep breath. 'It was a long time ago. Antonio Marx is no longer my agent.'

'Do you have an agent now?'

'For God's sake, is all this necessary? Let the lady sing.' An American accent cuts through our conversation. It is Dino Scrugli's production of Tosca and although he is almost sixty he looks nearer to forty. His hair is neatly cropped and his designer jacket casually scruffy.

'Go on then.' Nico waves his arm.

I smile at Dino, pleased to have his support. I have worked with him many times. We have been to receptions, galas, sponsored concerts, and private parties. Once we sailed on a yacht together around the Caribbean. There was a group of thirty on board and it had been a happy time in my life. I was famous and single. It was before my fall.

'Bene,' Cesare calls to me.

I compose myself, inhaling, pushing my lungs out and my stomach down, and my chest swells. My voice grows in confidence. *Casta diva* is a mezzo soprano. I am comfortable. My dramatic training is stirred. It is, as if I have never left the stage. I sing as if I am making my debut at the Royal Opera House with an adoring audience where I once received twelve curtain calls. I am aware of my gestures and filled with pleasure as I release the power of my voice. God's gift to me. I am soaring above them all. I am the voice. I am the airwaves. I am floating.

There is no applause.

My second aria, *Vissi d'arte* belongs to Tosca. It belongs to me. I expand my lungs and draw in air and lose myself. I am Tosca. I live the part; my lover Mario has been dragged to prison and I fight off the sexual advances of his captor, Baron Scarpia, the chief of police. When my lover is shot, I protest my fate to God. Having dedicated my life to art and love, tears fill my eyes. There is only one solution. I will kill myself. My final note expires.

Silence greets me.

I look toward Cesare and he nods back at me.

'Thank you, Signora Lavelle. We will be in touch.' Nico speaks but he doesn't look up.

Cesare holds my elbow and walks me down the steps. 'What was all that about?'

'Don't worry. It's just Nico being a prick!' I whisper. 'This new position has gone to his head.'

As we leave the stage Dino leans forward in his seat. He smiles and blows me a cheeky kiss. He was always an incorrigible flirt.

The following day I wake early. I drink herbal tea on the terrace and make a list of things I must do. I have slept well knowing my audition is over and I can do no more. Cesare believes they will decide quickly and notify us today. The rehearsals will begin immediately.

The opening night is under four weeks away. My diary is cleared to accommodate the rehearsals and press interviews. My agent, Carlotta Spitarzi has already telephoned. She is eager for me to meet her in Milan to discuss raising my image and profile, and to include pre-press interviews, magazine shoots and television appearances.

It reminds me of the past. When I was at my height of fame and I was in demand. Constantly busy. Always working. It prevented me from thinking. It stopped me dwelling on my past and the mistakes I made.

I write my list. I must contact Paulino the beauty therapist, shop for clothes, new shoes, makeup, hair appointment. The list is endless, and one that I haven't had to consider for a long time.

Before, in my previous life, I had a secretary, and a private chef in my home in Cologne. Now when I look around my apartment, I think that I may move from here, to somewhere more appropriate to entertain as I did before.

I make a list of guests I would like to invite.

Dino is first on my list. Andrei the conductor only asked if I was still acting the diva, after that, he didn't speak to me at all at the audition. We always worked well together but perhaps he is sceptical of my comeback. I wonder if he is courting Glorietta. Maybe she has manipulated him with her vivacious charm.

There are other names on my list; film stars, celebrities, actors, producers and conductors who I am keen to contact again. It has been too long. I have spent enough time in the wilderness. It is time for me to return with style, grace, humour and charm.

My day passes slowly.

I begin my daily ritual. I vocalise. I spend several hours working my vocal cords and scales, regulating my pitch and tone, and I look through music scores. In the afternoon I play the piano but as the day goes on I become more restless. I must make my comeback. It has to be now. Michael would be proud of me. He would want me to focus on this.

Cesare has been patient and kind but also ruthless and unrelenting. The past years have been a struggle and the past few weeks have been exhausting. Daily rehearsals, practising, honing and working. He has been my companion and my rock.

I am Tosca. I will sing for Michael. It will be my way of saying thank you. After the years of neglect. I must make it up to him. He is with me. I carry him in my broken heart.

It is a tragedy that he will not see me revive my career. He would be pleased and proud of me. In the years of my decline, I did not return his calls and I am filled with sadness and deep regret that I did not speak to him and that I did not hear his voice one last time. He would have been here for my opening night. Perhaps if I had seen him again, one last time, we may have laid some ghosts to rest.

It is only a week ago that I was rehearsing in church when Seán telephoned. It seems an eternity but I cannot think of the Golden Icon. I am restless. I wander from the terrace to the living room and check that my bag is wedged beside the pedals of the piano. I am hoping Padre

Paolo will have news for me soon and I can relax and rehearse in peace.

I wander onto the terrace and back again to the lounge. I imagine curtain calls, cheers of 'bravo' and 'encore' but I have to wait until late afternoon for the phone call.

And when my mobile does ring my heart skips.

A blackbird settles on the branches of the horse chestnut tree swaying in the breeze. He preens, in bright sunlight, pecking his chest with his yellow beak. He has a nest in the tree hidden by foliage. I take deep breath, savouring the moment of anticipation. My hand is shaking.

'It's not good news,' Cesare says by way of greeting.

'Glorietta?'

'Yes, she got the part of Tosca. But it was a good audition, Josephine, you sang well.'

'It was a fake.'

'Don't be too disappointed. There are other opportunities.'

'They wanted her. She manipulated them.'

'They want the right woman.'

'They wanted to humiliate me.'

'They wanted to hear you. You haven't sung in public for over three years. You were a success yesterday,' Cesare adds, 'You must be proud of your performance.'

'Maybe I'm not at that level any more.' I wrap my arm around my waist. 'I have worked so hard. I wanted it so badly. I thought I would open the Theatre Il Domo.'

'You deserve to sing in the theatre, and you will one day. It's just that Glorietta has the advantage.'

'She invited them all to dinner. She influenced them. I didn't stand a chance.'

'It was your first audition. Carlotta still wants to take you on. She's a good agent. She will find you the right roles.'

'I wanted to sing Tosca,' I whisper. 'The role is mine.'

'You will sing it one day and perhaps in the theatre. There will be other performances.'

'Not if Nico is the director.'

'It's gone to his head. You said it yourself.'

'This isn't about Nico. I wasn't good enough.'

Cesare inhales a deeply. 'We will not stop here, Josephine. This is just the start. I mentioned your name to Simone, and he wants you to record with the Philharmonic.'

Tears fall down my cheeks.

The blackbird flies away.

'Dino wanted you. I think he will do something next year. He mentioned Bellini's Norma. He likes you.'

I brush my hand across my face and pull a few strands of hair into the clip on my head. 'And Andrei? Did he say anything?'

'No.'

'Is he having an affair with Glorietta?'

'No. He's married and has three children.'

'Well, he will. He always sleeps with the leading lady.' There is silence between us and I realise my confession.

Cesare coughs politely.

'It was a long time ago,' I say.

'We must move on Josephine,' he sighs dramatically. 'Please. Let me come with you to Milan. Let's go and meet Carlotta Spitarzi. She is very good. She has the press lined up to speak with you about your comeback and she can change the angle of the interviews.'

I sniff.

'Josephine, don't cry. I am here for you. Call me later if you need me.'

I turn off the phone and throw it onto the table. My tears taste bitter. The dream to revive my career is over. Shattered like a broken mirror. I am an ageing, fading opera singer who once owned the world. I grab a handful of sheet music and throw it across the floor where it lands in crumpled piles, pages bent and twisted against the terrace wall.

I sit for a long time with my head in my hands. Sometimes my mind is blank and at other times I am on stage in costume under the glow of the lights. I feel the expectant hush of the audience. At the end of the performance they call my name, or 'bravo', and I remember all the curtain calls in Mexico, Italy, China and Germany.

As darkness falls, yellow lights from the villages across the lake twinkle teasingly like spotlights on a stage, one that I will no longer tread.

When I gaze up at the night-sky stars glisten like diamonds set in purple velvet and I wonder if they are the eyes of the dead staring down on me.

I open a bottle of Prosecco and drink it on the terrace, toasting the silent stars, the dead twinkling eyes, and the teasing stage footlights. I raise my glass to them all, drinking until my face is blotchy and my eyes are swollen. My body is heavy and lethargic and pains in my shoulder and neck have given me a headache.

On impulse I open my laptop. Perhaps Cesare made a mistake and Dino has sent me an email offering me the role.

There is an email from William with the details of Seán's funeral tomorrow. I think of the church in Ireland and of Michael's coffin. Now it is Seán's turn. He was once my husband and I think of how our lives could have turned out so differently. How things may have changed had we made other choices and how our paths lead us blindly into an abyss called the future.

I am filled with loss. All the people who mattered to me I have lost. This is my fate. It has turned on me. I am being repaid for my past mistake. For my secret. For my lies.

My fingers are too big for the keys. It takes time but I order a wreath of lilies to be sent to Monkstown church. I see Michael's coffin before the altar and Seán standing at the golden lectern, his foot in plaster, speaking proudly of his father's bravery during the war. How he saved lives. He never mentioned Michael was a thief.

Seán's dead. Michael's dead.

I think of Seán grabbing my throat when I tried to snatch my letter from him. Who, and how many, have read it since? Where is it? Then I think of Karl Blakey taunting me in the deserted Dublin street.

I imagine Glorietta's sparkling smile and her opening night on stage at the Teatro Il Domo. Her round blue eyes twinkling. Television cameras, the President, the curtain calls. Clapping and cheering. Then she is backstage receiving congratulations, flowers and gifts. Journalists, television crews from around the world and music critics from *Corriere della Sera* all praising her performance.

'Hail the new darling of the opera world,' I say aloud. My voice is slurred. I imagine the journalist's questions: What is it like to take the role from Josephine Lavelle? Will you and Raffaelle now get back together? Are you still in love with him?

I tap the computer keys and select a large and expensive bouquet of flowers. It is the right thing to do.

This is what matters now. It's about doing the right thing for the Golden Icon, for Glorietta.

Add a note? The screen prompts. I type in.

Congratulations Tosca. Every man's life is a fairy-tale written by God's fingers.

'Payment to your account?' Suggests the website

My finger hovers over the key. I brush a strand of hair from my eyes. My head thumps; a dull and persistent ache and my throat feels sore. A strangled cry escapes my lips and I slam the lid closed.

CHAPTER SIX

When thou hadst overcome the sharpness of death:
thou didst open the Kingdom of Heaven to all believers.
Te Deum, Tosca

Two weeks later.

It is Monday afternoon and I am sitting on the deck of
the slow ferry leaving Como enjoying the breeze against
my skin. I can barely look at the majestic Teatro Il Domo
as we pass. The crystal dome shimmers and reflects
colourful lights into the soft blue sky and I imagine
Glorietta and Andrei rehearsing for the opening night this
Saturday. I believe I can even hear the orchestra playing
Vissi de arte. I imagine Andrei's impatience as he taps his
baton irritably against the music stand, pushing his glasses
on his nose, calling the orchestra to order, the heat of the
stage lights, the smell of stage paint, and Glorietta's
radiant self-possessed smile.

She has been on every cover, of every important
magazine. Her superior smile has followed me from
bookstands to kiosks, to newsagents, and I have stopped
watching television for fear of having to watch another
report of her successful career.

The familiar villages along the lake, Moltrasio, Urio and Brienno, and on the far side, Torno, Careno and Nesso arouse in me my love for my adopted home and settle my sadness and anxiety. White clouds bubble over the Alps spreading wispy cirrus tails across the sky. Overhead a sea plane flies low before ascending high and over the forest covered hills.

This is a world far away from private yachts, planes, chauffeurs and mansions, where I was cared for by softly trodden staff who, for fear of disturbing my rest, whispered in corridors. That was another life. A life filled with music; operas in Edinburgh, Florence, Barcelona and Athens. I was booked up to two years in advance; for Liù in Turandot, Cio-Cio San in Madame Butterfly, and Mimì in La bohème.

Now I am a nobody.

I spent the morning in Milan with Cesare and my new agent Carlotta, who isn't nearly as enthusiastic as she was when she thought I would get the role of Tosca. Instead of feeling energised and optimistic I am resigned to my fate. Since I am no longer Tosca, I have diverted my energies to the ownership of the Golden Icon. I am determined to return it to its rightful owner and make amends for Michael's actions.

After my meeting today, I spent a few unproductive hours searching for information on the Golden Icon in the Brera Art Gallery. What possessed me to go there I am not sure, probably because it is two streets from Carlotta's office, and I wasn't in a hurry to get home.

But it is like my visits to the library. Each time I arrive at a brick wall. There are no facts, no details and almost no knowledge of the valuable statue but it is listed as being lost or destroyed in the war.

I have spent valuable hours scouring the internet, and I fear that the Italian Art Squad dedicated to the recovery of stolen artwork may discover that it is in my possession.

Perhaps I should hand it over to the *Comando Carabinieri per la Tutela del Patrimonio Culturale.* The website of the Art Squad and modern day Monuments Men, informs me that they deal with 'the theft and illicit trade in works of art,' and 'the illegal export of cultural property, and fakes,' as well as monitoring 'the activities of art and antique dealers, junk shops, and restorers,' but I hold back, because deep down, I want it to belong to Michael. Perhaps it should belong to his heirs.

I am hoping that I will find evidence to suggest that he didn't steal it. That he was the honourable man I knew, and that it has all been a terrible mistake.

But I am concerned. I keep reminding myself only two people know I have it: Dieter and Padre Paolo. I am terrified I will get caught with it in my possession and more dangerously, what if Maximilian goes in search of Dieter the only other man remaining alive out of the four young soldiers and finds out that it is in my possession?

Padre Paolo has been an enigma to me. I have visited or telephoned him constantly and each time he begs me to be patient. His good friend and assistant to the Cardinal, Padre Stefano has been posted abroad but he is due to arrive back in Rome this weekend. In precisely five days' time.

Each day I scour the newspapers online in Ireland and Germany scanning websites to see if there is any news or developments on Seán's murder. If there are any suspects or if the Turner was announced as a fake. I also check to make sure there is no news of Dieter in Munich's newspapers. He instilled a fear in me that I know is unreasonable but the fact that Seán died so soon after his warning about Maximilian has scared me and has made me fear for Dieter's life.

The shade of the boat's canopy provides welcome relief from the intense sun. I am exhausted and need a shower to revive my weary body.

It is late afternoon when I arrive in Comaso. The fountain in the square is spurting water and a few teenagers sit precariously on the edge. One boy splashes the dress of a girl. She flicks her blond hair and laughs before dipping her fingers into the water and splashing him back. He pulls her hand, dabs cold water on the tip of her nose before pressing his lips laughingly to hers.

I am absorbed with their youth and vitality. Their teasing humour is contagious, my heart feels lighter and my mouth spreads into a grin.

Carlo the manager of the small Alberge is clearing a table of debris. When he smiles he reveals crooked teeth. 'Josephine? Come and have a glass of Prosecco.'

'Another time, Carlo,' I call out. 'Milan has exhausted me. Perhaps tomorrow?'

'You just missed Raffaelle,' he calls.

I wave. I will telephone Raffaelle after a shower.

At the fountain the laughing boy has soft grey eyes, the teenage girl with the blond hair is Sandra, Santiago's daughter, Glorietta's niece. I know she recognises me. I smile but she turns quickly away.

Mario sits under the shade of a beige umbrella at the bodeguita. He is drinking coffee with Angelo the Mayor of Comaso and Santiago. Angelo and Mario raise their hands and smile. Santiago watches me and I feel his gaze on my legs. My heels clip across cobbles past crowded tables and from behind my sunglasses I give one last sweeping glance of the terrace and my heart misses a beat. My step falters. Karl Blakey looks out of place in this sun-filled village in a brown shirt and cotton jacket. He is hidden in a corner beside the wall. A shiver slides down my spine. I hurry past Georgio's pizzeria, past the gelateria and run up the steps. I am almost sprinting. I reach the corner and hear my name.

'Josephine! Josephine!' Raffaelle's voice is powerful and insistent. He is standing in the door way of the gelateria. He beckons me to him, and reluctantly I retrace my steps.

Karl doesn't move.

Raffaelle is standing with a cone in his hand and he licks the melting ice cream running down his finger. Over his shoulder, Santiago sits motionless. His head is tilted in my direction.

'There is chocolate on your moustache.'

'Lick it off,' he whispers.

I want to laugh. I want to play around like Sandra and the boy at the fountain but I remain rigid and cold. My hands are clammy and my blouse is sticking to my skin.

'I came to meet you from the ferry. How was Milan? How was Carlotta?' He kisses my cheek.

'You're not here for the ice cream?' I tease. I am determined that neither Karl Blakey nor Santiago will see they have affected me.

'Let me buy one for you.' He puts his arm around my waist and pulls me into his arms. His moustache tickles my neck. Inside the gelateria I admire the ice creams neatly laid out in labelled tubs and I am pleased Raffaelle's hand remains possessively on my hips. He makes me feel safe and secure.

'So many flavours,' I sigh.

'You will have peppermint, cara, I know you will. You always have the same.'

I read the tags aloud, 'Pistachio, mint, caramel…'

'Try the lemon,' suggests Nano, who stands with the scoop in one hand and a cone in the other.

'Hurry, or I will want another one,' Raffaelle jokes.

'This is a serious business,' I reply. 'It takes careful selection.'

Nano nods in agreement.

I take my time. I am frightened to step back into the square.

'Peppermint,' I say, and I feign surprise when the two men burst out laughing. I take the cone wrapped in a small serviette and relish the cool mint on my tongue.

I spend a few minutes chatting to Nano, delaying our exit, but when more customers arrive we head outside into the sunlight.

Karl Blakey has gone.

Perhaps I imagined him.

Sitting at his table in the shade are two foreign women dressed in skimpy vests with tanned skin.

I feel Santiago's eyes watching me, as I walk arm in arm, with Raffaelle up the steps toward my apartment. It may have been a trick of the light. Perhaps it wasn't Karl, I reason, but what if it was?

It is a steep climb. Raffaelle is panting as we arrive and I pat his stomach affectionately. 'You should spend more time at my apartment. It would do you good.'

'That is why I like you to come to my villa. It is beside

the harbour, there are no hills, and I don't waste valuable energy climbing all these steps.' He winks. I check the postbox on the wall. There are four yellow boxes. I am hoping there may be a note from Padre Paolo but there is no mail for me. I unlock the communal door. It is heavy and secure. The entrance is decorated with flowers and the patio is filled with the sweet aroma of jasmine.

We walk up a short flight of steps, past a security grill which I never bother to lock and I open the door. My apartment is in darkness. The ground floor is littered with an assortment of shoes and sandals and hooks of jackets and coats. As I walk along the corridor I close the door to the laundry room, and we climb the narrow stairs to the living room where I throw open the shutters, welcoming the breeze that comes in across the water.

Raffaelle unpacks a grocery bag that he brought from his villa. He puts cheese in the fridge and takes out a chilled bottle of Prosecco.

'I want to hear about Milan,' he calls, as I head upstairs.

I strip and shower quickly, then with wet hair and a cotton gown covering my naked body I wander outside onto the terrace where Raffaelle sits listening to Vivaldi's *Four Seasons*.

I place my feet on the chair opposite me, the nail polish on my toes is chipped, and I think I will leave it until tomorrow to remove.

Raffaelle's voice is soft. 'So? Any news?'

'No, but Carlotta seems to have good contacts.'

'Is she optimistic?'

'Yes.' I don't tell him that it is me, who isn't.

He nods and gazes across the lake.

'Any news on your exhibition?' I ask.

'I'm not sure they liked the paintings. They are from the old school. I think Van Gogh holding a mobile phone to his missing ear and a microwave beside Galileo, and a Caravaggio illuminated by spotlights, put them off,' he smiles. 'I think it was too surrealist for them.'

'Or too imaginative,' I add. 'I like them.'

We gaze out across the lake. Since the day I returned from Germany I have avoided talking about the Golden Icon. I haven't forgotten that Raffaelle didn't take me seriously. Besides I now believe it is my private quest. It is up to me to find out to whom it belongs. I also want to clear Michael's name.

So I don't mention my trip to the Brera Art Gallery, or my anxiety at waiting for news from Padre Paolo, or the fact that I think I saw Karl Blakey in the square a few minutes ago, or even, that I felt Santiago watching me.

'Have you heard from Glorietta?' I ask. 'I saw Sandra today. She was with a boy beside the fountain.'

He sips his Prosecco and looks out across the lake and seems to choose his words. 'I spoke to Sandra, she said she hadn't seen Glorietta. She is too busy with the rehearsals.' He says nothing more so I prompt.

'Who was the boy with her?'

'Alonso, Luigi's cousin's son. He says the boy is impossible. He doesn't want to study. He wants to be a shepherd and he's happy in the hills all day surrounded by sheep.'

'No news about how the rehearsals are going?'

'No,' he answers too quickly and I know he is lying to me.

It is still dark when I wake. The storm has passed and a chill wind comes in through the window. Raffaelle's body is tucked in to mine and his arm is heavy across my stomach. I snuggle further into his embrace, he half wakes and pulls me closer. His breath is full of sweet, stale Prosecco. I kiss his lips, pull on his moustache and he smiles sleepily. I wonder what he is dreaming.

There are no curtains at the bedroom window. Across the lake lights, from the villages on the far side of the water, twinkle back at me and the moon leaves a strip of shimmering light. I pull on my cotton robe, close the bedroom door and pad downstairs in bare feet.

In the living room I remove the cloth that covers my piano. I open my travel bag and remove the photograph. I spend a few minutes studying the faces in the faded picture of the four young British soldiers and think of how destiny and fate led their paths to cross and of the opportunity and risk they all took. I lean it against the book spines on the shelf.

Outside, under the starlit sky, I brush rain puddles from the chair and place the shoe box on the table.

I sit for a while thinking.

I know I will do the right thing. This is important to me. I missed my opportunity the last time but now, things are different, I have changed.

I am no longer Tosca.

Not this time. Not ever. I must look for another opera, perhaps something less ambitious and more low-key, or maybe I should return to Germany and sing some lieder or folksongs, or record some classical pop in London or Spain. Monserrat Caballé became very popular when she sang the duet *Barcelona* with Freddy Mercury. Perhaps I have to rethink my opportunities. Singing is my life. I was born to sing. It is my art, my passion, my life.

I will find myself.

Eventually sunlight eases over the hillside, rippling and shining like silk, and I marvel at the hues of purples, pinks and cerise that cast multiple shadows over the mountain. The sun is warm and I open the shoe box. It is the first time I have looked at the Golden Icon since I was in the church with Padre Paolo, over two weeks ago.

I need to look at it. I need to reassure myself that this has all happened.

Michael is dead. Seán is dead.

Karl Blakey has made me afraid. I need to be reminded of the beauty of the Golden Icon; its value and my responsibility.

I think of Dieter Guzman in Munich and his voice echoes in my head.

How did Michael die?

I pull my cotton gown tighter across my breasts, lift the lid of the tattered box, curl the frayed string into a ball and lift the golden statue. The Madonna's face is untroubled. Her downcast eyes are filled with sympathy, pain and love, and I scrutinise each feature. She knows the destiny of her son but she cannot help his fate.

My heart lurches.

The simplicity and detail is magnificent.

Sunlight catches its golden glow, yet it is cold against my fingers, and I trace the base underneath and read the papal seal.

Research has led me round in a small circle. I have discovered that the Vatican was concerned about the situation in Ireland. Pope Pius VIII signed his approval but it was the Cardinal and his wealthy merchant friends who really wanted the support of the Catholics. The Golden Icon was sculptured by an Italian goldsmith, Miguel Brindisi, a Spanish-Italian who lived in Rome and who had studied Michaelangelo's *The Madonna of Bruges*. That is as far as I could get with my research.

I am relying on information from Padre Paolo, and his contact Padre Stefano and I need it urgently. Perhaps I should telephone him and remind–

'Madre de dio.'

I turn quickly. I have been so engrossed in the Golden Icon that I haven't heard Raffaelle's footsteps, only his exclamation behind me. He stands in boxer shorts and bare feet, and holds out his hand.

'What is this?'

'The Golden Icon,' I reply. The seconds stretch into minutes until I press the statue into his palms making sure not to drop it.

His eyes screw up and he examines every detail as I have done. He has the eye of a painter and of an artist. His fingers trace the contours of the Madonna's face, the folds in her skirt, her hands, and eventually the face and legs of baby Jesus. He exhales loudly and his moustache vibrates.

'Is this a Cellini? No, no it is not ornate enough and it is a little later after 1550. Perhaps it is one of his pupils, in 1700 or maybe even 1800?'

'Cellini?'

'One of Italy's finest goldsmiths but he was also a sculptor and painter. He studied with Florence's famous goldsmiths. You must have heard of the Cellini Salt Cellar that he made for King Francis the first of France? They call him the Mona Lisa of Sculpture. It says on the base here 1829, perhaps it is a Miguel Brindisi?'

'It is.'

He looks at me. 'Why did you tell me you left it in a locker in Munich?'

'You didn't believe me when I came back from Germany and I was angry.'

'But - but this is priceless.' He sits and folds his arms.

Inside the kitchen I prepare rich, dark coffee and heat milk. The aroma fills the kitchen and floods though the apartment. Out of the back window I look up the valley where a new development of four burgundy-coloured villas are juxtaposed between several older palazzos and an apartment block. Bulldozers have made a clearing through the trees where a cluster of new homes will be built with a swimming pool and lake view. Beside them a narrow path from the car park leads through the forest, to where the old church of the Madonna of the Miracles is hidden, the Chiesa della Madonna dei miracoli. It is one of my favourite places. Undiscovered like a hidden jewel. It is like the Golden Icon tranquil and calm.

I place cups, coffee, bread, honey and butter on a tray and slices of fresh oranges and carry it outside.

Raffaelle watches me. Birds are chattering, there's the hum of morning traffic, the slam of a dustbin lid, and the barking of a dog.

He spoons sugar into his mug. His dark eyes, lit by sunlight, make him look young, happy and excited.

'You've had it for two weeks and never told me?' he laughs.

'Yes.'

'Cara, this is fantastic.' His voice is low and urgent. 'This will change our lives. We will be free. We can move to Florence. We will be wealthy.' He waves his arms. He is warming to his theme. 'It is what we have always wanted, no? It will be a new beginning for us. We can revive our careers. We will be in Florence amongst the greatest artists and singers.

'I will not have to give lessons to students. I can be with those who want to learn, whose passion in life is art, instead of putting up with silly children in Como who have no appreciation of beauty.

'We can buy a house overlooking the river. It will have a room where you can sing and you can perform all the great operas. You will be appreciated and adored by all your fans again, and I will buy you a Steinway.' I want to touch the laughter lines around his crinkled eyes. 'And my art will be appreciated. I will have exhibitions. All the artists will be there,' he laughs. 'They will be jealous of my success and envious of my achievements just as they were laughing at my failure. They will embrace me. Raffaelle Peverelli the most interesting and adventurous artist. You will sing and I will paint.'

'How will we do this?' I ask.

'It's simple. We will sell this. It is worth a fortune.' He holds it out in front of me. 'This is a replica of the marble statue by Michaelangelo, the *Madonna of Bruges* that he sculptured around 1500. It was notable for being the only sculpture to leave Italy during Michaelangelo's lifetime, once when Napoleon ordered it to be packed up and sent to France and the second time when Nazis were smuggling all the artwork to Germany.

'There were a group of men during the war who

tracked the stolen art. They recovered works by Rembrandt, Vermeer and Da Vinci. I believe that *Comando Carabinieri per la Tutela del Patrimonio Culturale*, is a result of these Monuments Men.'

'The Italian Art Squad,' I agree, 'they must know about the Golden Icon and they must be looking for it too?'

'It is one of the biggest police departments in the world set up to counter art and antique thefts.' He strokes his moustache thoughtfully.

'I Googled it on the internet. Would they know about the Golden Icon?' I insist, 'I spoke to a professor at Milan University. I even went to the Brera Museum and spoke to the curator, but there is no information about the Golden Icon, all the records seem to indicate that if it did exist then it was destroyed or went missing during the war. Presumably stolen from a convent in Holland.'

'It has been stolen but now it belongs to us. Will we begin a new future? We can begin again in Florence.'

'And what about your villa here in Comaso?'

'You know that I cannot sell it. That was the terms and conditions in my uncle's Will when he left it to me, he said it must be passed on to my eldest son.'

'Alberto?'

'Sí, Alberto will inherit it but I have left a condition in my Will that his mother may not live in it.'

'And your daughter?'

He shrugs. 'She will have to marry well or continue living with her mother in Bergamo.' He reaches for my fingers and places them to his lips. 'Will we go to Florence?'

After his sensual kiss I cannot pretend I am not tempted by the idea.

'It does not belong to us,' I whisper.

'The villa? We have spoken about this before. Alberto must inherit it.'

'I mean, the Golden Icon.'

'Of course it belongs to you. It is here on your table, no?'

'But it is not mine.'

'So who does it belong to?'

'I have to find out.'

'You said, you went to Munich to get it for Seán, but Seán is dead. So it is yours.'

I flinch. 'What about Barbara? Or Michael's heirs?'

'It doesn't belong to Barbara,' he says. 'You say, Michael stole it during the war. He was a thief.'

I swallow the surge of anger that swells in me, and speak slowly and deliberately. 'I must find out who it belongs to.'

'Listen to me. It is one of those pieces of art that belongs to the person in whose possession it rests. There are many dealers and collectors throughout the world. Please don't assume that each piece they buy and sell is paid for legally or even at the right price. Sometimes it is not paid for at all. It is stolen to order. A sculpture like this can never be owned. It is a work of art to be exhibited. If we don't sell it, someone else will. Who do you think owns it, if it's not you?'

'The Church?'

'Blah! The Church?'

'The Vatican.'

'The Church is too wealthy, besides they would lock it away inside the Vatican and no-one would see it again.'

'According to Dieter it was made in Rome and then

sent to fund an Irish rebellion against the British. Dieter mentioned the Catholic Relief Act, so I Googled it and it said that this Act disenfranchised the minor landholders of Ireland. This Act meant it raised, fivefold, the economic qualifications for voting…'

'So?'

'The Vatican wanted the support of the Catholics. They were ready to fund a rebellion in 1828 so they would be able to rely on them in the future. So maybe it belongs to the Irish people,' I say. 'It was made for them.'

Raffaelle looks doubtful. 'Maybe it was created to fund their revolution but it didn't happen, and the icon came back to Europe. Now it belongs here in Italy.'

I smile at his simplistic logic. 'Maybe it does belong to Barbara and the children. It will pay Seán's debts. Perhaps I should contact her?'

'An artwork as beautiful as this should not be used as a pawn to pay for a greedy builder's empire. It needs to be appreciated and to be seen. It has lain hidden for generations and it must be on show. We must sell it.'

'Barbara could sell it and it would go to a museum in Ireland,' I argue.

'It belongs in Italy. Here in my country if you obtain artwork you can keep it.'

'Only if you obtain it legally,' I say and he looks surprised. 'I have spent two weeks looking for information. I Googled it. In America, for example, the stolen artwork returns to the original owners even if the new owner obtained it legally, but I didn't get this legally.'

'But it is still yours,' he counters.

'What about William?'

'Who?'

'Seán's brother, William. He is Michael's other son. It did belong to Michael.'

'No, no, no, Michael stole it. It belongs to whoever possesses it.' He holds his arms wide. 'Be reasonable.'

'It does not belong to us. That would be stealing.'

'It is not stealing.'

I hold up my palm. 'Perhaps we should give it…?'

'Give? Why give it? There are many museums or collectors who would pay a handsome price for a rarity such as this. This is priceless, cara. This is something so special it must be on show and appreciated. We can sell it! Why are you so stubborn?'

'It is not mine to sell.' My voice rises. I move to the corner of my terrace where I can look down onto the street below. The smell of freshly baking bread wafts up from the bakery below.

Raffaelle stands behind me and wraps his arms around my waist. He kisses my ear and I lean back against him, feeling his warmth, security and love. 'You and me,' he whispers, 'in Florence. The most beautiful city in the world. We can live our dream together. I will get a divorce and we can marry.'

I feel my body stiffen and I turn from his embrace. 'I must wait and see what Padre Paolo says.'

'Padre Paolo?'

'Yes, I took the icon to him. He said he has a friend in the Vatican, Padre Stefano. He has been away but he is due back this weekend. He said he will help me find out who it belongs to.'

'You showed the Golden Icon to Padre Paolo and not to me? I can't believe you would do that.' He moves away. 'How could you do that? You trust Padre Paolo more than you trust me?'

'He was the only person I could think of…'

'The only person?'

'Yes.'

'And do you think I know nothing about Italian art?'

'It is not about art. It's about the church.'

'But you cannot trust Padre Paolo,' he says, 'he and Santiago are best friends. I don't believe you have been so stupid!' He turns his back to me and walks away.

'He is a man of God,' I argue.

Raffaelle laughs cynically. 'If Padre Paolo knows about the Golden Icon then believe me, the chief of police knows too. Did you not know that Paolo and Santiago went to school together, and that they feed information one to the other? That's how Santiago controls the area and knows what's going on. Did you not know that?'

I shake my head.

'Even the confessional isn't safe.' He runs his hand through his hair and turns to me. 'I don't believe this. It's just a matter of time until that police inspector comes knocking on your door. Santiago will want the Golden Icon. He will make it a police matter. He will come for it.'

I think of Santiago in the square. We both look over to the table to where the golden Madonna and her son glistens in the sunlight.

'It is stolen,' he says. 'It is a crime. You could be arrested. Imagine the newspapers. The headlines. You could go to prison.'

I grip the terrace railing and close my eyes. He is right. Not only do I not have the role of Tosca but I could be arrested for having stolen property; a valuable golden statue.

What am I thinking? What was Michael thinking?

Why haven't the police in Dublin who have been searching through Seán's documents found my letter? Have they evidence of my flight to Munich? They must wonder why I went there. What would I say?

My career may no longer be at its pinnacle but Seán was right. The press would still be interested in my downfall.

Had it been Karl Blakey in the village or was I mistaken?

I am suffocating. Although it is early, it is suddenly very warm. There is no air and I tug my cotton gown apart to feel a breeze on my chest. My mouth is dry and a trickle of perspiration meanders to my waist. I reach to wipe it with my fingers and I glance into the street below.

Looking up at me is Karl Blakey.

I gasp.

I duck back out of sight. I swallow hard. My heart is beating rapidly. I wait a few seconds and when I look again, he is gone.

'I think I am being followed,' I say to Raffaelle over my shoulder. I have to tell him. I fear now that things are closing in on me. I have been living on borrowed time but now I will be held to account. Padre Paolo is taking too long. I must do something.

Raffaelle stands beside me peering over the railing, and I think how ridiculous he looks in his shorts with his mass of dark chest hair and pale skin. 'Who would follow you?' he asks.

'He's a journalist,' I say, once I have controlled my breathing. 'I have just seen him down there in the street. His name is Karl Blakey. He was in the square when you met me from the ferry yesterday but I wasn't sure if it was definitely him.'

'Do you think he knows about the Golden Icon?' Raffaelle tugs his moustache. 'Is that why you think he is following you?' He is scanning the empty path below.

'I don't know,' I reply. 'He knows that Seán asked me to go to Munich but I don't think Seán would have told him why. He didn't want anyone to know about his family heirloom.'

'How do you know this journalist?'

'He wrote about me many years ago. He stalked me. He was determined to rake over my life and he treated me like a rotting corpse, picking over my bare bones, printing the smallest details, telling outrageous lies and sensationalising my decline.'

'We all make mistakes. Do not worry. He has nothing more to print about you now. There is no more scandal.'

I think of my letter to Michael and its contents, and the effect and repercussion that it could still have, but I remain silent. Now is not the time to confess my past. I will block it out and hide it away from my conscience as I have done all these years. I will focus on only doing the right thing. Finding the rightful owner of the Golden Icon, and in that way, I hope, I may clear Michael's name and finally make amends for my past.

'He could find out that the stolen Golden Icon is in my possession. It is only one of the world's greatest priceless treasures.' My tone is sarcastic. 'I would not under estimate Karl again.'

'Let's sell it.' He turns to me. 'Let's go now to Florence. I have a friend who will help us. He can be trusted. We can start a new life together.'

'Dieter said anyone who used the Golden Icon for their own means came to a bad end. They either died or were killed.'

'Pouff, this is crazy. He said it, to frighten you.'

'Even Michael never wanted to use it for his own gain. That is why he kept it hidden. He was afraid. It was only when Seán was going bankrupt and he was desperate for money that Michael began looking for someone to buy it, and Maximilian found out, and now look at what has happened to them. They're both dead.'

'It is a coincidence.'

'I must find out who it belongs to.' I begin wrapping the statue in the dirty linen with the frayed string. 'I must do this or I will never be able to live with myself.'

'You are making a mistake.'

'I don't trust Karl Blakey. My apartment is not safe I must hide the Golden Icon.' My body is shaking. I know the danger involved.

'Josephine, listen to me…'

'I have a good idea where I can hide it. Will you come with me?'

CHAPTER SEVEN

Thou sittest at the right hand of God:
In the glory of the Father.
We believe that thou shalt come: to be our judge.
Te Deum, Tosca

It is barely six o'clock. We throw on our clothes and leave
immediately taking advantage of the quiet early morning.
As I lock my apartment, church bells toll across the valley
and a donkey brays a greeting.

Raffaelle's footsteps and panting breath follow me. We
climb past the felled trees and the palazzos, and an
apartment block where an early swimmer stands under
the outdoor shower. We cross the car park and take the
narrow trail through the fir trees. The smell of rain in the
forest is damp and musky, the path is stained by rivulets of
mud and I taste moisture on my lips as we walk.

I walk quickly, passing sleeping homes and pathway
shrines whose paint is peeling and walls are crumbling:
cappella di san rocco and the *edicola con affresco della beata vergine
con bambino,* and I wait for Raffaelle to catch up with me. I
am studying the Virgin who holds her baby in her arms; a
loving mother and son.

'You should let me carry the rucksack,' he pants.

'You can barely carry yourself.'

'Why did we have to leave this early?'

'It will be too hot later on. There will be more people about.'

'No-one comes up here anyway.'

'Come on, or it will be dark by the time you get back.' I make my strides long. I straighten my back and breathe deeply relishing the beauty of the sunlight that shines through the dappled trees.

'I don't know why we couldn't drive.' Raffaelle speaks in short bursts. 'The track is narrow but it would be safe and much quicker.'

'I didn't want anyone to see your car has been moved.'

'No-one is following me. Are you sure you are not being irrational?'

I ignore him.

The path through the woods is steep and narrow, and in places, more than a forty-five degree angle. To my right, is a deep ravine where a ditch of naked trees have been chopped, and on my left, growing up the hillside is an abundance of wild blackberry and black current brambles. A yellow and white butterfly settles briefly on a branch and when it flies away I am left with a fleeting memory of its thick veins and velvet skin.

I cast my eyes over my shoulder and look down the trail to make sure there is no-one behind us. Karl Blakey is not to be seen but my heart beats frantically, not through exertion but through anxiety. When I saw him outside my apartment, staring up at me I panicked. I am usually controlled. I perform on stage, and I am used to adrenaline surging through my body, even if I sing badly or my performance isn't perfect, it is a disappointment but I have never felt fear, as I do now.

Karl Blakey could ruin my life. I can't let him find out about my affair with Michael or the Golden Icon, and as I walk the rhythm of my gait brings back more recent memories and I begin to repeat the familiar mantra revolving in my head.

Seán is dead. Michael is dead.

Seán died because of the Golden Icon. I am convinced of that. I believe it was Maximilian or his nephew who killed him and took the fake Turner painting. Had they thought it was valuable? Had they been looking for a painting?

I always assumed Michael died of old age or a heart attack but Dieter led me to believe it was something more sinister. Had he been trying to frighten me?

It has been over two weeks since I was in Munich and I don't know whether to feel lucky or scared that I have been left alone until now but Karl Blakey is definitely here in Comaso. I wonder too, if Santiago has been speaking to Padre Paolo. Perhaps the Padre is not helping me on Santiago's orders.

Who can I trust?

When I estimate we are half way up, I wait in the cool shadow of the beech trees. On the hillside opposite us the orange cable cars are yet to begin operating. The green gantries lay plotted up the hill like static iron soldiers. Over our head leaves flap in the early breeze and I watch them sway finding the movement relaxing and hypnotising. I pull a water bottle from the rucksack and drink deep long gulps.

Raffaelle perches beside me on a bench made of pine

logs. His breathing is heavy, his chest is heaving, and his hands grip his knees as he gazes down into the ravine. I pass him the water bottle.

'Are you okay?'

He shakes his head. 'No-one comes up here, cara.' He guzzles the water. 'There's probably wild boar down there, certainly deer.' He wipes his mouth with the back of his hand.

I survey the trail below. 'No-one is following us.'

'No-one would be so stupid as to hike up here. There are only sheep.'

We stand companionably listening to the bleating of the animals and their tinny bells, surveying the scene through the trees below us. The early sun glistens on the cross above the Santa Anna di Comaso church, and on fishing boats leaving the harbour. The lake looks green today, it's an illusion, only a reflection of the dark forest from the mountains.

'This is crazy,' he says. 'Why are you doing this?'

'It's the right thing to do.'

'For who? For you? For Seán or for Michael? Well, they are dead and this certainly isn't the right thing to do for me, or for us.'

I suppress my anger, ignore him and walk on.

'Since when were you so concerned about doing the right thing?' he calls.

I take a few paces back so I can look him in the eyes. 'I am not always right and I haven't always done the right thing but I intend to do it now.' My voice is harsh and my resolve resolute.

'Why? What's changed?'

'Me. Everything.'

'You are only thinking about yourself. Just because you didn't get Tosca you are taking it out on me. You don't think about me, or about us. Seán was your ex-husband. You owe him nothing.'

'That's why I haven't contacted Barbara,' I reply. 'Although I probably ought to. It would pay off her debts and at least give her and her children a decent life.'

'Forget them. What about us?'

'I've made my decision.'

'Well, it's the wrong one, the thing is with you is that...'

He is talking to himself because I turn and walk away. I block off and don't listen.

Some twenty minutes later I wait for him to turn the final bend and come into my view.

'Almost there,' I call encouragingly. I stand at a fork in the trail: to the right are stone steps that rise to the small garden belonging to the church, on the left is a steep grassy incline bordered by a stone wall with overgrown palms, ivy and fronds.

'I smell wild roses,' I call.

Raffaelle frowns. He is not impressed.

I take the stone steps two at a time as fast as I can until I reach the top then I am breathless. I stand with my hands on my hips, panting and gazing at the Chiesa della Madonna dei miracoli. Like so many Italian buildings it is faded okra, and the peeling paint only adds to its charm. At the front are three archways and two stone pillars. The roof is rounded with a small wooden spire. The grass is long and unkempt. There are old beech trees, wild orange buddleia and purple hydrangeas.

'You want to leave it here?'

I ignore him.

'Are you nuts?' he shouts.

'I cannot keep it at home. Karl Blakey will find it. He broke into my apartment once before.'

'Your apartment in Comaso?' He bites his moustache.

'No. When I lived in Germany.'

'What did he want?'

'He wanted evidence.'

'Evidence of what?' Raffaelle's eyes are dark brown.

'Evidence that I was taking cocaine.'

He scratches his cheek and I continue speaking, 'He followed me constantly. He took photographs and published them in magazines.'

'He was responsible for your downfall?'

'No, I was responsible for my behaviour but he was responsible for telling everyone how bad I was, and how I was struggling under pressure, and how I couldn't cope.'

'But I thought Guntar...'

'Guntar was my opera coach and my agent was Antonio Marx. They knew I was at the height of my fame and they kept pushing me and touring me until I was exhausted. I couldn't handle the pressure.'

Raffaelle is staring at me. 'You never spoke much about it.'

'I was a mess,' I say.

'I remember.' He reaches out and rubs my shoulder which I find comforting.

'Stay there.' I point to a rocky wall at the edge of the tangled garden. 'Turn your back, sit and look at the view.'

'How long are you going to hide it here for?'

'Just a few days, until I get news from Padre Stefano, Padre Paolo's friend.'

'We could have hidden it in the garden in my villa. It

would be safe there.'

'Under the wisteria?' I joke.

'You don't trust me. You don't want me to know where you hide it?' His voice is pained but I ignore him. 'Why did you bring me with you, if you don't trust me?'

'In case we were followed. I could pretend we were lovers out walking.'

'Great. That makes me feel good.'

I laugh. 'I'll be back in a minute. No peeking.'

I walk to the back of the church and along the grassy track. Half way along I find the remnants of a rocky wall but it is safe and secure. It comes to the height of my hip. I pull aside dried twigs, ferns and rampant ivy. Sweet aroma from a fig tree tickles my nose and I push aside bamboo roots. Over my head hangs a blue buddleia, its branches are swaying in the breeze and its petals catch in my hair.

I pull the rucksack from my shoulder, take out a trowel and begin to dig. The earth is damp, loose and pliable. The hole is easy to make. I toss aside rocks and stones and make sure it is dug deep. When I place the shoe box into the small hollow, it fits easily.

I cross myself, say a small prayer to the Madonna, and make her a promise that I will return her to her rightful place. As I cover her with earth I realise that if I die, the Golden Icon may remain hidden for years.

It takes a few minutes to cover the box, pressing soil into place, tucking and replanting the ferns, spreading the ivy and throwing leaves over my buried treasure.

My forehead is damp, I am perspiring. The muscles in my arm aches and my fingers are sore from gripping the trowel handle. When I open my palm I see red patches at the base of my fingers and I know the skin will blister.

I take my time to rinse my fingers with bottled water, replace the trowel and the bottle in the rucksack and hoist it onto my back. I am pleased to be relieved of the burden. I retrace my steps to the back of the church and pause to catch my breath listening to sheep bleating across the valley. My heart beats furiously but I am relieved. No-one will find it.

I walk around to the front of the church and across the small garden, Raffaelle is sitting with his back to me. He is perched on a rock gazing at the scene below and crouching at his feet is a familiar looking boy. His skin is smooth and silky like an olive, and he doesn't yet shave. On the hillside below is a flock of dirty grey sheep, their eyes barely focus as they graze and munch contentedly, their bells tinkle as they roam.

'But why don't you go to school?' Raffaelle says insistently.

'I'm not interested. I'm happy here. I love the views, and the sheep and it gives me time to think.'

'But you must learn. You must be educated.'

The boy shrugs.

'You are too young to be isolated from the world,' Raffaelle insists.

They both turn at the sound of my footsteps.

'This is Alonso,' he says. 'He's the son of Luigi's cousin.'

I smile. 'Hello.'

He nods back and I remember his soft grey eyes.

'Didn't I see you with Sandra beside the fountain?' I ask.

He shrugs.

'Is she your girlfriend?' Raffaelle nudges him with his

knee.

Alonso blushes.

'He doesn't want to tell you. Come on, let's go.' I pull on his hand.

'Women! They drag you up the hill for a romantic moment to watch the dawn then they need to pee,' Raffaelle says. 'Be warned, women are nothing but trouble.'

The boy laughs revealing a gap between his front teeth.

Raffaelle pats the boy on his shoulder. 'Think about what I said Alonso. There's so much to learn in life, so much to see, lots of girls–'

'Leave the poor boy alone,' I say, eager to be gone.

Raffaelle stands. 'Vai con Dio,' he says, and we walk hand in hand back down the empty trail. 'All done?'

'Yes.'

'I still think we could have hidden it in the villa.' I don't reply. 'We could have put it in the well. There's a small shelf half way down.'

'Too obvious,' I laugh. 'It's the first place Santiago would look.' From the valley comes the soft swell of gently rustling leaves like invisible waves ebbing in and out, and as the rhythmic calming sounds swoosh around us and I have a sudden urge to laugh.

Raffaelle mistakes my happiness, and he chuckles, pulling me closer. 'We can still sell it. Think about it. Why are you always so stubborn and selfish?'

I release his hand and quicken my pace. 'Let's get some hot bread from the bakery.' I lengthen my stride.

'Perhaps you don't love me enough,' he calls.

'Walking back will be easier,' I shout. 'Especially if you save your breath.'

In the afternoon I finish my vocalisation to a cacophony of a storm that blows in from the North. Black ominous clouds come rumbling from the Alps and I am distracted by the beauty of the ragged lightening that splits dark cumulus clouds, and the rolling rumble of thunder that echoes and bounces from the hillside until it recedes into silence and there is only the sound of rain thundering against my patio.

I wait for the clouds to break and to see a slice of blue sky before I venture outside onto the terrace. I sweep it dry trying not to think about the Golden Icon buried in the earth. I tip water from the candle holders, replace the cushions, and cut back the geraniums. It is cooler. It's a welcome relief from the heat.

I have telephoned Padre Paolo three times and I dial his number again. It goes unanswered so I leave another message.

To calm myself I play the piano. First I play Wagner, then Bach, and I end with Schubert's, *Symphony No. 8 in B minor*, his *Unfinished Symphony.*

Raffaelle telephones and we agree to meet in Luigi's for supper later this evening.

An hour later my terrace table is littered with opera scores and I am thinking I may take Cesare's advice and meet his producer friend Simone in London who wants me to sing with the Philharmonic. I telephone him but there is no answer. Frustrated I return my concentration to my music. I am marking scores and I am lost in my art and my love when the sound of my mobile phone startles me. I do not recognise the number and it is an unwelcome interruption so I ignore it.

I mark a note. A simple detail that I know will make a difference if I ever audition again, and a few seconds later my mobile rings again. I glare as it vibrates on the table its green light flashing. Dusk is falling. I flick on a lamp and answer it.

'Josephine?' She speaks as though we are good friends. 'Would you open the door? I'm downstairs. I have to speak to you.'

'Barbara?' I reply. My hands are suddenly clammy and my voice is hoarse.

'Just open the feckin' door. I know you're up there.'

I move on automatic pilot. I walk from the terrace, through the lounge, downstairs and along the corridor, closing the laundry room door as I pass. At the front door I take a deep breath, pull the lock aside and push the handle down.

Barbara wears a powder blue designer suit, her blond hair is tied in a clip on the back of her head and her dark eyes are unsmiling. Her teeth are whiter, her face browner, her body thinner.

'How are ya?' she says with a strong Irish accent, 'Aren't you going to let me in?'

I stand aside and she pushes past me.

'Is it straight on?'

'Yes, up the stairs.' I lock the front door and follow her. She doesn't wait and I find her standing on the terrace with her back to me.

'Nice view.' She whistles and picks up a handful of music scores. 'You didn't get Tosca did you? But you don't give up, do you? You'd better get me a glass of something. I could do with a cold drink.'

'Water?'

'Anything alcoholic.'

'Prosecco?'

'That'll do.'

From my kitchen window I watch her on the terrace. She stands motionless. Her hands on the railings as she gazes across the lake watching the twinkling lights, just as I have done many, many times. I take my time. I wonder if she has the letter. Would I swap the letter for the Golden Icon?

I clear away the music scores and place a chilled bottle, in an ice sleeve, on the table with two glasses. I empty green olives into a ceramic dish and salted almonds onto a plate, conscious that we don't speak but she is watching me. She leans her back against the rails like a boxer waiting for the bell ready to lunge into the ring at her opponent.

'Seán trusted you,' she says.

I pour the sparkling liquid and pass her a glass.

It wasn't a question so I don't feel obliged to answer.

'Slainte.' She sips and leaves a smear of red lipstick along the fluted crystal. 'He told you about our financial problems, didn't he?'

'Yes.' I sit down.

'Seán was very ambitious, but then again, you know that. Sometimes I forget that you were married to him. How long were you together?'

I shrug.

'How long did your marriage last? A year? Was it a year or less before you ran off with that Romanian?'

'Three years,' I reply. She mustn't know about Michael and I feel the tension easing from my body.

'What was his name?'

I raise an eyebrow.

'The fella who sang with you in Carmen in Barcelona. What was his name?'

'José..., José Raminov.' I don't add that he had comforted me after my affair with Michael was over and I was reeling with sadness and confusion.

'Oh? He's still going. I heard an interview with him on the radio a few months ago. Seán couldn't stand the man.' She raises her glass. 'But then you didn't care what Seán thought, did you? You haven't been very lucky as far as men are concerned. You've never managed to keep one of your own, have you?'

'I divorced Seán as soon as it was legally possible in Ireland so that you could marry him. You have two lovely children and I hardly think my life is relevant enough to come under such scrutiny. Move on Barbara, it's all in the past.'

'Ah?' She pulls out a seat and sits across the table from me. Her eyes flash green like a speckled egg. 'Michael was good to you too, wasn't he?'

My heart skips. 'It's no secret that he helped me.'

'He paid your sponsorship to go to Frankfurt.'

'Scholarship,' I correct her.

'If it wasn't for Michael you wouldn't be where you are today.'

I remain silent.

'Seán blamed him for breaking up your marriage. Michael encouraged you to sing.'

'We married too quickly. We were young. Seán knew I was born to sing.'

'He says you'd never had met that Raminov if you had

stayed at home.'

'Don't make a big deal of the past Barbara, Seán didn't. He quickly moved on and found you.' I look directly into her eyes. 'He had the integrity to keep the respect between us,' I lie.

She mustn't have the letter or she would have used it against me by now. I feel my confidence growing.

Her eyes are like shards of flint. 'Well, that's the thing, now Josephine, isn't it? It's your integrity that I am questioning. Seán hadn't seen you for years but he did trust you. He asked you to do something for him and he trusted you to do it. Even though he's dead you've let him down again. You've let us all down this time.'

I raise my eyebrow.

'I'm not stupid. I know what Seán asked you to do. So where is it?'

'What?'

'The family heirloom. The one he asked you to get for him. You know? The reason you went to Munich. The reason he paid for your ticket. The real reason he wanted you to sing at Michaels's funeral.'

'He asked me to sing at Michael's funeral because it meant so much.'

'To who?'

'To him, to me - to Michael.'

Her laugh is a grunt. 'Michael loved you to the end. He never stopped listening to your music but you soon forgot him when you hit the big time. Jetting around the world, singing, socialising and hob-nobbing with the rich and famous in your coke-fuelled life. You never had time for him then, did you?'

An image of Michael sitting listening to my music

comes into my mind. He has a head of white curly hair, his grey eyes are closed and he has a half smile on his lips.

'Is that why you think Seán asked you to come to Ireland,' she insists, 'to sing?'

'He said it's what Michael wanted and I think that he thought if I sang at the funeral it would add extra credit to his business circle.'

Her laugh is sarcastic and it irks me. 'Seán's bankrupt. Do you really think that asking a *has-been* opera singer to sing at his father's funeral would make a difference? No. As always you have delusions, Josephine. You've always had them. You think you're better than you are.'

I don't move. I don't flinch and I barely breathe.

'So where is it?'

I don't reply.

'Why do you think he asked you to go to Munich? Did you believe that he trusted you more than anyone; more than me, or his children? Did you not put two and two together or did your ego get in the way again? Josephine the superstar. The opera diva who thinks no-one can live without her. The world needs you, is that what you think? Seán needed you?'

She reaches for the bottle and refills her glass. The bubbles rise quickly to the top and spill onto the table. 'Seán's leg was in plaster,' she says. 'He…'

'He fell!'

'He told you that and you believed him.' She gulps Prosecco and her glass rattles when she smacks it down on the table. 'It was a hit and run. They were after him. They had threatened Michael and then they came after Seán.'

'Who?' I inhale through my nose and out through my mouth; slowly and deeply.

'Don't pretend you don't know.'

I shake my head.

'One of Michael's old war friends, Maximilian Strong. Well, they were no longer friends. They all fell out after the war.' She leans across the table. 'Michael told Seán that they found the treasure, hidden in a barn, somewhere near Germany at the end of the war. Family heirlooms he called them. Each time Seán needed money Michael managed to sell something to bail Seán out.' She has manicured fingers and soft hands. 'But this time Michael was frightened.'

'Why?'

'Whatever it was that Michael wanted to sell, Maximilian wanted it.'

'So why didn't Michael sell it to Maximilian?'

'I'm not sure. I think there was something in the past that happened and Maximilian threatened Michael's family when the boys were young. I know William has a burn on his forehead as a result of a fire.' She shrugs and frowns. 'I think this piece of treasure is worth a fortune and Michael pretended he didn't have it to save the family but when Seán got into financial difficulties Michael wanted to help.'

'Couldn't he have sold it through a third party?' I am thinking of Dieter.

'Presumably whatever it is, brings no-one any luck if they use it for their own gain, but Seán said it's a scary rumour that someone invented to stop people using it for their own means.' She gives a tight laugh. There are dark circles under her eyes. 'But it can't be worse than what I've been through already.'

'How did Michael die?' I ask.

'It was a heart-attack but a neighbour told Seán an old man with a younger man had left his house earlier. Seán thought they had threatened Michael, put the fear of God into him. He had become quite frail.'

'Did you tell the police?'

'Do you think I'm stupid?'

'But why now after all these years?'

'Seán thought it was to do with him being bankrupt and needing the money. He couldn't go himself because of the plaster on his leg, and he wouldn't let me or the kids go. He said it was too dangerous. When Michael died and Seán was almost run over and killed, he decided he wasn't going to involve any of the family. You were the only person he could think of who he could trust to go and get the family heirloom, and besides he said, you were dispensable.'

I sit in silence. My demeanour must fool her. My back is straight and my facial muscles don't move as the anger and fear rise in me. Her words are going around in my head travelling at chaotic speed, cascading in mini images: Seán in Dublin, Dieter in Munich, and the Golden Icon. I am dispensable.

A motorbike buzzes past along the coast road and a horn honks, church bells toll across the ravine and it all seems a world away.

'Seán was prepared to risk my life?' When I look up Barbara is staring at me. There is no sympathy in her eyes.

'So where is it?' she says. 'Our family heirloom. It belongs to me and our children.'

'I don't have it.'

She picks up an olive. The colour matches her eyes and she places it between her lips. 'I don't believe you.' She speaks with her mouthful. 'Seán has left me in debt. We need the money. On the night of Michael's funeral most people had gone home. Seán was upset and more than a little drunk. A young man with a shaved head arrived and they went into Seán's study. He beat him before he shot him.' Her eyes are filling with tears. 'Have you ever lost anyone you love?'

If only she knew.

'Seán said, he didn't trust you,' I say.

She stands turns her back on me and gazes across the lake. She is silent for a while and when she faces me I see the tears are dried and her eyes are black with anger.

'If you don't cooperate with me, things will get very rough for you. William suspects that there's an heirloom or something valuable and he has hired a journalist, a friend of Seán's to find out what it is.' She steps toward me. 'And do you remember Seán's friend David Mallory?'

I raise an eyebrow but say nothing.

'He's the Irish Consul in Milan. He was at Michael's funeral. He's working with the Gardaí and they have found documents of Michael's when he was in the war, and also your flight ticket on Seán's computer. They know Seán wanted you to go to Germany for him. They know you phoned him from Munich'

'I didn't know Seán was dead.'

'Maybe you're working with Maximilian Strong?'

'No!'

'David tells me that they are checking the flight register to see if you took that flight but I wasn't going to wait. I know you did. Seán told me after you left. He was excited. You were bringing back the family heirloom and all our financial problems would be solved.'

A trickle of perspiration runs down the spine of my back.

'So let me tell you something. I know Dieter Guzman lives in Munich. He is an art collector and was a friend of Michael's during the war and was looking after something valuable for Michael. Something we could sell to pay off our debts. I must have it Josephine. It is not yours. Give it to me. Let me take it home and save our house and Seán's business. It is what Seán and Michael would have wanted. Let their hard work not all have gone to waste.'

'You're right,' I say, 'but I don't have it.'

'Where is it?'

'Dieter has it.' The lie falls from my mouth and I feel no sense of shame or guilt. Seán jeopardised my life and my entire career. It was because of his blackmail that I missed my rehearsals and flunked my audition. I am dispensable.

'Dieter wouldn't give it to you?'

I shake my head. 'He wanted to give it to me but I wouldn't take it.'

'Why?'

'I didn't want to carry a stolen art treasure to Dublin.'

'What is it? A painting?'

'No, a statue.'

'A statue,' she says with surprise and then with distain. 'A statue.'

'A Golden Icon.' I think of it lying in the earth.

'You saw it?'

'Yes.'

Her eyes look haunted and tired. 'I must have it.'

'Then you must get it yourself.'

'I don't believe you.'

'Phone Dieter,' I challenge, wondering why she hadn't

already.

'He doesn't answer his phone.'

'That's why I phoned Seán's mobile the night he died. I had just left Dieter's apartment and I wanted to tell Seán that I wasn't carrying it through customs.'

'So, you never flew back to Ireland?'

'There was no point. That's why I was ringing Seán, to tell him I was catching the train home to Italy.'

'But you saw this statue? Dieter showed it to you?'

'Yes.'

'So it does exist? There is a family heirloom.'

'Yes.' I barely hesitate.

'What's it like?'

'It's a Golden Icon. It's beautiful. It's priceless. It is an icon of the Madonna and child sculptured with infinite detail. It is art in its purest form. It is the most amazing piece of treasure I have ever seen. It is based on Michaelangelo's *Madonna of Bruges*. It is exquisite.'

'My God,' she gasps. Her green eyes sparkle, her hand flies to her mouth and in a revered voice she says, 'It must be worth a feckin' fortune.'

I shower quickly, dress in a cotton skirt and blouse and add lipstick to my pale face. Barbara's visit has disturbed me and I have sent her to Munich for no reason. I stand arguing with my reflection in the mirror. 'Stop looking at me like that. I need time.' My eyes look tired. 'Three days. That's all I need,' I say aloud.

I don't envy Barbara going to Dieter's apartment.

'You lied,' I say.

'I had to,' I argue back.

I brush my hair add drop-pearl earrings, and ten minutes later I am heading down the steep steps to the village square.

Luigi's restaurant is on the corner, on the bend of the main road. It is a blend of stone, oak wood and steel olive green shutters that are tied back to reveal long open windows with views of the pontoon and the lake.

The terrace tables are full, and inside there are glowing candle lanterns, colourful dried sunflowers, rows of neatly laid wine bottles and a large wall clock.

I am thirty minutes late.

Raffaelle sits at our usual table in the corner. He stands and kisses me, pulls out my chair and I settle opposite. He wears a T-shirt and beige trousers, his hair is unruly and his eyes sparkle.

'I was getting worried–'

'You'll never believe who was here - and who came to my apartment this afternoon,' I interrupt. Fleetingly I wonder if Barbara left on the last ferry as I advised her to do and I glance around the busy tables to make sure she is not amongst the diners.

'Prosecco?' He frowns, and lifts the half empty bottle from an ice bucket and pours the clear bubbling liquid.

We clink glasses. Soft samba music plays a tune I recognise, *The Girl from Ipanema*, and I smile back at him.

'Let's order first and then you can tell me. I hope you are hungry. I spoke to Luigi and as well as the usual pizzas he has fresh *Salmerino* and *Alborello*.'

I reach for the menu and we are still discussing the merits of each dish when Luigi comes to our table.

'You're busy tonight?' I say.

'It will be worse at the weekend with the opening of the

143

Theatro Il Domo. In Como it is very busy. Everywhere is full. There are television crews, reporters, film stars, everyone has come for the opening. There is no accommodation and all the restaurants are full.'

'Ah yes,' Raffaelle doesn't look at me. 'Tosca.'

I study the menu.

'It's very exciting,' Luigi continues. 'Santiago is beside himself. He is so proud of his sister. We are all delighted for her.'

'I'll have the sun dried *Missoltini*,' I say.

Raffaelle orders fresh *Salmerino*, as well as anti pasta, garlic bread and rocket salad.

After Luigi leaves Raffaelle leans across the table and takes my hand. 'There is something I must tell you,' he says. 'Things aren't right.'

'Like what?'

'At the villa this afternoon, there was a man hanging around.'

'Why didn't you phone me?'

'I didn't want to frighten you. I have been thinking what you said about this journalist fellow. I thought maybe it was him but this man did not look like a journalist.'

'How do you know?'

'He was wearing a dark suit and looked very out of place. He is young and bald. He had a shaved head.'

'Police?'

He shrugs. 'I probably wouldn't have taken any notice but he was watching the villa and this afternoon he was here in the square.'

'Only Padre Paolo and Dieter know I have the Golden Icon.'

'Could Dieter have told them, or perhaps–' He breaks

off mid-sentence.

I wait and we regard each other silently.

'Padre Paolo, might have mentioned it to someone,' he says.

'Padre Paolo? Don't be crazy,' I lower my voice. 'He wouldn't tell anyone. I know you are upset I confided in him, but he was the only lifeline I had, and he still is. He may be the only one who can make sense of all this.'

'Listen to me. None of this makes sense. Someone else must know you have the icon.'

'Why?'

'You said you saw the journalist Karl here in Comaso, and now this man is watching my villa.'

'But why is he watching your villa and not my apartment?'

'They must know we are together. It's getting dangerous, cara. You must be careful.'

I shake my head. Is he deliberately trying to frighten me?

'Padre Paolo says that he will speak to Padre Stefano on Saturday. I only have three days to wait.'

'Ay!' He leans back against his chair and shakes his head. 'You are so stubborn. Let's just take the icon and leave here. We will have money to do what we want, and we can begin a new life together. Why are you so unreasonable?' His voice modulates from caressing to anger. Then he hisses loudly. 'Why are you so stubborn?'

'It's not stubbornness.'

'It's dangerous.' He leans across the table and I look at the dark hairs on his wrists. 'I don't like it. Beside I have made some enquiries of my own.'

'You what?'

'Shush, it's not like that.'

'Enquiries? Who have you told?'

'I haven't told anyone. All I did was to contact Sergio, my friend in Lenno.'

'What for?' I snatch my hand away.

'He's an art dealer and he's very discreet.'

'Oh Raffaelle, I don't want the art world knowing about the Golden Icon. That's precisely why I haven't been to anyone.'

His face is filled with disbelief. 'But you need information. I want to help.'

'I don't want help from an art dealer I can't trust.'

'I didn't tell him you have it. I talked generally and he says it would be worth a great deal, hypothetically, if it did exist. He could broker a deal for us. The Serbs and the Armenians are willing to buy anything on the black market. No-one else need know. It doesn't have to be traced back to us.'

'I'm not selling it.'

'Sergio also said that if this Golden Icon was found during the war and no-one knows who it really belongs to, then it is ours and we have the right to sell it.'

'No! Oh Raffaelle I can't believe you have spoken to someone about this.' I hold my head in my hands.

'Sergio can be trusted. It is what he does. He is used to business like this. Besides, you must act quickly. I think Santiago knows something is going on. Padre Paolo must have said something.'

'Why do you say that?'

'He has been in the village square the past two mornings drinking coffee.'

'So?'

'Chief Inspectors do not sit drinking coffee watching who gets on and comes off the ferry. He was there yesterday when you came back from Milan. Did you not see him?'

Raffaelle is making me panic and I wonder if this is his intention. I stare at him. I control my breathing and I take a deep breath.

'Listen, I need Padre Paolo to get me the information. I must do the right thing. We've been over this before. It does not belong to us. We must be patient.'

'The man at my villa did not look very nice. Perhaps he works with that man, the one Dieter warned you about, Maximilian Strong. Did you not say he had a nephew? He looked like a criminal. We must be careful. We cannot hide this Golden Icon forever. We've left it buried near the church and it's a waste.'

'Shush,' I turn to look over my shoulder. 'I can't believe you are so indiscreet. Anyone could hear you.'

'No one listens to our conversation. You are becoming obsessed about doing the right thing.'

'It is not an obsession.'

'You have changed. In the past two weeks you have hardly spoken to me. You have been on bad form since you lost the role of Tosca. You are constantly angry with me. You won't listen and you are very difficult.'

I sigh. He is right. I have wanted to be alone to sort out my thoughts and my feelings. I have also been grieving for Michael although I cannot tell him this. 'I'm sorry Raffaelle but—'

'Is this about Glorietta getting Tosca? Is it because I had lunch in her villa and you think I supported her instead of you? Is this why you are punishing me?'

'No.'

Luigi places steaming plates of mushroom spaghetti and salad on the table and I pick up my fork. From the speakers a Portuguese girl sings a medley of Bosa Novas which I try to concentrate on; the rhythm, notes and tone.

Raffaelle leans his elbows on the table and pours oil over his bread.

'Barbara came to visit me this afternoon,' I say.

'Barbara?' His mouth is open in shock. 'Seán's wife? From Ireland?'

'Yes.'

'Well?' He tugs his moustache.

'She wanted the family heirloom to pay off his debts.'

'And what did you say?'

'I told her I didn't have it. I told her that I didn't take it from Dieter. I said, I wouldn't carry it through customs to Ireland.'

He forks pasta into his mouth then dabs his lips with the napkin. 'Did she believe you?'

'She has gone to Munich.'

'If she had phoned Dieter first, she would know you were lying.'

'She did phone him, but he didn't pick up.'

'She will know you have lied when she gets there. You have sent her to Germany for no reason.'

'It was to give me more time. I need until Saturday. I must wait for Padre Paolo to find out some information for me. There must be a record of it in the Vatican.'

'Why are you so keen to give this to the church?'

'I'm not!'

'Padre Paolo has done nothing for you in these past weeks. He is deliberately not helping you. I believe he has told Santiago about your secret, and he is now watching us too.'

I shake my head but Raffaelle continues speaking. 'You are unreasonable. You have not been yourself recently. Cesare has phoned you with other opportunities. He even asked you to sing with the Philharmonic in London and you turn him down.'

'I said I would think about it.'

'You should be out there looking for more roles or other operas. You have been avoiding everyone. You have shut yourself in your apartment and you do nothing. You are feeling sorry for yourself and you are becoming dull, cara; very, very dull.' He twirls pasta on his fork.

I push my plate aside. The pasta remains untouched and I reach for my glass.

'We could have a new life,' he urges. 'New friends and mix in the right social circle. We could change our lives but you are not interested.' He places his fork on his plate and takes my hand in his. My palm is perspiring. He traces the finely etched lines that lead to my wrist.

'This icon could change our destiny. You hold our future in the palm of your hand. I will be with you. We will be together in Florence, Italy's most beautiful city. All you have to do is say, yes. We can leave in the morning.'

'No!' I pull my hand away. 'Just because you have squandered your inheritance.'

His cheeks are red as if I have just slapped him.

'That is why you have taken the teaching job you hate so much,' I say.

'The art world is very unpredictable. My paintings have not sold. I need a prestigious exhibition to raise my profile. I can do that with your help with a little finance.'

'You are lazy, Raffaelle. You have been given everything on a plate and you have taken responsibility for nothing. The only thing you have left is your Uncle's villa which you are not allowed to sell,' I lower my voice, 'I will not subsidise your career.'

'You are very hard with me, Josephine.'

'You are incredible. You don't think Barbara has any right to the icon. You don't believe I should give it to her so that she can pay off Seán's debts. Her children have lost a father and grandfather in the space of a few weeks. Their mother now faces bankruptcy and they could be forced to leave their home. Yet you think it is right for me to sell a stolen art treasure to finance your career.'

His voice is strained when he replies, 'I think that the man who was in my garden this afternoon is with Maximilian Strong. I think they are after the Golden Icon. I am worried about you.'

'Are you deliberately trying to scare me?'

'Your time is running out.'

My throat is dry. My head begins to throb. I rub my eyes conscious that mascara comes off on my fingers. I wipe the smudges onto the napkin.

'No, Raffaelle. Our time is running out. Maybe you should decide if it's me you want or the Golden Icon.'

Luigi is busy behind the bar and a young waiter I have not seen before removes our plates. We remain silent until he leaves the table.

'I saw Glorietta this afternoon. She came off the ferry,' he says.

My glass hovers half way to my lips.

'So Glorietta was here? How is she? How are the rehearsals? What did she want?'

150

'She was with Bruno.' Raffaelle won't look at me.

'The handsome toy-boy dancer?'

He frowns at me. 'He's too skinny.'

'You mean he is too young. Don't be jealous,' I tease. 'She probably likes her men skinny now that she is not with you.' I nod at Raffaelle's waist to make my point.

'It was a long time ago.'

'What?'

'You know what I am saying. We split up a long time ago.'

'She's still in love with you,' I say. I also think he is still in love with her.

'She threw me out.'

'Probably because of that young art student.'

'It was nothing.'

'It was to her.'

He shrugs. He doesn't deny he still loves her.

'She invited me, well, she invited us both to the opening night on Saturday. She said she will send tickets.' He has the grace and sensitivity to pause.

Samba music plays softly in the background. The thought of going to the opening night unsettles me and my pulse races.

'You should go on your own without me. I know you would like to see it,' I say. 'I would not be brave enough to see her singing my role. I doubt I would have the composure to sit through the performance.'

He nods and shrugs, so I continue speaking. 'She will gain international fame and recognition,' I say. 'It will be televised around the world and attended by anyone who is anyone. It is the first opera in the new theatre and a showcase to the world but also, it is an amazing opportunity for her. A major step in her career.'

He refills our glasses.

'Don't be hasty. You do not have to decide tonight. Let us see, nearer the time,' he suggests. 'You may change your mind.' His dark eyes smile at me.

The tension leaves my shoulders but I cannot help imagining the opening night; the thrill, the rush of adrenaline, the orchestra, and the lights.

The waiter brings our food and we eat and for the rest of the meal we talk about nothing of any importance. It is superficial chat and I am sure that Raffaelle, like me, is busy with his own thoughts and feelings.

Our conversation flows easily and after the meal he insists on ordering limoncello with our coffee.

'It will help us sleep,' he says suggestively, as if sleep is the last thing he wants to do. He leans toward me and I kiss his lips. Then he freezes. He is looking over my shoulder. He pulls away and his face turns to a scowl and when I turn around, standing in the doorway is Santiago Bareldo, the local police chief, Glorietta's brother.

He selects a table across the room. He nods and smiles at a few diners and raises his hand to us. Raffaelle holds up his glass in response, like a toast, to his health.

'He's like a skinny pig,' Raffaelle says.

'He was almost your brother in law,' I reply.

'He's arrogant.'

'You didn't think that when you were with Glorietta.'

He laughs. 'I had to be nice then. I don't now.'

'Yes, you do.'

He looks stubbornly at me. 'You don't like him either.'

'He is pompous,' I agree.

Raffaelle takes my hand he begins whispering how he

would like to be pompous with me in his bedroom and we both giggle. We clink limoncello glasses and our heads are bent together across the table when I hear a voice beside us.

'I was hoping I might see you.' Santiago has jet black hair with patches of grey above his ears. His nose is long and pointed as if sniffing for clues and his eyes are hooded as if guarding a secret.

We lean apart and Raffaelle glares at him.

Without being asked Santiago pulls out a chair and sits down. He rubs the palms of his hands together and appears to be selecting his words carefully. 'Signora Lavelle I hope you feel you can come to me for any, should we say, police matters. If you feel that there is anything that I can help you with, please do know that you can come to me.'

I smile graciously and before I can reply Raffaelle says.

'And why would she need your help?'

I raise a warning eyebrow at him.

Santiago looks expectantly at me and I meet his gaze with an inquisitive smile.

'Perhaps Signora Lavelle, would know better than you?'

'Know what?' I reply.

'Why you may need me.'

'I'm not aware of any reason.'

'I have had a telephone call from the police in Ireland concerning you. The Gardaí, is that what they are called? They were looking for you and wanted to know where you lived. And then I had a call from the Irish Consul. It seems that they are very concerned about you. Presumably your ex-husband was murdered - but then, I think that you must know that.'

My heart skips a beat then does more rapid beats in quick succession. I begin twisting a paper serviette between my fingers, winding it over my index finger, round and round making it tighter and tighter.

'Padre Paolo is also behaving strangely,' Santiago continues. 'He has been very guarded with me, as if he had a secret, and now, it seems, he is avoiding me.' Santiago scratches his nose. 'And I am beginning to wonder if the events aren't linked in some way; the police in Ireland, the Irish Consul and Padre Paolo. The thing is, is that Padre Paolo and I were at school together and he can't keep a secret from me for very long.'

'That's not very ethical for a Priest, is it?' Raffaelle says, 'Surely one can go to Padre Paolo in confidence?' He tugs his moustache. 'Isn't that the whole point of confession?'

I kick Raffaelle under the table.

'In the confessional Padre Paolo is discreet.' Santiago's nose points toward me. 'But if matters are not discussed in the confessional there are ways of saying that something requires attention or that someone needs help.'

I am twisting the serviette. It splits and I pull it from my index finger and throw the mess onto the table.

'Tell me Signora Lavelle, did the man from the Irish Consul find you?'

I shake my head.

He smiles confidently as if he knows everything. 'He will. I'm sure he will. He was very insistent. I think his name was David Mallery or Mallory or something similar. He seemed very concerned about your welfare. He says he met you recently in Ireland and that you sang at the funeral of your ex-father in law.'

I don't reply. I am thinking about the letter. Have the

police found it? Where is it? Who has it?

Santiago scratches his nose. 'Bene, I will leave you to finish your meal in peace but please remember Signora, should you need any help or assistance, the Italian police are here to help you. Please contact me.' He stands up.

I think he is about to walk away but he stops and turns as if he has remembered something important.

'Will you be going to the opening night of Tosca on Saturday?' Although Santiago's question is directed at Raffaelle, he is watching me. 'We are all very excited about the opera and the opening of the Teatro.'

I pick up my limoncello and wonder if I will be arrested if I throw it over this odious little man.

'I think not,' Raffaelle says. He places his hand over mine. 'I believe Josephine and I will be on a romantic weekend exploring Florence. We are thinking of moving.'

CHAPTER EIGHT

O Lord, in thee have I trusted:
let me never be confounded.
Te Deum, Tosca

On Wednesday I wake with a sense of urgency. I am
determined to speak to Padre Paolo. I want him to
reassure me that he has not broken his confidence and
trust to me. Why is he avoiding me and Santiago?

The small market in the port is busy. I push my way
between locals and tourists, and stalls laden with fresh
fruit, vegetables, flowers, and handmade souvenirs. Rich
ripening cheeses heave a pungent smell and the aroma of
fresh coffee from the lakeside cafe tempts me to sit beside
the water and relax.

The early breeze is cool against my skin, the water is
deep blue, and the sun is already hot on my back. On the
slipway beneath the waterside cafe a drake and his family
are bobbing on the lapping waves.

I stop in my tracks.

Air explodes from my chest, sitting on the stone wall
gazing out at the lake, as if waiting for me, is Karl Blakey.
His legs are crossed at the ankles and his stomach hangs

over baggy jeans.

'I was hoping to bump into you. I rang your bell a few times but you didn't answer the door.' His chin wobbles when he speaks. His gerbil eyes are hidden behind square sunglasses, and his pudgy hands hold an expensive-looking camera.

'Get lost,' I reply. I walk around him toward the church.

'I've got a message from William.'

'So you're working for him now?'

He smiles. 'He knows that you can't be trusted.'

I continue walking.

'I told him you were probably back on the coke.'

I stop, remove my sunglasses and stare hard at him. 'If you print any lies I will go for you. My lawyer will sue you for everything you have, and–'

'You don't have a lawyer. You couldn't afford to pay the last one.'

I stare at him.

'Unless you've come into some money recently, have you?' He speaks quickly. 'William seems to think there's a family heirloom and you've stolen it. Of course, I defended you. I told him that wasn't your style. I did say that you normally only steal other women's husbands, but he insists that you have something belonging to him. Something that's very valuable.'

'My friend here, is the local chief of police, and if you harass me I'll get a court order and make your life difficult like the last time.'

Karl stands. He is as tall as my shoulder. 'He wants it back,' he says, 'and I've promised to help him, and you know how good I am about keeping my promises.'

I turn and walk away.

'I know you went to Munich,' he calls. 'I know Seán was blackmailing you, and I'm going to find out about your secret Josephine. I promise you.'

My back is hot but it isn't from the relentless July sunshine. Now it is from invisible trackers who are watching, monitoring and closing in on me. Karl Blakey is, once again, my shadow. He stirs unpleasant memories of my past life, but much worse, he threatens the safety of my future. His presence in my village that has been far removed and remote from prying journalists, inquisitive public and demanding agents now makes me feel threatened.

I walk quickly to the church where I take refuge. Sitting in the shadows in the back pew I concentrate on breathing, pushing my stomach down, raising my lungs, regulating my erratic heartbeat. My hands are still shaking as a result of my encounter with Karl.

Who has my letter?

I gaze at the Madonna with the son in her arms. She is serene. I envy her peace and solitude. I say a prayer, thinking of the Golden Icon buried in the earth on the hill behind the village, hoping for a miracle.

A retired foreign couple are studying the church paintings, taking photographs and whispering quietly. Behind me the door opens and the stone floor is bathed in sunlight. A young couple wearing cut-off shorts and creased T-shirts stand at the top of the aisle then begin to walk silently down the aisle as if it were their wedding day. I am attracted to them by their vivacity and youth. Seán and I must have been that age when we married.

The wooden pew is hard against my back.

Michael had understood me better than Seán. He was an avid opera fan. He recognised my talent and knew the opportunity I had at my fingertips, and although I was married to his son, he encouraged me to fulfil my destiny, he guided me. He nurtured me and he loved me.

After I sang in Covent Garden I was regaled as the new opera star destined to be as famous as Maria Callas. My performance of Tosca altered my life and my destiny. Until then I would have sacrificed everything for Michael.

As I lean forward in the pew, and lay my face in the palm of my hands, I hear Michael's voice, *Life never works out how you plan it. Different things are important to you at different stages of your life. You will thank me one day.*

I raise my eyes and look up at the Virgin.

Pure serenity.

I want her to understand. I want to explain to her. Divorce wasn't possible then. Rural Ireland wasn't like the seventies in England or in America. There was no divorce. No contraception. No abortion. I was an American. These constraints were like chains around my throat. I was a caged animal. I was living in foreign territory, a land that no longer welcomed my funny American mannerisms and my cute accent. It was a country that stifled my art, my creativity and my passion. Only Michael had understood.

The young couple stop to take a photograph of my Madonna.

It had been Michael who had travelled with me to London for the first audition. Not Seán. Michael had taken a few days off and we had flown over the Irish sea and enjoyed afternoon tea in the Savoy to celebrate my success. I look up at the Madonna pleading for her to understand. I have lost the two men I once loved, I say silently to her.

An old man wearing a yellow corduroy jacket shuffles into the church. He settles nosily in a pew then bows his head as if apologising for disturbing my thoughts. He stands and walks with his shoulders hunched and head bent to the back of the church. He rattles loose change in his pocket.

Raffaelle's words from last night still echo in my head.

You lost Tosca. You're stubborn. You're selfish. We could start a new life together.

Padre Paolo appears from the vestry. The door closes quietly behind him. He treads softly and quickly, his cassock swirling against his legs and a large jewel encrusted cross hanging around his neck. In his haste he almost passes me by. If I had not hailed him, things may have all worked out differently, but he stops at my bequest, halting mid stride. His brown eyes are filled with anticipated excitement but when he sees me in the pew his enthusiasm is replaced with one of guarded wariness.

'Ah, Josephine.' He holds out a hand. 'What a delightful surprise. One I wasn't expecting.'

'I need to talk to you Padre.' My voice is soft. I want to indicate to him that I am serious and that I need help. 'It's urgent. You haven't returned my calls.'

'I have been busy.' He looks over his shoulder and around the church as if searching for someone. The retired tourists, the young couple and the old man have disappeared.

Reluctantly Padre Paolo sits beside me and the wood groans under our weight as it has creaked for years though masses, funerals, weddings and baptisms.

'Santiago was here,' he says. 'We are preparing for the September fiesta and discussing the route of the procession this year and who will head it. Angelo is very keen to take an active part and you know how insistent the Mayor can be.' He spreads his hands apart. 'I am hoping the Arch Bishop will be here, but–' he pauses and sighs as if this is a weighty problem that only he alone can solve. 'We will have to see. Has Angelo asked you to sing this year?' he asks.

I shake my head. 'Not yet, Padre.' I don't say, I don't care about the procession.

'I know you didn't get Tosca but you are still popular in the village. You have a good voice. Do not be discouraged that Glorietta's voice is better than yours. She is younger and she has a career ahead of her. This is a fantastic opportunity for her to be recognised around the world.'

'Padre, do you have any news for me?'

I sense him choosing his words. 'I am waiting.' He looks at me and folds his fingers together as if in prayer.

'Waiting for what, Padre?' My head is screaming at him.

'The Cardinal doesn't return to the Vatican until Friday. I have told you this Josephine. I am unable to do more.'

'I thought you were waiting for Padre Stefano?'

'He is with the Cardinal.'

I am impatient and I speak quickly. 'I think my life is in danger, Padre,' I say. 'I believe that there are people who want the Golden Icon and they are willing to kill to get it.'

Opera and drama are my art and my passion, and he smiles at me as he would smile at a child in the street with a *gelato*.

I explain slowly, 'My ex-husband Seán is dead. His father Michael is dead. Someone wants the Golden Icon and they are prepared to murder for it. I need to know if you will be able to find any information for me. I may not be able to keep it for much longer.'

He replies carefully 'Why do you not give it up to the police?'

My mouth falls open.

He continues speaking. 'It is the most natural thing to do, no? When you are given an item of such obvious wealth and value that does not belong to you. You should give it to the police.'

I raise an eyebrow.

'Padre, I came to you, a man of the church because I trust you.' I emphasise my sentences deliberately. 'I need information and you promised to *help* me. My life could be in danger. I have nowhere to go and no-one to turn to, only you, Padre. You are my saviour.'

His eyelashes flick quickly. 'Signora Lavelle while I am waiting for an answer from the Cardinal I insist that you seek protection. Please, please go to Santiago. He will protect you.'

'What is taking so long? Why don't you have any news for me? Does the Cardinal or Padre Stefano not have a telephone? Can you not speak to someone else in the Vatican?'

'It is not that simple.'

'Are you not willing to help me?'

'It's not like that.'

'I think I made a mistake in coming to you. I thought you above all people would help me to do the right thing. I assumed that I had your confidence and your trust, and that you would–' I cannot continue. I stand knocking my knee on the pew. He reaches out and places his hand on my arm.

'I know that Santiago is Glorietta's brother and that you lost the role of Tosca to her, but don't let pride stand in your way. Think about your situation Signora Lavelle. The Golden Icon is not yours. It is stolen.'

'Stolen? I told you it concerns a friend of mine. I asked you to find out about it for me. I want to know who it belongs to, so I may return it. I came to you for help.' It dawns on me that Raffaelle may have been right all along. Perhaps Padre Paolo has betrayed me. That is why Santiago stopped at our table last night in Luigi's restaurant. It had not been a coincidence that he was eating in that restaurant. Perhaps Santiago knows about the Golden Icon and the threat of the Gardaí and the Irish Consul was only to frighten me.

'I thought I could trust you, Padre.' I hear a catch in my throat. 'I don't think you have even contacted anyone in the Vatican, have you? Instead you went running to Santiago and you betrayed me.' I don't squeeze past his knees instead I turn away from him and walk along the pew. It is ungainly and awkward but I want to get away from him.

'Signora Lavelle,' he calls, 'Josephine!'

My body is shaking. I am at the door and I reach out to touch the iron handle but from the corner of my eye a figure moves in the shadow. It is the old man with the yellow corduroy jacket. His eyes are like black holes and a half smile hovers on his cracked lips.

I slam the door behind me and run.

My feet won't carry me fast enough. I have to get home. I need the sanctuary of my apartment and I need to think. I am propelled by urgency and fear. It is the same feeling I had four years ago when I was hunted by the press. When I was betrayed and humiliated. But its familiarity shocks me. It grows inside me, gnawing at my fears, doubts and insecurities like a vicious and vindictive disease. I stumble through the village realising all my judgements have been in error.

Why did I agree to go back to Dublin to sing at Michael's funeral? I should have stayed away and never seen Seán or Karl Blakey again. Why did I go to Germany? Seán hated me so much he was prepared to sacrifice me. I am disposable. Where is my letter? Does Barbara know I lied?

It is midday. I am hot and my head thumps. Perhaps Karl Blakey is watching me. Maybe Maximilian Strong's nephew is in the village watching Raffaelle's villa. Alarm propels me. I take the long route to my apartment avoiding the main square and the fountain. Turning constantly to look over my shoulder. I pass familiar alleyways that seem darker, stone houses that were once quaint now seem sinister, and at the bakery the steps seem steeper than usual. My muscles tire, I slow down, breathing hard. I stop and lean against the wall. It is cool on my back and the jagged edges prick my skin. It is my penance.

My eyes are closed, my face is damp and perspiration clings to my skin. A film of uncomfortable moisture covers me like a clammy shroud. I fumble in my handbag for the key and open the wooden communal door. I glance at my mail box and in that instance I decide I will get the Golden Icon. I will dig it up and I will take it to the museum in Milan, the Refectory of the *Santa Maria della Grazie church*. There will be queues of tourists waiting to see Leonardo's *Last Supper* but I will be patient. I will wait. I will give it to the Curator.

Why should I risk my life? Why did I bury it up in the hills? Why didn't I put it in the safety of a bank deposit box? Why didn't Raffaelle advise me to put it somewhere safer?

I stop half way on the stairs to my apartment. My front door hangs ajar. The broken lock dangles from the split wood. Very slowly and with the tip of my finger I push the door open. The corridor is filled with my discarded shoes and my outdoor jackets hang untouched. I remove my shoes. The laundry room is untouched. I walk in bare feet and at the bottom of the stairs I hear a voice. I grab a rolled up umbrella.

Music?

Step by step I slowly go up to my living room. Music scores have been pulled apart and are strewn across the floor. The wooden bookcase has been forced from the wall and lies like a crooked and broken giant, books are torn, pages ripped, spines are broken. Chairs are scattered and broken. The sofa is slashed and white stuffing hangs loose and lays in clumps across the floor. My piano has been daubed with gold paint, and not unlike graffiti on Italian trains, it is sprayed with obscenities.

In the kitchen, cupboards and shelves have been emptied and scattered; food, plates and glasses are smashed on the floor.

Music?

I grip the rolled umbrella. Upstairs in my bedroom the arc shaped window lies open. Views of the lake and mountains remain the same but the sheets, duvet and pillows are slashed and ripped. The contents of my wardrobe are strewn over the floor like the entrails of a dark monster, and from the CD player beside my bed, Tosca sings.

I live for love, I live for art. I live for love, I live for art.

Raffaelle arrives in less than fifteen minutes. 'I was in the square,' he says. 'Drinking coffee with Angelo. Santiago is on his way.'

We are standing in the doorway looking at the mess in the lounge. 'It's best not to touch anything. The police may want to take fingerprints. Who would have done this?'

Santiago's voice rings out from downstairs.

'Come on up,' I shout down.

'Are you all right?' he asks. 'You are not hurt?'

'I'm fine. I came home to find this.' I open my arms to the disorder around me.

'Have you touched anything?' His voice is sharp and his ferret eyes travel over me first, then over my home. He thrusts out his nose and tiptoes through the debris to the terrace. He is accompanied by a uniformed police officer who takes photographs and makes notes.

Santiago calls to me from outside.

'Is anything missing?'

'How would she know, with all this mess?' Raffaelle shouts back.

I ignore Raffaelle and tiptoe through the debris to stand

beside Santiago who is staring into the street below, more interested in the terrace than the destruction to my home.

'They forced the lock but they could have climbed up, here,' he says pointing.

I am shaking. My knees cannot support me and I slump onto a chair. Raffaelle rummages inside the kitchen and finds a half bottle of brandy. He pours a generous measure and I sip, holding it with both hands. The afternoon breeze encompasses my body like a thin gauze and it causes my hair to stick to the back of my neck. I am fighting the nausea rising in my chest, a bile tide in the claustrophobic cabin of my body.

I am frightened.

'It is shock.' Raffaelle stands beside me. 'It's normal.' He places his hand on my shoulder reassuringly and I am grateful for his presence.

I respond automatically to Santiago's questions. What time did I leave? Where did I go? How long was I gone for? Did I see anyone? Do I have any reason to think why someone would do this? I don't mention Karl Blakey and he doesn't react when I say I spoke to Padre Paolo.

'For heaven's sake Santiago, can't you see the state she's in? Can't these questions wait?' Raffaelle explodes and I wonder why he is so antagonistic toward a man who, for many years, was virtually his brother-in-law.

Santiago moves around the apartment. He flicks music scores with his feet, turning them to see what lies underneath. Glass crunches under his foot. He leans down as if something catches his eye and when he stands he is clutching a black and white photograph.

I curse myself. It is the print of the British soldiers in the war; the thieves, the looters and the murderer. I had forgotten I left it resting on the shelf against the books.

'It would appear that whoever did this was a professional. He or they picked the lock of the communal door downstairs but then used force to enter your apartment. What were they looking for? What were they after? We need to establish if anything is missing.' He leans against the doorframe looking into the lounge and turning to gaze at me on the terrace. His secretive eyes travel over my face and then rest on the photograph in his hand.

He says to Raffaelle. 'I understand she is in shock but this is the scene of a crime.'

'I have nothing of any real value,' I say.

'No? A wealthy, and once famous opera singer, must have something valuable. Jewellery?'

'Only a sapphire necklace. I usually keep it in the bedroom, in a drawer beside the bed.'

Santiago nods at the uniformed officer who disappears upstairs.

'Money? Did you keep cash?'

I shake my head.

'What a stupid question.' Raffaelle begins pacing up and down and I am grateful he is here to act as an intermediary between me and Santiago.

'Who would break in here during daylight hours? If you have nothing of value what were they looking for? Who are they? Or were they working alone?' Santiago nonchalantly taps the photograph on the palm of his hands.

'What are you going to do?' Raffaelle asks.

When Santiago crouches down beside me his nose is level with mine. There are tiny blackheads on his cheeks and lines at the corner of his eyes. He holds the photograph between his index finger and his thumb and I refuse to look at it.

'Padre Paolo is concerned about your safety. He has been concerned about your welfare. Is there anyone who you may think is responsible for this? Can you think of anyone who would cause damage to your property? What are they looking for?'

I am shaking my head but my mind is working frantically. I dare not glance at the photograph in his hand. He is taunting me.

I think of the man at Raffaelle's villa. Karl Blakey in Comaso who once broke into my home in Germany. Barbara whom I sent on a wild goose chase. The Golden Icon buried in the woods, and Maximilian Strong and his nephew.

Michael and Seán are dead. Michael and Seán are dead.

I am shaking. I cannot speak.

Raffaelle places his hand on my head and strokes my hair. 'There was a man at my villa yesterday. I don't know who he is but he is not from here. He wore a suit and sunglasses and he has a shaved head.'

The uniformed man returns holding my sapphire necklace in his hand. I take it from him and hold it to my chest. It was my last gift from Michael.

'It was under some clothes, so they were looking for something else,' he says.

'What time?' Santiago rises to his feet and stares at Raffaelle.

'About four o'clock and then early evening.'

'Last night I met you in Luigi's. I asked you if you needed help but you didn't say anything.'

'I didn't know he was going to do this, did I?' Raffaelle replies.

'You still don't know it was him, Signor Peverelli.' The man in the police uniform says. 'It is not a normal robbery. They did not take your necklace, and they have damaged your property. It is more of a warning.'

'Are you sure nothing is missing?' Santiago insists. His eyes are inquisitive. It's as if an invisible current runs between us and I am locked in his gaze. I cannot tear my eyes from his. Does he know?

'Give her a chance to tidy the apartment.' Raffaelle pushes himself between me and Santiago as if to snip our invisible contact. 'Perhaps something is missing, she just doesn't know yet.'

'I will get to the bottom of this.' Santiago places the photograph on the table beside my elbow and pauses at the door. 'I'm not sure what it is you want to hide, Signora Lavelle, I only hope that whatever it is, that it is more important than your life. Whoever these people are or whatever they want, they are determined. They have done this damage but it could have been far worse. Consider the possibility that you may have been here. Do you think they would be too polite to harm you?'

Raffaelle's grip tightens on my shoulder and Santiago continues speaking.

'If they haven't found what they are looking for this time. They will be back and believe me, there will be a next time. You are playing a very dangerous game and they will not stop until they find it. These people will show you no mercy. Are you sure it is worth risking your life?'

Raffaelle helps me tidy the apartment. We fill countless rubbish bags that he carries down to the bin and I sweep the floor. I refuse to stay at his villa so he brings me plates and glasses from his home and food supplies from the village.

'I wish you would stay with me,' he says on his return. 'It is crazy for you to be here on your own.'

'I will not be intimidated.' I know he is thinking I am stubborn. 'Karl Blakey did this. I saw him this morning down at the harbour and he told me that William, Seán's brother, is now after the family heirloom.'

I do not mention that Karl wants to find out why and how Seán was blackmailing me and would do anything to rattle me.

I hand Raffaelle books to place on the shelves.

'He would do this damage?'

'And worse! Nothing will stop him. He bugged my house once.'

'And what about the thug hanging around the villa? Do you not think it could have been him?'

'Dieter said that Maximilian and his nephew Ian are dangerous. They import women from eastern Europe, and he forces them to work in brothels. Just supposing, it was Ian who killed Seán. He didn't know what he was looking for, that's why he stole the copy of the Turner from his study but when they realised it was a fake they decided to watch the house and follow Barbara. That would have led them here, to me.' I hand him more books which he places randomly on different shelves.

I continue, 'I think they followed Barbara here, to Comaso. It's obvious. They didn't know about me until this week.'

'So, you think they are still following her?'

'I don't know. He was here yesterday at your villa, the same time Barbara was here with me. If she left on the last ferry last night and, if he hasn't been around today, maybe they followed her and they both went to Munich.'

'Barbara would be there by now. She will know that you are lying. Dieter will have told her that you took the Golden Icon. She will come back here but you don't want to give her the icon now, do you?'

'It's about doing what is right.'

'So what are you going to do? It is getting dangerous. Look at this mess. You could have been here. You could have been hurt.'

It was something I didn't want to think about.

Raffaelle slams down the books. 'What if you are wrong and it wasn't Karl Blakey who trashed your apartment? What if it is Maximilian and Ian? You are in danger.'

I stare at the debris on the floor and my tainted piano. 'I think I will take the icon to the refectory of the *Santa Maria della Grazie.*'

'The church?' Raffaelle tugs on his moustache. 'Ah, Josephine, you fill me with despair. You won't let me take it to my friend Sergio in Lenno?'

'It would never bring us any luck. Anyone who wants to use it for their own gain…'

'Yes, yes, I know. But your life is in danger. Your flat has been ransacked and all you want to do is to take the most valuable and priceless icon in Europe and give it to the church.'

'It isn't the church exactly. It's more of a museum. They will know what to do with it. I can leave it anonymously I don't want to get involved with the Italian Art Squad. I don't want them asking questions about Dieter and Michael, and the past.'

'And what about this Maximilian and Ian? Do you think they are going to just go away and leave you alone?'

'He will when he realises I haven't got it.'

'You are delusional! I don't understand you.' He throws the few remaining books onto the shelf. 'I have had enough. You care nothing for me. There is no point in speaking to you any more. You are beyond reason. You are selfish and difficult.'

'Raffaelle–'

'It is simple.' He holds up his hand in protest to me. 'You don't love me. That is the truth in all of this.'

'Raffaelle, wait…'

But he is gone. I listen to his footsteps receding down the stairs, the slam of the front door and this time I know he won't be back. I am on my own.

CHAPTER NINE

The stars were shining,
And the earth was scented.
The gate of the garden creaked
And a footstep touched the sand...
E lucevan le stelle, Tosca

I spend all afternoon scrubbing golden paint from my battered piano and sorting through music scores; my leather bound copies are torn, pages are ripped and others merely screwed up and creased. Now I am flattening each page, each score, remembering each opera. It is a lifetime ago and my sadness is overwhelming. I was another woman then; younger, reckless and filled with positive energy and spirit. Now I am defeated. I am no longer me. I am undecided and confused.

The front door bell rings.

I tie a knot in the belt of my silk gown and hasten down the stairs, along the corridor, closing the laundry room door. The front door has been mended by Raffaelle's neighbour who owns the local carpenter shop. I have a new lock and chain.

When I peer through the spy-hole I am rewarded with a

distorted vision of a sandy-headed man in a white shirt and open collar. He looks vaguely familiar.

I partly open the door.

'Josephine Lavelle?' His accent is Irish. 'David Mallory, Irish Consul.' He holds out a business card. I take it through the gap. 'I met you at Michael's funeral. I'm sorry I didn't telephone first, but I was told you didn't have a secretary or a press office any more. I've come from Milan to see you.'

'Hold on.' I close the door, remove the chain and open the door.

There is a sheen of perspiration on his pale forehead. The jacket of his suit hangs over his arm.

'You'd better come in,' I say.

He is tall and slim, and his handshake is firm. I am aware of him following me upstairs. I point through the lounge to the terrace. 'Make yourself comfortable while I dress.'

I pull on white cut-offs and a cotton printed blouse. The view across the lake is magnificent and I lean out of the bedroom window inhaling the sweet aroma of jasmine. Below me David Mallory has dragged his chair into the shade of the evening sun. He sits with his legs crossed whistling a slow sad tune that I don't recognise.

He stands up when I walk onto the terrace.

'Drink? Water, beer, coffee?' I ask.

'Beer, thank you.'

I wave my hand for him to sit.

In the kitchen I rummage for a glass but David Mallory prefers to drink beer from the bottle and I sip sparkling water.

'Beautiful view.' His sandy head nods toward the lake.

'Yes.'

'It's a long way from Ireland.'

'A different life,' I agree.

'Michael's death was very sad.' He wipes beer from his lips. 'He was still a very fit man even though he was almost ninety.'

I cannot imagine Michael that old. He was sixty when our affair began.

'You knew Shona?' he continues.

'She died shortly after our wedding. Only a few months later. They didn't tell us how ill she was until afterwards. She didn't want to ruin our day.'

'That's Shona,' he smiles. 'They were friends of our family for years. I was at school with Seán, and William went out with my sister Brigid, they were together a few years.'

I pick up my glass and the bubbles tickle my tongue.

'We were all close but then I lost touch. I was abroad. That's why I wasn't at your wedding. I went to Canada. I–'

'Mr Mallory.' I put my glass back on the table. 'I–'

He smiles and holds up his beer bottle. 'I'm sorry. It's been a very difficult few weeks as you can imagine. I called you a few times and Inspector Bareldo was kind enough to tell me where you lived, but then I thought it would be better that I came to see you in person.' He looks around appreciatively. 'I'm so pleased that I did. This is far more convivial than the heat in Milan, and besides a change of scene clears the head and gives a different perspective on life.

'You sang very well at Michael's funeral. It was beautiful and you were missed at Seán's. It was a shame that you couldn't come over for it.'

'I sent flowers.'

'You understand this has all been devastating for Barbara and the children. It has been such a shock. Did you know it was a burglary too?' He pulls his chair further into the shade.

'William told me.'

David Mallory looks away. He looks tired like a man who wants to get home; home to a cooler climate. Home to a place with no problems.

'We don't really know what he was looking for,' he says, 'although he stole the Turner. You remember the one hanging in Seán's study? It's unusual. You see, Seán thought he was a mourner and a friend of Michael's and so they went to his study but it doesn't seem likely that he killed Seán for a fake painting.' His pale eyes focus on my face. 'Perhaps you can help us?'

'Us?'

'I'm working with the Gardaí in Ireland.'

In Luigi's restaurant Santiago told us David Mallory was working with the Gardaí, and although I knew it would just be a matter of time until they tracked me down, my pulse races. I am conscious that I must regulate my breathing but my palms begin to perspire.

Does David Mallory have my letter? Does he know my secret?

I tilt my face in what I consider to be an enquiring manner and he continues speaking.

'You see, the thing is, the police think that Seán was killed because the burglar was looking for something; something very valuable. We know that you had a lengthy conversation with Seán after the funeral and we need to know if he mentioned anything to you. Did he say anything about a valuable painting or a piece of artwork to help him pay off his debts? The thing is–' He holds up his hand and his golden wedding band glistens in the sunlight. 'We know he asked you to go to Germany. We found the receipt for your plane ticket on Seán's computer. We are trying to establish if there is a link between Seán's murder, the stolen painting and your trip to Munich.'

I sip water and the bubbles are salty on my lips. Although my movements are slow and deliberate I am thinking quickly.

'The strange thing is,' he continues. 'Seán booked a return ticket for you, but you didn't travel back to Ireland. Did you? Why would Seán pay for your return ticket to Germany? Unless you were doing something for him?'

'I went to visit someone.'

He takes a crumpled piece of paper from the pocket in the top of his shirt. 'Dieter Guzman?'

'Yes.' I know now, that he knows more than he is telling me. He is trying to trap me.

'Dieter Guzman is a collector of artefacts, paintings and hidden treasures,' he says, 'unfortunately for him, they are not all his. Most of them are stolen or they are forgeries, but there is one piece that I am looking for Miss Lavelle, I don't care about anything else. I am looking for a solid gold icon of the Madonna and her child. It's called The Golden Icon.'

'Does it belong to Seán?' I ask.

'It belongs to Ireland. Let me tell you something of our Irish history; on the fifth of April 1829, Pope Pius VIII was ordained as Pope. He was sixty-seven years old. He was feeble and afflicted with terrible and painful sores on his back. He was so ill, all he could do was sign papers presented to him by his Cardinal, Giuseppe Albani who ruled the Papal States autocratically as if he were the Pope himself.

'At this time there were many events happening in England, Ireland and in Europe as it was then divided. Many people in England believed in the divine right of Kings; the legitimacy of hereditary nobility, and the right and privileges of the Anglican church and there was a vigorous campaign which led to the Roman Catholic Relief Act.

'Although the Home Secretary Sir Robert Peel opposed emancipation, he knew that civil strife would be an even greater danger and would cause a revolution in Ireland. Basically, they feared an uprising. They feared a rebellion.' He swigs from his beer bottle and wipes his lip. 'You see, Miss Lavelle, this Act allowed members of the Catholic church to sit in parliament at Westminster but it was a compromise. What it really did was to deprive the minor landlords of Ireland. Any man who owned or rented land was permitted to vote but–' He waves his finger. 'Here's the catch, they raised the price they had to pay, from forty shillings to ten pounds. Now, if you don't understand our old currency, forty shillings was equal to two pounds, so it was a mere rise of 400 percent.'

I raise an eyebrow. 'That wouldn't have made the British popular,' I say.

'Exactly! So, the Golden Icon was sent to Ireland to fund an Irish Rebellion in 1830 but it was stolen from the Bishop's house without ever reaching the rebels and it ended up back in Europe.' He leans back and folds his arms.

'Why are the Gardaí working with you, Mr Mallory?'

'Why?' He looks surprised. 'Because I am Seán's friend and I am also the Irish Consul in Milan, and, I am working on behalf of the Irish government.'

'I wouldn't think this is normally the role of the Irish Consul.'

'No, but this is a delicate matter, Miss Lavelle and one that we wish to resolve quickly. If the Italians realise that the Golden Icon is in Italy, it would, as they say, be a whole new ball-game. No-one wants to involve the infamous Italian Art Squad.'

'Did Barbara visit you in Milan?' I ask.

'Barbara?'

'Yes, she came here yesterday to this apartment to see me. She is in Italy. I'm sure you know that. She was asking me similar questions to you, and I told her I didn't take the Golden Icon. I left it in Germany. When I saw it I decided I wasn't going to carry it through customs. A stolen Golden Icon in my possession would do me no favours if I was caught, Mr Mallory. Also, at that time, I was attempting to resuscitate my career but Seán hired Karl Blakey, a journalist who wrote about my downfall four years ago, to blackmail me into going to Germany. He threatened to tell Karl where I lived. The thing is, Mr Mallory, it doesn't make sense that you're working with the Gardaí. Why is the Golden Icon important to you? Are you doing this for the Irish government as you say, or simply for Barbara? Because it could only have been Barbara who told you that the family heirloom is the Golden Icon, no-one else knows. Are you here because you want to reclaim it for her?'

David Mallory rubs his face. 'Barbara did come to my

office in Milan. So I researched what she told me and I spoke to the Gardaí. There are many people interested in its recovery. It doesn't belong to Barbara but it does belong to the Irish government.'

'I hope you told Barbara that?'

'I did, but there's something else. Something far worse.' His pale eyes are fixed on me. 'Dieter Guzman is dead.'

My body is rigid. My mouth dry. I block out the humming engines of the cars below on the lake road but there is a scream of a crying baby from the street that startles me.

'You didn't know?'

I shake my head. A black bird bounces on a branch in the horse chestnut tree. He begins to twill. The sunlight on his feathers makes him look so black he looks almost purple like liquid ink.

'How? When?' I ask.

David Mallory's eyes scan the tree then he looks back at me. 'A few days ago.'

'How?'

'He was murdered - strangled.'

I am back in Dieter's apartment. I hear his heavy breathing, see his yellow teeth and dirty hair.

'Barbara was detained by the German police for questioning.'

'But she—'

'She had nothing to do with it, I know. He was already dead. His apartment had been broken into, but she was seen calling at his home.' He begins to peel the label from the beer bottle, scratching it with his index finger. 'The thing is Miss Lavelle, is that there is one combining factor to all these deaths. A man called Maximilian Strong, and the police suspect he has been involved with Seán's death, and now with Dieter's murder. They fear he is not going to stop until he gets what he wants, and he wants the Golden Icon, at any price.'

'You think he is the murderer?'

'He is almost ninety but he has a nephew who unfortunately is as ruthless as he is. Ian Strong began dealing drugs in London and after a spell in prison, he deals in drug trafficking and child prostitution. It seems Maximilian Strong has found a lucrative market to sell stolen art work in Eastern Europe. He finances drugs, prostitution and people-trafficking, using stolen art work to sell or barter with eastern European dealers.'

I raise my eyebrows. David Mallory continues speaking.

'Unfortunately Ian is not as refined as his uncle. He promises young girls job opportunities, drugs them, takes their passports and forces them into prostitution. He has no regard for human life. He is not just a dangerous criminal but a murderer and,' he pauses, 'we think that you are next on his list.'

'Me? Why?'

'Because apart from Barbara you were the last person to speak to Dieter. It won't be long until the German police, the Italian police and the Gardaí all want to speak with you. You see, the thing is Miss Lavelle, is that everyone has been looking for the Golden Icon for years. It isn't just Maximilian Strong who wants it. The Italians think it belongs to them. The Vatican is especially interested as they made it and paid for it, and now the Germans believe it is theirs, and of course, the Irish want it back as it was originally given to them by the Pope.'

'So you are here on behalf of the Irish Government?'

'I am here because of Seán and Michael. I don't want the same thing to happen to you. Maximilian Strong found Dieter before we did. I have come here to warn you - to help you.'

I imagine Dieter's wrinkled neck and a shiver passes through me and a trickle of perspiration slides down my spine.

'It is just a matter of time until he finds you, Miss Lavelle. He's a very determined man and like me, he wants the Golden Icon. He may already know where you are.'

'I don't have it.'

'It's Maximilian you have to worry about. If he didn't find what he was looking for in Munich then he will come here. You are the only one left.'

'He can't kill me for something I don't have.'

'He can and he will. I am here to help you. I can take the Golden Icon and return it to its rightful owners—'

'Who are?'

'The Irish government. It will go on display in Ireland. It belongs to the Irish people. I am here to recover the Golden Icon and bring it home.'

'And Barbara?'

'Barbara?' he says.

'Yes, if it was Michael's wish to pay off Seán's debts surely it belongs to Barbara.'

'It is a national treasure.'

'She went to you in good faith, Mr Mallory. She trusted you. Seán and Michael have been friends of your family for years and I thought you were here as a family friend. Shame on you.' I stand up. 'I wish you lots of luck but I'm sorry I cannot be of more help.'

The table is strewn with pieces of ripped beer label. He rises wearily and throws his jacket over his arm.

'Please think about this very carefully Miss Lavelle. You probably don't have much time left.'

'I don't have the Golden Icon, and I will tell Maximilian Strong that, when he gets here.'

'You may have sent Barbara on a wild goose chase to Munich but no-one else believes you. None of us are that gullible or desperate.'

'Mr Mallory let me show you something. My apartment was ransacked this morning while I was out, look.' I pick up my mobile phone and show him the photographs. 'I have only just finished cleaning and I am still sorting these music scores. If there was anything of any value they would have found it.' It's only a white lie that I am telling. In the lounge I point to the piano, the slashed sofa and torn cushions.

'What they couldn't break or smash they ripped apart. They left nothing unturned.'

I follow him down the steps to the front door, almost pushing him out. He takes the door handle and pauses on the steps in the hallway. 'Think this through carefully but quickly, Miss Lavelle. Your time is running out.'

'Dieter showed me the Golden Icon,' I say, as if mustering patience needed to speak to an errant schoolboy. 'Although he showed it to me, I didn't take it.'

'I hope you are not attempting to mislead me. It belongs to the Irish Government. I don't want to alarm you but the net is closing in. Please don't think about keeping it for your own private gain. Apart from an unlucky story attached to it, if you attempt to use it for your private use, we know you filed for bankruptcy four years ago. We would soon know if there was an elevated change in your financial status. Unless of course, you find a private buyer, who would only give you a fraction of its true value. You will never be able to sell it without repercussions and that certainly wouldn't benefit your already flagging career.'

I want to slap his face but he moves quickly, down the stairs toward the communal patio. He is standing on the bottom step when I speak and I am looking down on him.

'If it was in my possession Mr Mallory, I would certainly not give it to the Irish, they didn't seem very capable of looking after it, the first time.'

'And I could also say the same about you, and the fortune and the fame that you failed to maintain.' He lifts his hand. 'Goodbye Miss Lavelle.'

On Thursday morning I wake after only a few hours' sleep. I am drained of energy. I have spent the night thinking and I have considered my options. I cannot go back to Padre Paolo. I will not go to Santiago. I will not give the Golden Icon to Barbara or to David Mallory and as much as I love Raffaelle I cannot contemplate a new life with him in Florence. But I must make a decision. The hour glass of my life is dwindling. If Maximilian and his son Ian killed Dieter, then they will be here for me soon. I must leave. I must escape. The right thing to do is to take the Golden Icon to Milan, go to London and disappear.

Raffaelle is in the villa when I phone him and he agrees to meet me for a drink in the bodeguita in the square beside the fountain at nine this evening. I don't tell him I am leaving Comaso tomorrow.

The rest of the day passes quickly. I pack and clean the

apartment trying to erase the presence of my burglar Karl Blakey. He has invaded my space, my privacy and I feel violated. He has searched through my cupboards and drawers, sniffing, feeling and touching my clothes and my music. Nothing is sacred. I know it is him who has done this damage. Maximilian and Ian were following Barbara. They were in Munich.

I will collect the Golden Icon first thing tomorrow morning. My bags will be packed and I will leave on the early morning ferry.

It is almost dark when I venture from the safety and security of my apartment. I negotiate the steep steps under the yellow glow of the street lamps and I am struck with the realisation that my life in Comaso is almost at an end. This is the last time I will run down the steep steps to meet Raffaelle. I will not have time to say goodbye to the Mayor Angelo and his wife, Carlo, Luisa, or Nano in the gelateria or Luigi. My step falters, I swallow and blink back tears.

Raffaelle is waiting for me. He is sitting at a terrace table outside the bodeguita. He greets me with a distant kiss on my cheek, orders white wine and sits back with his legs crossed.

I lean across the table and speak quietly. I tell him about David Mallory's visit and my decision to leave Comaso. Afterwards I tap my foot in nervous rhythm to the music from the restaurant across the square where a dark Italian girl sings romantic pop songs. She is accompanied by an older handsome man playing an electric piano. Several notes are flat and I cringe in anticipation of the repetitive chorus and the same mistake. Surrounding the singers is a wedding party. The guests are jovial and their spirits are high. The bride and groom are still in their wedding attire. They look young, far too young, for marriage.

My emotions have drained me. Raffaelle's wine lays untouched on the table. He is digesting what I have said. Now when he leans forward to speak I move the glass away from his elbow and gesticulating hand.

'We have it in our possession. What difference does it make if Barbara thinks it belongs to her or that the Irish Consul shows up and says it belongs to the Irish government. Pouff.' He puffs out hot breath and his moustache quivers.

'She has more claim to it than the Irish Government.'

'What does it matter what I say or think? You seem to have made up your own mind without consulting me. You don't love me enough,' he says. 'It could be a new beginning for us together but you are not interested.'

I recoil at the false note that drifts across the fountain. The bride and groom are each standing with a different group of people, and for as long as I have been watching them, they haven't yet spoken to each other.

'We cannot live a lie.' I sip my wine. 'We cannot live using someone else's fortune. It is not right. I'm still aware of the caution that comes with the icon.'

'Caution? It is a sham designed to frighten everyone,' he sighs. 'Well, Padre Paolo hasn't been of much use to you. So much for trusting him before me.'

'He told Santiago he was worried for my safety.'

'He probably told him about the Golden Icon too.'

'I'm not sure, maybe it was the phone call from the Gardaí or David Mallory that made Santiago aware of my situation.'

'The Irish government want it. Barbara wants the icon

to pay off Seán's debts. Santiago is sniffing around like a dog hunting truffles and worse of all is that Maximilian Strong or his nephew will kill you for it.'

'Maybe I should give it to Santiago. He is the chief of police here in Lombardy. He will know what to do. It would be safer than me carrying it to Milan.'

Raffaelle raises his palm. 'No, no, no, cara, no!'

I raise an eyebrow at his outburst.

'He cannot have it. That man is a philistine. He has no appreciation of art.'

'Maybe not, but he has a sense of what is right and wrong. He will do the right thing and he will liaise with the Italian Art Squad. It came to me by default but it is my responsibility. I must put the wrong right.'

'This is crazy. It isn't your wrong to put right. It was Michael who stole it. He is the thief. It has nothing to do with you.'

I look at him thoughtfully and say nothing.

'You are not responsible for what Michael did,' he insists, 'during the war, nearly seventy years ago.'

It's something about the casualness of the bride and groom that unsettles me, or the group of people laughing and talking, or perhaps the way Raffaelle looks at me, but I have the feeling that someone is watching us. I glance around at the other tables. I think of Karl Blakey. Is he hiding behind a wall or window spying, reporting back to William or making notes for the lies he will tell? I take a deep breath. My mind is made up.

'I'm leaving tomorrow,' I say. 'I will get the Golden Icon first thing in the morning and give it to Santiago. I can't live like this. I cannot live in fear, hiding around every corner, wondering who will come knocking on my door or who will trash my apartment next.'

'And what about your music? What about opera? And what about Cesare?'

'Cesare will always be my friend but even he cannot perform miracles. My reputation as a difficult diva precedes me. It always will. It is my legacy. It is all I have left.'

'Where will you go?'

'London, or maybe back to America.'

'America?' He raises his voice and I raise my palm to silence him. 'But your brother is the only family you have there.'

'I know.'

'You have no other family. You will be alone again like you were when I met you.'

'Yes.'

'You are not happy alone.'

I shrug. I cannot look at the bridal party.

'Will you come back?' he asks.

'Perhaps, when this is all over.' I pull a serviette from a plastic container on the table with a picture of three holy-looking women and underneath the words *Tre Marie*.

'I will wait for you.'

'You are an attractive man, Raffaelle. You have many pretty art students. I don't expect miracles.' He doesn't reply and I realise I am expecting him to put up more of a fight to keep me. I flinch as the piano player misses three notes, and I wrap the serviette tight around my index finger.

'What about Tosca?' he asks. 'Glorietta sent us tickets for the opening on Saturday.'

I shake my head. 'Tomorrow is Friday. I will go early

and get the icon and I will give it to Santiago. Then I will leave here.'

'It is a waste.'

I am not sure if he is referring to our relationship or the fact that I have decided to give the Golden Icon to Santiago. 'Perhaps you will still go to Florence one day?' I say.

'And perhaps one day, you will sing Tosca in the Teatro Il Domo.'

I raise an eyebrow at his audacity but I smile.

'Will we not spend our last night together?' he says.

'No, that would only make me more sad. Come and meet me in the early morning,' I say, 'before five, when it is getting light. Come with me to get the Golden Icon, please?'

He nods and I lean over and place my mouth against his cheek.

'Fino a domani,' I whisper. When I stand up Raffaelle reaches out and his fingers brush my hand. Then without a backward glance I head for the stone steps and the sanctuary of my apartment for the last time. I climb the steps, turn the corner and tears are falling down my cheeks. My dreams are as far from me as the stars are in the night-sky. Everything is over. I have no-one. I stumble up the ill-lit rocky steps when a bony hand grabs my wrist. I squeal. A brutal slap cuts across my mouth and my head is smacked against the stone wall. I have a fleeting image of a shaven headed man and an old man whose eyes are pink-rimmed like those of a repulsive reptile. He wears a yellow corduroy jacket.

His skeletal fingers are hooked around my elbow. A fist comes out of the dark and smacks my cheek. I crack the back of my skull on the wall. I fight the hands that hold me but strong fingers press against my windpipe. My cough turns to a choke.

My handbag spills to the floor. The contents tumble onto the street. A black shoe stamps on my mobile. A hand grabs my hair and my face is pushed against the wall. The skin scrapes open and blood pours down my cheek. I release a scream but the stone wall rips my lip and scrapes my teeth.

Sour breath assails my nose. 'It is time we had a chat, Miss Lavelle. You know who I am, and why I am here. Let's not waste any time. Where is the Golden Icon? I know it isn't in your apartment and I know that you haven't given it to Padre Paolo.'

'Padre Pao…' My speech is muffled. My lips graze the wall and a rock is poking into my eye.

'You should never trust a man like that with a secret.'

I move my head but a hand grabs my neck.

'I don't have much time and my patience is running out. My nephew Ian has always liked you. Haven't you Ian? Why don't you show her?'

Ian's hand travels across my body and he squeezes my breasts then he caresses my stomach and his fingers rest between my legs. My scream is muffled.

'Where is the Golden Icon?'

I grunt. I cannot breathe.

'This is not a game. Tell me.' The grip tightens. 'Ian? Let's show Miss Lavelle just how much you like her. We can do it here in the street or we could go to your apartment and take all night. The choice is yours.'

Ian tugs my skirt and bunches it around my waist. I wriggle and strain away from him. He rips my underwear. He has iron-like fingers that are pushing and probing.

'Hey! Polizia! Polizia!' There are running footsteps. A voice shouts. 'Hey!'

The grip on my body recedes. 'You have twenty-four hours to give it to me or we kill you and Raffaelle.'

'Polizia! Polizia!' The voice shouts.

I am released. I sink to the ground, breathless and aware of my semi-naked state. I pull my skirt and cover my knees. Blood trickles down my cheek, my head is throbbing, my chest heaving. I lean with my back against the wall aware that someone is bending over me. I want to cry. I have been saved.

'Still alive then?'

When I open my eyes Karl Blakey is smiling down at me.

Karl Blakey reaches down and helps me to my feet. I lean against the wall for support. He picks up my bag from the floor and inspects each item: purse, lipstick, tissues, coins. He's like a lizard. His tongue flicks as he places them in my handbag.

'You were lucky I was passing,' he says.

'You've been following me.' My voice is thick and my lip sore.

He pulls a tissue from the pack and passes me one. I dab my face.

'I've been looking out for you,' he says. 'It's just as well that I was around. This could have been a very nasty incident.'

He bends to pick up the pieces of my smashed mobile phone. 'I saved you. He was going to rape you.'

'You're not a hero Karl. You're a scumbag.'

His laugh is an octave too high. 'Is that all the thanks I get? I could have photographed it. That would have made a good story.'

A group of teenagers pass us on the way to the village. 'Buonasera,' they call.

'Buonanotte,' he replies. 'They probably think we are old friends or even lovers, stopping to kiss on the steps.'

Their laughter follows them down to the square below.

'Why are you following me? Seán is dead there is no story now. Why don't you go home?' I snatch my handbag from his inspecting fingers and prying eyes.

'Well, you see, there's something that still doesn't make sense.' He stands too close to me. 'And it's still a mystery to me. Why was Seán so interested in blackmailing you?'

'He wasn't.'

'He had something on you. Something I missed. There's a bigger story and I've got a hunch I missed it four years ago.'

'Is that why you trashed my apartment?'

His piggy eyes and gerbil cheeks shine ghoulishly under the yellow lamplight.

'You're an arsehole,' I say.

'Look, I know about the Golden Icon,' he says. 'Barbara told William that when she got to Munich the police detained her. So, we know you have it. The thing is, so do those guys who just assaulted you.'

'I don't need you to tell me that,' I mumble. I am rummaging for the key to my apartment. My knuckles are scraped and bleeding.

'He said you've got twenty-four hours. That's not long.' He scratches his ear. 'I wouldn't want to be in your shoes.'

'When have you ever wanted to be in my shoes, dick-head?' I turn my back on him and hobble to my front gate.

'You are very ungrateful.' He holds out my front door key and I snatch it from his grasp. 'You're still acting the prima donna, Josephine. You're a real diva. I'll give you that.'

I slam the wooden communal door in his face and lock it behind me.

My nerves and fear overtake my sense of reasoning and I call Raffaelle from my home phone. My mobile is dead.

An hour later I have cleaned my face and we are sitting on the terrace. The sky is like a black velvet cushion. It looks soft against the bright stars and half-moon. My top lip is split, my cheek and forehead is grazed, and I have a lump on the back of my head.

Raffaelle has listened to the story twice, in detail, including Maximilian's rancid breath, Ian's attempt to violate me, and his threat to kill us both.

He is leaning against the railing, his arms folded, gazing up at the moon when I speak.

'They have given me twenty-four hours to give them the Golden Icon. You must leave with me,' I insist. 'They will kill you. Ian was going to rape me. They could have brought me in here to my apartment and no-one would have known.' I shudder at the thought. My hands are shaking and I am drinking my second brandy.

'There was no-one else around?' Raffaelle pulls the

corner of his moustache.

'No,' I lie. I don't tell him about Karl Blakey because I can't face the fact that Karl is determined to unearth my secret.

'You're sure he's the same old man you saw in church when you were talking to Padre Paolo?'

I nod.

'Same yellow jacket?'

'Yes, I suppose so. Oh, Raffaelle, how do I know?'

'You said it was a minute ago.'

'Okay, I think so.' I stretch my aching shoulder. I am looking at the broken remnants of my mobile phone laid out on the table.

'I think you will need a new one,' he says.

'Raffaelle, stop it! Please, listen to me. They have given me twenty-four hours. Let's get the Golden Icon first thing and give it to Santiago. He can protect us both.'

'You won't need protecting. You won't be here. You are going back to the States, remember?'

'I'm worried about you.'

'Worried?' His laugh is sarcastic. 'Worried about me? No, Josephine. You are not worried about me, any more than you have been worried about anyone in your life. You are selfish and stubborn. You only ever think of yourself and what matters to you. I don't think you've ever done anything for anyone unless you have benefitted from it. If you cared about me we could use the Golden Icon and get out of here. We could move to Florence and start a new life together but you won't.'

'Raffaelle, please. Please listen to me. This isn't about us selling the icon and living off the proceeds.' I stand and move toward him. 'Come with me?'

'I am not going with you. I can't! This is my home. This villa which has been in my family for generations is my home. Even though you tell me I have squandered my inheritance, I still have my art studio and my students. It isn't always what I want, but it is mine. It is my life and the only one I have, and I am happy with it. Yes, I want to go to Florence and yes, I have dreams. You are not the only one who dreams of art and lives for their passion. I dream of these things too. We could be happy together.'

'It may mean nothing to you but I have my dignity.' He reaches out and strokes the softness of my cheek, touching the side that isn't bruised. 'I love you, but you don't love me.' He moves away and stands at the railing. 'Maximilian has given you twenty-four hours to deliver the statue to him. That's tomorrow night - Friday, so if you give the Golden Icon to Santiago, he will give us protection in return and we can go to the opening night of Tosca on Saturday. Then if your mind is made up and you are still determined to go, you can leave Comaso.

'Be honest with me Josephine, you will not be happy unless you see Glorietta playing Tosca. Tell the truth, cara, will you?'

'Tosca is me.' I am exhausted. 'I am Tosca. The role is mine and to see Glorietta on the stage would destroy me.'

'It will not kill you, cara. It will help you,' he says. 'It will be closure.'

I put my face in my hands. I have spent weeks imagining Glorietta rehearsing; the stage direction; the orchestra; the production. I can even feel the dress she wears. It is not jealousy or envy but simply that they made a mistake in casting her.

'The role should be mine,' I say.

'But it isn't! She is good. She is better than good. She will be a superstar after Saturday night. You want to be seen by the public to support her. You need to be seen by the critics in the theatre. It will be seen as a gracious gesture toward her. It would make you more popular.'

I look at the passion and sincerity in Raffaelle's eyes.

'You're right, they didn't make a mistake at all,' I say. 'Her voice is beautiful. Its tone, its sound and its quality will bring a spiritual depth to the role. I have to see her. I want to see her. I must see her.' My salty tears sting the graze on my cheek causing me to wince but although my face hurts, it is nothing compared to the torture in my soul and the sadness in my heart.

'These are tears of relief and joy. Everything will be all right. You will see.' He rubs my shoulder and I look up at him as I reply.

'I will go to the Teatro Il Domo with you, Raffaelle. I will be there on the opening night regardless of the press and what they say or my humiliation. I will go with you. I will give my support to Glorietta and publicly endorse her as my successor. She deserves that much. It is time for me to stand aside.'

Raffaelle kneels beside me. 'I'll come with you first thing in the morning. We will go up the hill and get the Golden Icon and give it to Santiago.'

'Thank you. I appreciate that, but you hate Santiago, so much. You haven't said a good word about him in all the years I have known you. Why is that?'

'We are not friends.'

'You were once.'

Raffaelle nods. 'It is difficult to explain.'

'So are most things. Try me.'

'He told Glorietta about the art student.'

'And?'

'Well, I would still be with her if he hadn't said anything. He betrayed me.'

'You betrayed her.'

'It was only for a few nights.'

'I think you still love her Raffaelle. You should tell her.'

He shakes his head. 'She has Bruno now.'

'He's just for show,' I smile. 'Eye-candy, they call it.'

'Really?' His eyes light up and there is a softness in his face that I haven't seen for a very long time.

CHAPTER TEN

Oh, sweet kisses and languorous caresses,
While feverishly I stripped the beautiful form
of its veils!
E lucevan le stelle, Tosca

My main concern through the night is not my throbbing head, my split cheek nor the bruising over my eye but the Golden Icon lying buried in the grounds of the Chiesa della Madonna dei miracoli.

The events of the evening leave me lying awake wondering who to be afraid of the most. Maximilian Strong and Ian who threatened to kill me, Raffaelle or Karl Blakey who will stop at nothing to uncover my secret.

My thoughts are jumbled. Tiredness holds me prisoner to my fears and my insecurities. Returning to London or the States fills me with agitation and I am awake to watch the dawn yawn over the lake. I stare for a long time from my bedroom window memorising the view and logging its details in my mind. It will be the last time I watch the sunrise from my apartment.

When Raffaelle arrives he pulls me into his arms but I push him away. He stares at the open luggage lying on the floor.

'Your mind is made up then.'

'You know it is. I will catch the first ferry.' I resist the urge to stroke his cheek and kiss his lips. 'Come on. Let's go and get the icon,' I urge. 'We must hurry.'

'Let's drive,' he says.

'No.'

'Why not?'

'Because–' I don't finish the sentence.

I can't explain the growing foreboding that spreads and seeps through my body like moving quicksand. It is engulfing me, suffocating my senses, and I resist the urge to throw myself into his arms and tell him that we will go to Florence. Instead, I grab my rucksack and wedge a sharp kitchen knife into the front pocket.

'What do you want that for?' His dark eyes flash.

'In case–' I lift the bag onto my back. 'Ian will not get near me again.'

He bites the corner of his moustache but says nothing.

I lock the door behind me and I walk as fast as my tired body will allow me. I am anxious. I will not be at ease until I hold the Golden Icon in the palm of my hands again.

We walk up the steep hill, past the snug secret gardens hidden in villas, the apartment block, and passed the gated entrance to the palazzo where palm trees stir in the early breeze. We cross the car park and wind our way through the narrow forest path.

I bless myself at the shrines but I barely stop. Once we are half way up I glimpse the lake glittering below and I pause, drink water and wait for Raffaelle to sink onto the log bench before I pass him the bottle.

'You will miss all this,' he says, between gulps.

I realise my life will change irrevocably. This sleepy village has been my refuge and my haven but it is my destiny to move on. I will find other operatic roles, perhaps less important, and in venues less known, but at least I will sing. I will return to the stage where I belong.

'Come on, let's go,' I say.

The few cars on the coast road look like children's toys, they snake and disappear in the bend behind the church of Santa Anna di Comaso. I imagine the sleepy village stirring below; Carlo preparing breakfast in the Alberge, the ferry-master swapping tickets for money on the pontoon; the waitress with the butterfly tattoo flinging open terrace doors in the cafe on the lakeside, and the bakery grinding into a busy day.

I picture trays of hot rolls and fresh ciabatta and the comforting smell of baking flour that has greeted me each morning for the past four years, and my stomach growls.

'I'll get fresh bread on the way back,' I whisper and Raffaelle nods.

I know he's conserving his energy. His hands are on his hips and he lengthens his stride attempting to match my gazelle-like pace.

The church bells toll and I stop periodically to wait for Rafael. We walk comfortably sometimes side by side, and sometimes when it narrows through the forest between the trees, we walk in single file.

The humid smell of the beech trees, the pines, the firs and the olive trees fill my senses as we wind our way higher. Below us is tinkling sound of tinny bells and sheep bleating and in the ravine a donkey brays.

'Isn't it beautiful?' he says.

'If only my life was always this peaceful,' I reply.

'The beauty of nature is in your soul,' Raffaelle says between panting breaths, 'and reflected in your eyes.'

'That isn't what you told me last night.' He looks at me questioningly. 'You said I was selfish and stubborn.'

'Yes, but you still appreciate nature,' he smiles. This time he is first to take the lead and he walks ahead of me and I let him go. I look back down to the village, the calmness of the lake and the serenity of the hills leave me with a sense of wonderment and awe at God's creation. Across the valley a dog barks, and I turn and walk quickly away, satisfied that we are not followed.

We reach the fork in the path below the Chiesa della Madonna dei miracoli and we both pause. I have deliberately walked slowly to make sure no-one comes behind us, and when I draw alongside Raffaelle I reach out for his hand. I am sad but I have a clear picture of what I must do.

'Are you okay?' he says.

'I am on a path toward a destiny I have neglected and denied for too long. It is time to go back.'

'Cesare says that you will do well with the Philharmonic. He says they are booked into the Carnegie Hall in October.'

'It won't be the same.'

'It's a start.'

'I'm not sure I have the energy to start again.' My fingers reach up and touch my sensitive wounds, my lip is swollen and my cheek is raw. Only the wind on my face seems to smooth my sores but inside my soul I am seething with anger and rage. I still feel Ian's body pressing against mine. His fingers probing. His breath in my face.

'You will be strong, cara. Look at you now. You are a different woman to the one who arrived in Comaso. You have resolve.'

'Not many people get a second chance,' I say.

'You will, and you won't make the same mistakes next time around.'

We walk up the rocky steps together and when we reach the garden of the church I pull him in the direction of the path.

'Don't you want me to sit on the rock?' He points to where he sat last Tuesday, the day I hid the icon.

'Come with me. It is no longer a secret where it is buried.' I take his hand.

We walk to the back of the church following the overgrown pathway to the hiding place. It has been buried for three days, yet it feels longer, and I am excited at the prospect of regaining my treasure.

I scan the ground identifying the area where I buried it. I recognise the fig tree, the overhanging buddleia and the palm fronds. Leaning over the low wall I push them aside. The ivy seems thicker and I tug its roots, but the fern lays already pulled from the damp soil. I don't use my trowel. Instead I scrape damp earth with my fingers and the soil falls away into a hole. A deep hole, one the size of a shoe box.

'It doesn't make sense.' I am digging frantically.

'What's wrong?'

'It's not here.'

'It must be. Where did you bury it?'

'Here. Right here. Under this!' I lift the fern in my hand.

'There's a hole but here's no box,' he says, stating the

obvious.

'It's gone.' I look around. There is no sign of anything. No indication that it has moved because of the storm or rain disturbing the earth, so I climb the wall and move further into the undergrowth, crawling on my hands and knees. Nothing else seems out of place.

'It's gone,' I repeat.

Raffaelle continues to stare at the empty hole tugging his moustache.

I don't know how long I crouch in the dirt, on my knees but eventually he takes my arm and lifts me to my feet. I pull away from his grip. I walk slowly at first, methodically looking at every small detail then I broaden the circle, taking bigger steps, casting my eyes further beyond the wall and up the hill to the ill-kept woods beyond. Then I run. First in one direction and then another until I no longer know what I am looking for, and sometime later, Raffaelle catches me in his arms and holds me tight.

'Shush, cara, shhhh.'

'It's gone.' His shirt is wet from my tears. I rub my eyes and mascara stings my irises. My torn lip is swollen, my grazed cheeks burn with my salty tears, and my head thumps.

'Who would have taken it? No-one knew it was here.' I push him from me.

'Raffaelle? Did you…'

'No, cara, please don't think I took it.'

'Maximilian has given me twenty-four hours. I barely have twelve left. You seem very calm.' I pull a tissue from my pocket.

'I will tell Santiago,' he says.

'You are the only one who knew where it was hidden.

You are the only one who came up here with me to hide it.'

He turns away. I am screaming at him.

'When did you come back up here? When did you steal it? Did you come back up here after Barbara came to Comaso? Were you frightened I would give it to her? Do you think you can sell it - take the money and run to Florence? Or did you come here last night after Maximilian and Ian had beaten me?'

He does not turn to face me. Instead he speaks with his back to me gazing up the slope toward the church.

'Someone has followed us here,' his voice is calm and measured.

'No-one followed us. I have been careful.' I grab his arm. 'I should never have trusted you. You are like all the other men I have met, motivated by greed and money. You are despicable. I trusted you.'

'Maybe you took it!' His eyes are dark when he faces me. 'Maybe you were frightened that I would steal your precious Golden Icon? Maybe you think you can take it from Lake Como by pretending it has been stolen, to fool me and to fool Santiago. Maybe—'

I slap his cheek hard with the palm of my hand.

'You have it,' I scream. 'You have stolen it!'

He grabs my wrists. His face is close to mine and his voice hisses when he speaks. 'You're the one leaving Comaso. You're the one who is going away. You're the one ending our relationship. Maybe it is in your suitcase and this is all a game or a decoy to fool me.'

He releases my wrists, pushes me away and I stumble, exhausted and drained of emotion. I watch his receding back as he disappears down the path. I wait a while then follow him, but I do not take my eyes from his back.

On our way down to the village we don't speak. We don't hold hands, and we don't look at each other, and when we part company we say nothing. We never get the opportunity again.

CHAPTER ELEVEN

Forever, my dream of love has vanished.
That moment has fled, and I die in
desperation.
E lucevan le stelle, Tosca

My suitcase lays open on the bed. Somewhere in a foggy distance the persistent sound of the phone rings in the lounge. It is my home phone. My mobile is smashed. Then it stops. Outside a strimmer shrieks through the gardens. The raw noise comes from the hills above my apartment. Someone is cutting hedges and slicing my head into pieces, severing my disjointed thoughts and emotions into shards of fragmented rationality.

The Madonna and her child was crafted, sculptured and moulded over two hundred years ago. She has been stolen and hidden ever since. She was created to bring balance to a situation, and to make a difference in the world, as I believed I once was. It seems as if she has been let down all her life. I am filled with despair. I too, have let her down.

The midday sun reflects on the hills across the lake. It is deep green. I haven't stirred from my vantage point, sitting on my bed, staring out of the window. My body is thick and lethargic. Although I know the minutes are ticking past and the twenty-four hours promised to me are slipping away, I cannot move. I missed the first ferry, and the next and the next.

I look at my watch. I must leave. I still blame myself. I pack the last few items into my case. Of course Raffaelle knew where I had hidden the Golden Icon. Although I had left him sitting on a rock he could easily have followed me and spied on me digging the hole. He must have gone up alone one morning, or perhaps even later that day, I know he has it.

My cheek is sore. My eye is half closed. My lip feels thick. I yawn with difficulty. I am exhausted. I have not slept. Only worry and fear propel my weary frame. Maximilian will be back tonight looking for me, if he is not already nearby and waiting. Suddenly I am filled with energy and a desire to leave. I slam the lid of the suitcase shut but my movements are sluggish. I am pulling them from quicksand of my lethargy but not fast enough.

Raffaelle is probably in Lenno with his friend Sergio. I imagine him unveiling the Golden Icon casting the frayed string aside and the linen cloth falling to the floor as Sergio's thick fingers and dirty nails trace the Madonna's face.

I hear my phone or is it the doorbell downstairs? I am too tired to move. I don't care. There is no-one I want to speak to. I am being dragged into darkness and into sleep. I yawn. I should finish packing and leave but instead I lay on the bed and lie against my leather case. A breeze comes through the open window and the sound of a baby crying in the apartment below makes me think of the

Madonna and her child. The smell of baking bread wafts up through the window and my stomach rumbles. I have not eaten today.

My eye lids close. Bells tinkle; sheep, goats, cows, church bells? Telephone? The doorbell? They all lull me to sleep.

I awake with a start not knowing where I am. The sun is no longer shining in through the bedroom window. I am dizzy. Perspiring in my clothes. My face is crumpled, my cheek swollen, the lines on my face ingrained, my lip sore.

The doorbell rings. I pull matted hair from my neck and push it into a makeshift bun, welcoming the gentle wind from the open window on my neck.

The doorbell.

It is persistent. My legs are heavy when I swing them to the floor. The bell rings as if someone is pressing it and will not let go. I stagger downstairs hoping it will be Raffaelle with the Golden Icon in his hands and an apology on his lips, but through the spyglass, I see my friend and opera coach, Cesare Serratore.

I pull the door open and collapse into his arms sobbing. My cries come from somewhere deep inside; my fear; my loss; and the uselessness. I am blabbering and incoherent.

'Josephine, what? What? What is wrong?' He grabs me by the shoulders. I take a deep breath and pull away from him, wiping my tears with the back of my hand.

'Madre mia, what have you done to your face? What has happened?' His eyes crease in concern, and when he touches my cheek, I flinch.

'When did this happen? Raffaelle?'

'No! Raffaelle would never hit me.' I think of how I slapped Raffaelle's cheek. Was that only this morning?

'Cesare, I have so much to tell you,' I say. 'I cannot

believe you are here. I need to speak to you.'

'I have been trying to phone you. What's happened?'

'My mobile is broken.'

He links his arm though mine and I flinch at the pain in my shoulder. But when we walk up the stairs I decide I will tell Cesare the truth. I will tell him everything. He is my friend. I will start from the beginning. I will leave out no details and I will tell the truth and unburden myself of this secret then I will tell him that I am leaving Comaso and I will sing with the Philharmonic in New York or London or wherever he wants. I will be safe with him.

'So tell me, what happened to you?'

'I tripped,' I lie, and I am reminded of Seán telling me how he fell when it was a hit and run. I know by his eyes that Cesare doesn't believe me.

I find a bottle of Prosecco, some cashew nuts and olives.

'Salud, cara.' Cesare raises his glass to mine. His smile is broad and his hair falls across his eyes. He brushes it aside with the back of his hand with customary care. As I watch, I realise how much I owe him and what a large part he has played in my life; he brought me to live in Comaso, and helped me to focus on my singing.

'Congratulations, Josephine,' he laughs, staring at my bruised face and swollen lip. 'It is just a shame you look as if you have just stepped out of a boxing ring.'

I pause with my glass midway to my lips.

'Yes. It is the right decision. New York and London will do me good. I know there is a demand for pop opera and I have resisted for so long but now I know. I have no choice. It is the right thing to do.'

'Have you not spoken to Nico? Or to Dino?'

'Nico? Why? No, not since my audition. He was a pig.

Do you not remember? He reminded me of the time I walked out of Carmen? He humiliated me.'

Cesare leans forward, takes the glass from my hand and wraps his fingers around my cut and bruised knuckles.

'The role is yours. Tomorrow night at the opening of the Teatro Il Domo. You are Tosca.'

'Mine? Me?'

'Yes, Glorietta is ill. She has strep. She fell sick yesterday and she cannot perform tomorrow. Nico wants you to replace her for the opening performance, tomorrow night.'

I cannot think. 'Glorietta is sick? Her throat?'

He nods in confirmation. 'Unfortunately it happens, as you know. It is a shame for Glorietta but this is your chance. Your opportunity to–'

'But Nico hates me.'

'He does not hate you. He needs you. Dino is adamant that you replace her. It is the first time he is producing a performance as big as this, and as it is the grand opening of the Teatro Il Domo, he is calling the shots. They want you.'

I think of Glorietta. All her hard work, her training, her hopes and her ambitions. I know how disappointed I would feel if I were in her place now.

'I can't.'

'You must. Everyone is relying on you.'

'But the opening night is tomorrow.'

'That is why we must hurry. No-one could contact you so I have come here to take you to Como. Nico said he would keep trying to telephone you. We must leave at once. Perhaps we can go over some of the directions and the production tonight in the hotel. You have a dress fitting first thing tomorrow morning, and a dress rehearsal with the orchestra after that.'

'But my voice?'

'It is strong.'

'My face.'

'Makeup.'

'There isn't enough time.'

'There is, and besides, you know the role perfectly. It is just stage direction for this performance but that will come naturally to you.'

'Look at my face and my lip.'

'It looks sore, but with some makeup, no-one will notice.'

'I'm not prepared. I haven't even finished packing.'

'That is why I am here.' He looks at his watch. 'We have forty-five minutes to throw everything into a suitcase Josephine. Let's not miss the boat this time.'

In the end Nico telephones me on Cesare's mobile phone, he is kind and professional, filling my ego with compliments and reassurances. I do not question his motives instead my chest swells and I push my shoulders back, as he begs me to replace Glorietta at such short notice.

'If you insist,' I reply. 'I would never let you down.'

'It is for one night only. The doctor says Glorietta will be better on Sunday.'

'I understand,' I say.

Cesare has placed my bags at the door. I take the black and white photograph of the four young soldiers from the book shelf and place it in my purse. Then we are running as if we are in training for the Olympics, only with each step I am fragile and weak. I haven't eaten all day.

I insist that we take another path to the pontoon, I don't want to pass the fountain. I don't want to see anyone. I don't want anyone to know I am leaving. There will be no goodbyes - only memories.

I grab Cesare's arm, tugging him past the bakery and down the back steps behind the carpenter's shop.

I have left a note to the cleaner with money and instructions for closing up my apartment. I will send for my clothes and my broken piano and books. I telephoned Raffaelle and left a message to say I am singing Tosca but realise I am foolish. He will already know. He probably knows Glorietta is ill. He may even be in her villa, at her bedside. Maybe they have the Golden Icon with them.

As we descend the steps, I trip but Cesare catches my elbow, he is half carrying and half wheeling my suitcases. I carry two smaller bags. We pause to cross the road. It is busy with summer traffic and I am breathing heavily.

'Come on.' Cesare pulls me. 'We must go, look! The ferry is arriving.'

The boat arrives with its legs splayed wide. It is the fast ferry and it leaves a wake in the water.

I wait in the crowd while people disembark. My head is filled with Tosca. My head is humming; *I lived for art. I lived for love. I lived for art. I lived for love.* I am infused with passion, with love and joy, and hiding behind my customary dark glasses. No-one would see or understand my range of complex emotions.

The cool breeze is lifting my spirits. I am pleased to be going. I want to leave. I want to run. I am ready to go. When I look at the strangers on the pontoon I realise that

I have always run away. I have always avoided the truth and the consequences. I have always left behind those I love to fend for themselves.

I am impatient waiting for passengers to disembark.

I don't want to think about Raffaelle but I see his face with my red-hand print on his cheek and the humility in his eyes.

It reminds me of Seán's face on the day I told him I was going to sing Carmen at Covent Garden. Then I see Michael's face when I tell him I have been accepted for a scholarship in Germany, and the smile of love and warmth he gave me.

'Josephine?' I turn at the sound of my name. People are embarking, jostling me to get on the ferry.

'What happened to your face?' Barbara stands beside me on the quay. She has disembarked. She looks drawn, tired and exhausted. She glances at the suitcases at my feet then at Cesare standing beside me.

'You sent me on a goose chase to Munich. Dieter was dead and I spent three hours with the German police. The Golden Icon belongs to me. Do you not think I have lost enough? Seán was murdered. We are on the verge of bankruptcy and we need the money. I am not going to lose my house too!'

I move away. I must get on the ferry.

'I know about your letter,' she calls. 'The press will pay a fortune for this. Karl Blakey is practically biting my hand off and I'm going to give it to him but the choice is yours.'

'You can't. I am singing Tosca tomorrow. You will ruin me.'

'You are destroying me and my family.'

'I don't have the Golden Icon.'

'Josephine, hurry! Quick, the boat is leaving,' Cesare shouts.

'You sent me to Munich but you have the Golden Icon here.'

'I buried it in the hills behind my apartment. It's the truth. I buried it there three days ago, at the Chiesa della Madonna dei miracoli, the church of the Madonna of the Miracles,' I explain. 'But when I went to get it this morning, it was gone. Look at my face. Maximilian was here last night and this is what his nephew did to me. They have given me twenty-four hours, until tonight to get it, but I don't have it.'

We are alone on the quay, apart from two of the crew, who are staring at us.

'I came to give you this.' She reaches into her handbag and holds out an envelope. 'After Munich I went back to Ireland. I knew Seán was blackmailing you but I didn't know how or why. It took me a long time to find it. He had it well hidden.'

'Thank you, Barbara.' I am filled with surprise at her generosity. I want to hug her to me. 'This is a gift to me. You're very kind.' I peer inside the envelope. It is a copy of my letter.

'I have kept the original and I will give it to the press if I don't get the Golden Icon.'

I am frozen, rooted to the quay.

'Come on, Josephine!' Cesare has moved forward with the crowd. He is boarding the ferry taking my suitcases with him.

'You can't do this,' I say.

'I know you fucked Michael.'

'Signora?' One of the crew calls out.

'Your fans will love your letter.' She nods at the yellow envelope clutched in my hand. 'The opera world with be very impressed with your sexual revelations.'

'You can't print this. Have you no compassion? The newspapers will crucify me. Especially now. Don't do it.'

'Seán knew about your affair. Do you think his humiliation was any less than yours will be?'

'Josephine?' Cesare calls out to me. 'Hurry!'

I take two steps toward the ferry. 'Please,' I shout.

Her eyes glisten like green icicles.

'You're a slut.' She spits the words at me.

'Signora?' One of the crews call to me.

The gangplank is moving.

'A whore,' she shouts.

The boat men are casting off and I move quickly. I jump onto the gangplank and the waiting sailor catches my arm. I fall against him and he stabilises me against the rail before he pulls on the rope and closes the steel gate.

The envelope is clutched in my perspiring palm. My throat is dry. I shall never be able to sing.

The boat moves away and when I turn to look, Barbara is staring back at me and I stand looking at her until she is the smallest dot on the horizon.

Comaso recedes into the distance. My village with its colourful houses built into the hillside, its railings adorned with red geraniums, the sleepy Alberge and lakeside cafe.

I can see Raffaelle's okra-coloured villa behind the harbour wall, its green shutters are open and I imagine the refuge of his secret garden, the covered well brimming with potted geraniums, the gently swinging hammock and gnarled wisteria branches over the rickety bistro table.

My eyes follow the ravine where we walked to the Chiesa della Madonna dei miracoli, where I had foolishly buried the Golden Icon, and where I slapped Raffaelle's cheek.

Over my shoulder Cesare sits with my bags at his feet. He is speaking into his mobile phone and I am reassured by his presence, amazed that he still has faith in me.

I am about to replace Glorietta Bareldo in the most coveted production of Tosca, in Italy's new and famous Teatro Il Domo, but if the press find out the theatre will be rocked by the revelations of my past, I will be humiliated and my life will be finished.

I lean against the railing, close my eyes and lift my face to the evening breeze dazed by my confrontation with Barbara. She will destroy me but I must not think. I am exhausted. I must focus on tomorrow. I must block out my feelings and my fear.

I spend the ferry journey contemplating the shape of the wake left behind in the water, watching my village fade until Comaso disappears completely. Then, as the ferry turns into the bottom end of the Y-shaped lake rising majestically from the water, radiating and sparkling in the sunlight is the Teatro Il Domo.

On the quay television trucks, delivery lorries, workmen's vans and an assortment of cars line the pathway leading to the wooden walkway that spans the water to the glass fronted reception. I make out the shapes of the bronze statues and wonder if my likeness may now one day take its rightful place amongst the great and talented. Apprehension seeps into my body which I welcome. It means I am alive. I am no longer frightened, and my tiredness subsides.

It is almost dark when we step onto the quay in Como. I am thinking of Raffaelle at Glorietta's bedside, comforting her. Will he give the Golden Icon to Santiago for protection or will he risk selling it?

Mistaking my deliberations for weakness Cesare takes my bags and guides me through the throng of people departing the ferry to a waiting taxi. We haven't spoken on the boat. He has left me to contemplate not knowing about the Golden Icon.

He has said nothing about my confrontation with Barbara. He must have heard it all and I know, I must give him an explanation. I also want to unburden myself.

He lifts my cases into the trunk of the car and I turn to smile gratefully at him.

'Cesare, I want to tell you the truth. Tell you everything—' I am about to step into the taxi but I stumble and hold onto the roof. Across the road is a man wearing a yellow corduroy jacket, standing with him is Ian.

I gasp and duck inside. I fall onto the seat. Perspiration trickles down my spine. My legs are crumpled beneath me. As the taxi speeds off I turn to look out of the rear window. Ian's right hand is cupping his balls, the other is pointing at me and he is laughing.

We are in the *Villa Il Domo* in Cernobbio. From the window of my hotel room the crystal dome of the Teatro Il Domo gleams and shimmers under the moonlight.

I have eaten well and showered, and I turn from the hypnotic view and lay on the bed, gazing at the dusky pink velvet drapes. My head is filled with an assortment of feelings and memories: Tosca, Raffaelle, the Golden Icon, Glorietta sick and missing her opening debut, Maximilian and Ian. Barbara shouting I am a whore. My letter, in the draw beside my bed, filled with secrets that Karl Blakey is waiting to get his hands on, and Michael. I haven't trusted myself to read my letter to him almost thirty years ago.

There is a knock on the door and Cesare stands with a bottle of chilled Prosecco.

'You should not speak,' he says. 'You should be resting.'

I move aside to let him in. 'I need to talk to you.'

'Did you get hold of Raffaelle?' He places the bottle on the small table in the alcove of the bay window.

'There is still no answer at the villa and he doesn't answer his mobile.'

'Are you worried?'

'I telephoned Luigi and he told me that Raffaelle ate dinner there tonight.'

'So, he is not returning your calls.'

'I assume he is with Glorietta and he is not speaking to me.'

Cesare pours the sparkling wine, kicks off his shoes and sits beside the bed on the small sofa.

'To Tosca.' He holds up his glass.

'Tosca,' I reply. I lay on the bed, push a pillow behind my back and take the envelope from the bedside table. I pass it to Cesare.

'You should know about this,' I say. 'Within the next few days everyone will know.'

He reads carefully and slowly his head moving from side to side. He flicks his hair from his eyes and when he eventually looks up at me I see disappointment in his eyes.

'When was this?'

'A long time ago. I was a different woman at twenty-three than I am today. I cannot excuse what I did or why I did it.' I close my eyes. 'It is all such a long time ago.'

'Times have changed, circumstances have changed, but morals and judgements haven't.' Cesare adds with a sigh. 'The public can do what they like but unfortunately they expect their diva to stay on a pedestal of perfection and when they don't they take great delight in bringing them down to earth.'

'As I already know, to my own cost.'

'It will be very embarrassing. How did you manage to keep Michael a secret for so long?'

'You mean, why did this not all come out four years ago?'

Cesare tosses the papers aside and I replace them in the envelope.

'Seán said he found the letter after Michael died but I guess if he had known earlier it wouldn't have made much difference. He wanted Michael's money. Michael was funding him or bailing him out. We married too young. I had no experience and Seán didn't understand my needs or even listen to me.'

'Ah, so when Michael died, Seán decided to blackmail you?'

'That is the real reason why I went to Munich. When I sang at Michael's funeral, Seán blackmailed me with the letter. He threatened to give it to the press. So I was forced to go to Munich to collect his family heirloom which would pay off their debts. But when I saw the Golden Icon I knew I couldn't take stolen property through the customs. So I went to the nearest hotel and phoned Seán.

That's when William told me he had been murdered.'

'It was stolen property?' he says.

'Yes, the Golden Icon was stolen.' I explain about Michael, Dieter and Maximilian and Terry during the War. I take the faded black and white picture from my purse. I tell him how I brought the Golden Icon back to Comaso, how I went to Padre Paolo for help and about Raffaelle wanting to start a new life in Florence. I explain how I buried the Golden Icon in the grounds of the Chiesa della Madonna dei miracoli, then Barbara's first visit and finally David Mallory's visit.

'Then you saw Barbara in Comaso this afternoon. She has the original letter and will go to the press.'

Cesare doesn't speak but he watches me carefully.

I tell him how I have been followed and that my apartment was ransacked by Karl Blakey the journalist who hunted me down four years ago. Then I tell him what happened last night and how Maximilian and Ian threatened me. How my face got bruised, how I was almost raped and that Karl Blakey saved me.

I talk and talk. I tell him how Raffaelle and I went up to the hiding place this morning but the Golden Icon was missing and how I accused him and smacked his face. Finally I yawn. I am drained. My confession has made me weary.

'Madre mia,' he says. 'How is this all possible?'

'I have no idea, Cesare.'

'Why did you just not give it to Santiago?'

'I should have done, but I wanted to do the right thing. That is why I went to Padre Paolo. I wanted to make amends for what Michael did. I didn't want him to be a thief. I wanted to do the right thing for the Golden Icon, and give it to whom it belongs.'

'So Maximilian is after you and Barbara is blackmailing you?' he says. He stretches his legs and raises long arms above his head. 'What a mess. The only good thing is that you will be safe here in the hotel and in the Theatre tomorrow. With all the television cameras and security there will be no problems, you will be safe. Don't worry.'

I stare up at the ceiling and study the reflecting lights shining from the chandelier.

'How badly do I want to sing Tosca, Cesare? How important is my life, my privacy and for how long can I keep my secret?'

'I think it is too late.'

'There is one journalist, Karl Blakey. He has been following me. He is now working for William who is obviously in competition with Barbara for the Golden Icon. He would sacrifice me without a moment's hesitation, and he would take great delight in doing so.'

Cesare stretches his legs and folds his arms behind his neck.

'What can we do?'

'How can I explain love, Cesare? How can I justify my actions and explain to the world? How will they judge me? How could they understand? Must I explain? How can I tell them that I loved my husband's father more than my husband? How can I say he loved me, that he listened to me, he understood me and he loved me enough to let me go, to fulfil my dream? Would anyone understand?

'Michael wasn't like Seán. Michael was never like Seán. Michael was kind, generous and loving. He helped me follow my dream and pursue my destiny. He paid for my sponsorship with Guntar. He sent me to France, Belgium,

Italy and Germany. He encouraged me. He recognised my talent and gave me the freedom to follow my passion and my art. He helped me develop and grow. He was happy for my success.'

Cesare refills my glass and says nothing. He leans back on the upholstered gilt sofa.

'Sitting there like that, you could be King Herod,' I say.

'Your sense of drama is returning, Josephine. You will be excellent tomorrow,' he smiles.

'Tomorrow seems a long way off, first, I must deal with today and my past. I want you to understand, Cesare. For every step of encouragement I received from Michael, I received anger and resentment from Seán. Every time I travelled Seán was annoyed. Every time I sang Seán expected me to be at home, and the more the public demanded my voice and the more I was commissioned to sing, the more jealous and demanding Seán became.

'It didn't take me long to realise Seán wanted a pretty wife to entertain his business clients. He was happy for me to sing at small dinner parties, so long as it was all for Seán, but he didn't want to share me. He wanted to control me. He wanted to possess me. Michael tried to explain to Seán that if I was free to pursue my career I would return home.

'At first, Michael encouraged me to be the dutiful wife. He had lost his wife Shona, and when he took an interest in my career Seán was pleased. I was a hobby for Michael. He was sixty and just retired. I was his project, his interest, his hope—'

'You were a hobby?' Cesare's dark eyes are understanding and they encourage me to continue.

'I was more than a hobby. Michael wanted to know the

real me. I was only twenty-three. I had been married less than a year. I was flattered.'

'So, you wrote a letter to Michael that Barbara now has. And in return for the Golden Icon she will give you, your original letter,' he muses. 'So, who do you think has the Golden Icon?'

'Raffaelle must have it. He is the only one who knew where it was hidden.'

'You were not followed?'

'No, we went up very early and I made sure, each time that there was no-one else around.'

'Perhaps Maximilian or Karl Blakey followed you?'

'They have no idea. Last night they were looking for it. That is why they threatened me.'

His sigh is long and drawn out. 'Well, so long as Raffaelle is sensible, he will give it to Santiago. Do you want to telephone Santiago?'

'I hadn't thought of that. Maybe I should, but what if Raffaelle decides to keep the Golden Icon? I don't want to betray him to Santiago. They hate each other as it is.'

'Would he risk Maximilian coming after him?'

'I don't know, Cesare. I can't think. I am so tired. I barely slept last night.'

'Bene, I will go now. Tomorrow you have a day of rehearsal followed by the opening night, Josephine. Let's wait and see what happens. You need to rest, relax and sleep. It will be a long day. Do not fill your head with your past, instead concentrate on the present, and dream of the future.' He stretches and stands up.

It is good advice. At the door Cesare hugs me.

'Do you think Raffaelle is all right?' I ask.

'You have left him messages and you know he ate in

Luigi's tonight. Go to sleep and stop worrying.' He kisses me gingerly on the cheek, careful not to hurt me, and I close the door behind him.

When I am alone I realise I will go to London. There is something important I must do that I cannot deny any longer.

I am weary but underneath a torrent of emotions there is bubbling excitement. I will be on stage tomorrow in one of the world's most important and prestigious theatres. I will feel the lights on my face, the stage under my feet and the natural acoustics of the theatre in the glass dome above my head.

The door to the balcony is open and the evening air fills me with calm. In the distance the lake is dark like black ink, and the theatre's sparkling crystal dome reflects the white moonlight.

The air is still, and heavy clouds scurry across the sky as if preparing for an imminent storm. I imagine the theatre tomorrow night; the stream of cars, the chatter of the audience dressed in their fine evening clothes greeting each other, air kissing; the powerful, the wealthy, the famous. The wealthy society that keeps the wheels of the opera world turning. The red carpet laid out from the quay along the walkway to the glass foyer of the reception. The pre performance gatherings; parties and interviews, television cameras, and the expectant hum of anticipation just before the curtain rises and the moment I step onto the stage.

I am back.

I am Tosca.

I remove my gown and lay naked against the crisp cotton sheets pulling the pillow under my neck. I yawn stretching my cheeks and I wince. My eyelids are heavy, very heavy, and the hands of the clock move slowly through the night. I lay awake until dawn not thinking about my stage presence, nor the dramatic requirements of the opera, or my voice. Instead I practice and rehearse questions that journalists will ask and I worry what the critics will say. I examine every conceivable nuance, hidden meaning, double edged question that a reporter will trap me into confessing, and decide I will not be on the defensive. I will not make a confession.

It is time to face up to my past and to take responsibility for my actions. I must face my destiny and my fate, whatever it may be. In the eye of the public, I will be the diva again, but I know in my heart that there is only one person I cannot fool any longer.

CHAPTER TWELVE

Fragrant, she entered
And fell into my arms.
E lucevan le stelle, Tosca

It is the first Saturday in August. The opening night of
Tosca. My comeback.

In the dressing room my hands are shaking. Nerves are
propelling me through each second and each minute as
they have been through each hour of the day. Through
fittings, rehearsals and interviews. I have vocalised and
after a short nap I now sip camomile tea. I breathe deeply
trying to appear calm to those around me. Although the
air conditioning works perfectly and the room is at the
ideal temperature, perspiration is running down my spine.

The dressing room is large. It smells faintly of paint,
fresh flowers and cologne. A long mirror lines one wall
under which is a shelf with jars and pots of creams. There
are two television monitors; one showing live coverage of
the guests arriving, the other, the interior of the
auditorium.

All day I have been consumed with the enormity of the
architecture and the acoustics. The theatre is tiered

around a horseshoe shaped stage. Its interior, unlike the ornate Teatro alla Scala a Milano, is minimalist and luxurious.

Above the stage is the glass dome; round, magnificent and perfect. The orchestra sit to the south of the stage, and we enter and exit from the north, and the audience spans from east to west.

The rehearsals went well. I know the part by heart. Dino, Massimo my lead man, and Andrei the conductor all greeted me with enthusiasm and assisted with stage directions and encouragement.

There was a fifteen minute meeting with Carlotta Spitarzi my new agent and I am scheduled for a live interview on Italian television after the performance plus several interviews tomorrow morning with the international press.

Cesare sits with me drinking herbal tea. He has been my confidante and friend. I could never have managed these past twenty-four hours without him.

'This is the benefit of your professional training, Josephine. All the hours of discipline, breathing techniques, stamina building, poise and drama. You are a world class soprano singer. You have been amazing today.' He smiles at my reflection in the mirror. 'You should feel proud of yourself.'

'I will feel better if all goes to plan, with no hitches in the performance tonight.' I rub cream onto my face avoiding the cuts and sores.

'Nothing will go wrong. You are a true professional.'

Nina, the dress fitter has been in and out of the dressing room all afternoon and she arrives to make the final adjustments to my costume. I have been measured, pulled and pushed into my gowns, and tied like a turkey at Thanksgiving. The dressing room door opens and closes continually; stage hands come and go, changes of scripts, notes, messages and instructions. Amid the chaos Cesare fields all enquiries while I sip my tea and attempt to relax.

Dario, the theatre's public relations manager who has been dealing with the press is hosting a reception in one of the suites. He is flamboyant and flies around as if he glides on ice. His dyed blond head of hair comes around the door.

'Josephine?' he calls. 'The performance was sold out when Glorietta was the lead star, but now they know you are opening tonight's show, it is crazy out there,' he laughs.

He waves an arm almost knocking Nina in the face as she returns with a mended seam. 'Oops, sorry Nina my darling, I'm trying so desperately to keep calm but it's impossible. My phone rings non-stop. They all want to see you and talk to you, Josephine, and between you and me, Nico can't believe any of this either.'

His phone rings and he gives a dramatic sigh of desperation. He speaks to me, but holding the mobile. 'I've got to take this call. It's important, but there's a friend of yours who wants a ticket for tonight.'

'A friend? Who?' I ask.

'He's a journalist. He says he knows you. Oh, hold on.' He begins speaking into his phone and our conversation hangs in the air as he goes out and into the corridor.

Cesare looks at me through the mirror. He is dressed in his tuxedo. His hair falls around his chiselled features, curls hang to his shoulder. His long legs pace across the room from the sofa to the dressing table and back. Meanwhile he watches both television screens giving me a commentary of events outside; who is arriving with who, what they are wearing, and to which pre-performance party they have been invited.

I sip my tea, grateful for his reassuring presence, and the calm and safety he provides.

'This is probably my final opportunity to prove to the world that I have not lost my talent or my voice,' I say to him, 'I am grateful to you Cesare. I have dreamed of this moment for four years. After the audition I never thought for one moment that it would happen.' I look at my reflection in the mirror and study my swollen cheek and grazed temple. I watch Cesare striding around the room. 'After I lost the role to Glorietta, I thought I would never sing on the stage again. I thought I would never know what it was like to perform at this level. I thought I had lost everything.'

I sit at the dressing table and add powder to my bruised cheek.

'It is because you had faith in me, Cesare. After I had lost everything and everyone you still believed in me. I had nothing. But you came to Germany and found me. I was like a broken sparrow curled up in bed, sick and alone, abandoned by my friends, admirers and fans. It was you who encouraged me to come and live in Comaso. It was a health spa for me; fresh air, good food, rest, and good friends.'

He returns my smile in the mirror.

'I will never be able to thank you enough, because not only did you help me regain my confidence and my singing techniques, you were my friend and you listened to me. You understood my need for music, my love of art and my desire to sing.' I meet his gaze in the mirror. 'Why did you do it?'

The door opens. 'What will I do about this journalist? Let him backstage?' asks Dario.

'Who is he?'

He checks a piece of paper. 'I think he said Charley Blake?'

My hand flies to my mouth. 'It must be Karl Blakey. He is no friend of mine. Don't let him anywhere near me, or the stage. Don't let him in with the press. The man is dangerous.'

'Keep an eye on him. Warn security that he wants to get too close to Signora Lavelle so that they keep an eye out for him,' Cesare says. 'Don't let him into the theatre.'

'Okay, will do.' Dario backs out of the room.

I sigh.

'He is very clever, Cesare. You don't think he will get backstage?'

'Not a chance.'

There is a knock on the door. 'Makeup in two minutes,' a voice calls.

On the wall beside me the plasma screen shows images of the audience arriving and taking their seats. I have the sound turned down. It will help when the opera starts and I am able to follow the performance and time my arrival on stage. My dressing room is barely a short walk to the stage, along a narrow corridor strewn with cables, busy stagehands, cast and crew.

'So why did you persevere with me? When everyone else had lost faith in me.'

'I like older women,' he jokes, 'they are easier to work with, and so....very, very grateful.'

I raise an eyebrow and smile. 'I need to know.'

Cesare pushes curls from his eyes and fold his arms. 'Guntar had no right to treat you as he did. I heard that he was jealous when you went to Olga Schomberg for training. He began to speak badly about you. I always assumed that you would have enough contacts to help you. I never realised for one minute that you were so alone and I didn't know that you had become such a diva. Yes, *bene*, I had heard that you missed a few performances, and that you sometimes forgot a line, and there were rumours that you were out of control but–'

'I was highly strung and exhausted. I had done back to back performances all around Europe; Madame Butterfly in Vienna, then Lucia di Lammermoor, La Traviata, Armida, La Sonnambula, Il Piratamedea and Anne Bolena in Saint Petersburg. I was exhausted. My agent, Antonio Marx was pushing me and my voice was changing. My tone was becoming dark and chesty so I cancelled a few dates in San Diego, the Met and another performance in Ghent.'

'You cancelled eight; you cancelled in Florence, Edinburgh and Athens as well, and the producers were losing money.'

'I couldn't keep my pitch on register, Cesare. I was exhausted.'

'You were replaced by an understudy more times than you sang.'

'Antonio kept pushing me.'

'Agents always maximise the potential of their client, it is their job.'

'I couldn't cope.' We are watching each other through the mirror.

'I know,' he replies.

'Is that why you rescued me?'

'I knew you would recover on the Italian Lakes. I knew that you would rest and recuperate, and probably more importantly, you would live in peace in Comaso. I was hoping that you would begin to lead a normal life and understand—'

There is a knock on the door. Cesare opens it. 'Another bouquet?' he says, and two dozen red roses are placed beside several other vases of flowers on the crowded table.

'Gina!' Cesare calls down the corridor. 'Do you have another vase?' He hands me the accompanying card which I read aloud.

'Wishing you all the success you deserve. From Nico.' I am smiling. I am reassured and more confident.

My dresser arrives. 'I have altered the panels,' Nina says. 'The dress should be more comfortable now.'

I stand, remove my dressing gown and step into the costume. Nina zips the back.

'Hair and makeup,' someone shouts. I am losing track of the names of the people who help me, laughing and fussing over me as I am dressing. I wear a thick, dark wig and makeup with heavy black eyeliner.

'Nasty bruise,' one says.

'The lip has gone down since this morning,' says another.

'We can cover this graze here and no one will be any the wiser.'

'Envelope for Signora Lavelle,' shouts a young boy. He stands gawping in the doorway. Cesare pulls it from his hands and pushes him firmly back into the corridor.

'It isn't an embossed card like the others,' he says. 'It's notepaper from our hotel, the Villa Il Domo.'

I take it from him.

'Be still,' Nina admonishes me. She stands with a thread and needle, sewing the ruffle at my waist.

The makeup girl is young. She is wearing a sleeveless T-shirt and a red heart tattoo covers her bicep. 'Nearly done,' she smiles.

I strain my eyes to read the entwined names drawn in ink on her arm. When she is finished she says, 'My parents adore you. I shouldn't say this but my father said that although Glorietta Bareldo is an excellent soprano, the role of Tosca is yours. It belongs to you. There is no-one in the world who has ever sung Tosca like you. Not even Maria Callas.'

I swallow hard, tears prick the back of my eyes. 'Thank you. Please tell your father he is very kind.'

I read the note in my hand, written on hotel note paper from my hotel.

If I don't have the Golden Icon by breakfast tomorrow, I will go to the press. Barbara.

Cesare is reading the note over my shoulder and I turn to look at him.

'She gives you enough time to get over tonight's performance and enough time for the reviews to be printed in the newspapers, and hopes that her revelations will be more sensational. If you perform like you have never performed before it will be even more effective. She wants to frighten you.'

'The press will be like hyenas,' I say.

'Josephine, the audience and the press here tonight are only interested in your performance. They look beyond affairs of the heart that happened many years ago. They are not interested. Tell me, who in Italy has not had an affair?' he laughs. 'It was all a long time ago and there are very few people interested in these stories. Who has not been linked to a romantic liaison? Who has never made mistakes? You can rise above it. Ride the wave and see it out. The scandal will pale in comparison to your amazing performance.'

'Oh, Cesare, thank you.' I grip his hand. 'If only I had the Golden Icon.'

'If you did, would you give it to her?'

I turn back to the mirror. 'I wouldn't want to. I don't like her, but do think that it is what Michael would have wanted. Now that Seán is dead it would protect his family from financial ruin. Barbara could live in peace with her children, after all, they are Michael's heirs.'

'But, you don't have the icon, and you cannot stop her from printing Seán's confessions. Look! Don't think about the Golden Icon now. Focus on tonight's performance and Tosca. Enjoy this moment…'

There is a sharp knock.

The door opens, a boy comes in carrying a bouquet of irises and lilies tied with a silver bow, he places them on the counter below the mirror. Cesare hands me the small card and I tear open the envelope.

Game Over. Your twenty-four hours has expired. MS.

'It is from Maximilian.' I run to the door and call down the corridor at the boy's departing back. 'Please remove these flowers. They are making me ill.'

'What will I do with them?'

'I don't care. Give them to a hospital. Take them home to your mother or throw them away. Just get rid of them.'

When he leaves I turn to Cesare.

'I have run out of time and I am running out of ideas. I

have no idea where the Golden Icon can be. I trusted Raffaelle. He was the only person who knew where it was hidden but somehow I don't think he would do that to me. I can't believe that he would steal it. But why doesn't he answer my calls? Why hasn't he been in touch with me? I know I treated him badly. I slapped his face–'

'Don't think about all this now,' Cesare urges. 'Please Josephine, relax. Breathe deeply and stay calm.'

'I don't think Raffaelle would be willing to risk his life by stealing the Golden Icon. Dieter told me that there is a story attached to the icon that if anyone attempts to use the icon for their own use then something bad will happen to them; they will die or be killed but Raffaelle didn't believe...'

'Josephine, please. Relax, stop thinking about all this.'

Nina returns with an assistant and my costume for the first Act. This time Cesare leaves the room. As she modifies my dress we are interrupted constantly with messages of good luck from fans; flowers arrive from Dino Scrugli who I know is hosting a post party celebration in my honour in the revolving bar upstairs after the show. I receive a cuddly teddy bear from Massimo Mallamo, my tenor friend and leading man. Hector Barrantes and Géorgios Papandu the shows sponsors have spoilt me with perfume, diamond earrings and a necklace.

But there is nothing from Raffaelle.

Another knock on the door.

Andrei Ferretti stands on the threshold. His grey hair and beard are neatly trimmed. He pushes black heavy framed glasses onto his nose and regards me thoughtfully through the reflection of the mirror before speaking

'Give me two minutes alone with Signora Lavelle.' His

voice holds no question of discussion, and Nina and her assistant leave, but not before voicing their opinion.

'No more than two minutes, we haven't got long.' Nina is not intimidated.

'We haven't time…' says the other.

'You've time enough. Close the door,' he tells them.

I stand and face him. Although I smile my hands are shaking.

We are the same height. He is a few years older than me, still slim, and still very attractive. 'This is a very important night for us both,' he says. 'You did very well today in rehearsals. It is good to be working with you again, Josephine. You are still very talented and you have worked hard.'

'This is high praise indeed from the maestro himself.'

He smiles. 'You have been through a great deal and it is good to see you back. It has been a long time. I have missed you.'

'It's been four years. You didn't bother to contact me.'

'Cesare always said to leave you alone until you were well, until you were ready.'

'You didn't speak in my defence at the audition when Nico was so rude to me.'

'I did afterwards. After you had left, but it fell on deaf ears, Nico was paranoid that you might do something to destroy his first performance here in the Teatro Il Domo.'

I take a deep breath. 'I would never do that. I would die before I ruined a performance here.'

'I know, but he is very nervous. Nico is very ambitious. It took him a long time to get Dino involved in this project, and fortunately Dino likes you.'

'Yes, but you still favoured Glorietta. She was your first

choice. You still thought her better than me, and she will be here tomorrow night.' I sit down and face the mirror. He perches on the dressing table, beside me, one foot on the floor the other leg dangling in the air.

'I had forgotten just how unmistakable your voice is. When I heard you this morning with the orchestra it was like,' he smiles, 'old times, in fact, I think you may even be better than before, if that is at all possible. Cesare has done a remarkable job and it will not go unnoticed. This is about you Josephine. You are still a very special and unique woman.'

'Thank you Andrei, and you are still a talented and charming conductor,' I reply and return his steady gaze.

He leans forward and briefly kisses my lips. It is a soft and gentle kiss. 'Good luck,' he whispers. 'Let's give them a night they will never forget.'

It is only after the door has closed behind him and Nina and her assistant are fussing with the hemline of my dress that I remember my letter to Michael and I wonder if he will still have the same respect for me when the truth comes out.

Nico knocks and enters.

'Josephine? How are you?' His dark eyebrows are creased like two fine moustaches. His tuxedo jacket covers a red waist coat and he wears a matching bow tie. 'Andrei is pleased with the rehearsal. You won't let me down, will you?'

'So far, so good, Nico,' I smile. 'I'm still here, and I still have the wig on my head, *and* I haven't stormed out yet.'

At my feet Nina, who is fixing my hem, smothers a giggle.

'Ah? So it would seem that the talented soprano is back

but not the diva. That is good news. Let us hope that this is a permanent character change and it's not just a temporary respite from your tantrums. Good Luck tonight Josephine, and please, no surprises,' he says. Then he is gone leaving in his wake the faint smell of spicy aftershave.

I raise an eyebrow as the door closes. 'Arsehole.'

The dressers splutter with laughter and Nina stands up smiling. 'I think you are finished,' she says.

'Yes, that's what Nico thought too.'

We laugh and she kisses me quickly. 'Ignore them all. Be you, be Tosca, be yourself.'

They wish me good luck and almost collide with Cesare as he enters the room.

'I've been outside watching the audience arrive. You have no idea of the big names here: Georgio Armani, Sophia Loren, George Clooney, and Brad Pitt and Angelina Jolie are making a film in Milan and they are here too; Berlusconi is here with that actress...'

He gives me a running commentary on who is coming into the theatre, faces he recognises on the plasma screen at my elbow. Famous actors, fashion designers, directors and people from the government but I am not listening.

I sip water my throat is dry. I take a deep breath. I am born to perform.

He turns up the volume on the television. The orchestra are in the pit tuning up. Each time my dressing room door opens their strings, drums and horns reach my ears, and I experience a surge of elation, waves of excitement flow around me and my pulse begins racing.

I am dressed.

My co-star arrives. Massimo kisses me. He is playing

the part of Cavaradossi, the lover of Tosca, a role he has played on many occasions all over the world.

'It is like old times,' he says. 'You, me and Andrei. Do you remember all the fun we had together?'

'I do Massimo. Just like it were yesterday.'

'When did we last sing Tosca together?'

'It must have been six years ago, in Barcelona?'

'Ah yes, the Liceu. Eighteen curtain calls, I think you had.'

I laugh. 'Fourteen, don't exaggerate.'

'Look.' Cesare is pointing to the plasma screen. 'Isn't that the chief inspector, Santiago and his wife?'

'You are drawing in a big crowd,' says Massimo, frowning at the screen.

'They were here for Glorietta. I am only the understudy. She will be here tomorrow and I am sure she will outshine me.'

There is a knock on the door and Massimo kisses me. 'See you on stage. Let's show them that we are still a magical team. You and me just as we always were.'

The door closes and I reach for my new mobile phone. I am dialling Raffaelle's number. The same boy who brought Maximilian's flowers stands on the threshold and Cesare goes to him.

Raffaelle's mobile clicks to answer phone, so I speak and leave a message. 'Raffaelle I am worried about you. Call me. I go on stage in a few minutes and this is not like you. I don't care about the Golden Icon. I just want to know that you are all right.'

The boy is leaning into the room hesitant to enter. 'Signora Lavelle, I've been asked to give you this.'

'By whom?'

'I must not give it to anyone else, only you.' He holds it away from Cesare's open palm.

I toss the phone onto the chair. I am reluctant to take it.

'Who gave it to you?' I ask.

'Signora Bareldo.' He holds out a small package. I take the small square gift box from his outstretched hand, thank him, and he leaves.

'It's from Glorietta? You must open it,' Cesare says.

'Why would she send me anything?' I pull at the red ribbon and lift the top off a silver box. Inside staring up at me is a small replica of the Madonna. It does not look like the Golden Icon but it reminds me of her. It is a golden charm of the Virgin sitting alone; sad yet triumphant as if she knows she will lose her son but the world will gain a God. Serenity and acceptance is written on her face. Sacrifice, love, joy and expectation. It is so beautiful. I cannot speak.

'She knows that this is your role. She has known all along that you are Tosca. That is why she specifically asked for you to replace her,' Cesare says.

I raise an eyebrow. 'Glorietta, asked for me?'

'She insisted. She told Nico and Dino that it must be you who took the part and no-one else. She was adamant.'

'I don't believe it. But why?'

'Because she knows what Tosca means to you. She knows that you are the best Tosca in the world, and more importantly, she understands generosity of spirit. She is a good person and I think that had you not been rivals, you would have been the best of friends.'

I am staring at Cesare but thinking of Glorietta. I last saw her at the audition in the studio not far from where I

241

now stand, when our paths crossed, and she had whispered to me. Now I remember the scene vividly and I know they had been words of good luck.

My eyes are moist. I am ashamed. But I cannot lose control.

I am Tosca. I command rage, jealousy and anger to flow through me but not before I hold the charm in my fingers, close my eyes and lift it to my lips murmuring a silent prayer.

The theatre's cameras switch from the audience to the orchestra then back again. Cesare is studying the crowd carefully, under my instruction, looking for Raffaelle.

'Glorietta sent him tickets so I am sure he would not miss my performance.' I am standing smoothing my costume at the hips.

'There's Santiago again.' Cesare points at the screen. 'Look! Isn't that Padre Paolo with a Cardinal?'

When I look up I am shocked to also see Barbara arriving with David Mallory from the Irish Consul. Is it a coincidence that they are both here together? Rivals to possess the Golden Icon or friends to blackmail and intimidate me. But behind them there is another row of seats that has my full attention. I have a fleeting glance of an old man. He has swapped his yellow corduroy for a black dinner jacket and bow tie, sitting beside his is his nephew, Ian.

'That's him!' I point them out to Cesare before the camera pans away to the balcony seats and we swap glances. 'That's Maximilian and Ian. Keep an eye on them. Tell security,' I say.

'I will. Stop worrying. Security is very strong here. A mouse couldn't get in.'

'I can't see Raffaelle.'

'Two minutes,' a voice calls around the door. I know now, that it is time.

Tosca.

It is Act One. The scene is the church of Sant A'ndrea della Valle in Rome and it is the year 1800. Cavaradossi, the tenor Massimo, is hiding an escaped political prisoner called Angelotti in the Attavanti private chapel.

I look at Andrei in front of the orchestra. He is lost in concentration, turning the score, his baton in the air, one eye on the strings and the other eye on Massimo singing the hidden harmony. *Recondita armonia.* Cavaradossi is painting a portrait of Mary Magdalene in the church, inspired by the Marchesa Attavanti and he compares the beautiful blond in his painting with the raven haired beauty of his lover Tosca.

The Sacristan grumbles disapproval and Angelotti ventures from his hiding place, and I begin calling out as I emerge on stage as Tosca.

The painting of Mary Magdalene hangs from the girders. A backdrop to the first Act. She is my blond rival. She is my Glorietta. Heavenly, spiritual and pure, and my jealousy explodes with renewed suspicions. Cavaradossi reassures me of his love, and I leave, but when I return Scarpia the baritone and chief of police, is in search of Angelotti. He shows me a fan with the Attavanti crest and I am consumed with vengeance. Thinking Cavaradossi to be unfaithful. I am distraught.

Scarpia, the chief of police is scheming to get the diva Tosca in his power. It is an emotional performance and I am unsettled. I know that something is wrong. Even if Raffaelle was with Glorietta, he would still have contacted me. He would be here. There was love between us. We were friends. Where is he?

At the end of Act One I leave the stage. I am walking to my dressing room. 'Cesare,' I call. 'Bring Santiago to my dressing room. Urgently.'

'But I can't. He is in the audience and there is so little time.'

'Then hurry. It's important.'

I am not embarrassed to change my costume in front of Santiago when he arrives. His inquisitive eyes takes in the details of my costume, my makeup and I am conscious that he is standing so close to me, he can see my beaten face.

'I am worried about Raffaelle.' I wipe perspiration from my lip. 'I don't know where he is.'

Santiago doesn't sit in the seat that I indicate to him. Instead he places his hands in his pockets and leans against the wall, taking in the opulent room; the flowers, the cards, the gifts and the small screens attached to the wall. Momentarily he is distracted as the camera angle shifts to the audience and he frowns.

'I think something may have happened to him,' I insist.

'Why would anything happen to him?'

'He is not here.'

Santiago shrugs.

'He had tickets for tonight. He would want to see my

performance. He was going to come and see Glorietta.'

'Maybe he changed his mind.'

I stare at him through the mirror. 'He wouldn't do that.'

Santiago's nose points at me but he remains tight-lipped.

'I know he wouldn't,' I insist, conscious that my voice is rising. 'You said we were to go to you if we had a problem, and so here I am, I have a problem. I need your help.'

'To find your boyfriend.'

'He's not my boyfriend,' I say too quickly.

'Ah, a lovers tiff. Signora Lavelle I am not employed to find truant lovers.'

'No, it is not like that,' I speak quickly. 'I have been intimidated. Look at my face. There is a man; Maximilian Strong and his nephew Ian. They are in the audience. Last night they beat me and threatened to kill me. They also threatened to kill Raffaelle.'

As I am speaking the girl with the red heart tattoo, attends to my face. She is retouching my eye liner.

'Do you not understand? They are in the audience. Raffaelle is not here and I am frightened they may have hurt him or done something to him, and I think I will be next.'

I pass him Maximilian's note. I am speaking quickly conscious of the little time I have left. 'They gave me twenty-four hours, and that time is up and I don't know where he is. I am worried.'

'Twenty-four hours for what?' His voice is low and he taps the card against his fingertips.

The tattooed girl backs off and it is the turn of the hairdresser.

I look at Santiago's reflection in the mirror. I am not

sure how much to tell him, and I don't have time for all the details. 'They think I have something but I don't.'

'I know about the Golden Icon,' he says. 'Just tell me where it is.'

'I don't have it. How do you know about it?'

'David Mallory, the Irish Consul came to me. He wanted to find out where you lived in Comaso, and Padre Paolo told me he was worried about your safety, but when I offered my services to you. You continued to deny its existence.'

A runner knocks on the door. 'Two minutes.'

He continues speaking, 'I have not called the Italian Art squad although it is my job to do so. I have been hoping that you would trust me and not do something stupid. I was hoping that Raffaelle would know better. I warned you, after your apartment was broken into, that these men would be back.'

I don't bother to tell him that they didn't break into my apartment and that it was Karl Blakey.

On the screen I see Andrei raising his baton.

'You must look for Raffaelle. Please.' I dab at my lipstick. My lip is still sore. The door opens. The runner, clipboard in hand, moves from one foot to the other glaring at Santiago.

'Signora Lavelle, quickly. Dino is frantic.'

'Where is the Golden Icon?' Santiago blocks my path but I push him away and sweep out of the room using my dignity as a shield. I climb across cables, push past set assistants, ladders and lights.

Tosca takes over me. I am transformed.

I must fight for what is right. I must rage against lust and greed and finally I must kill a man. Tosca turns from lover to killer. Music fills my heart. My head rises in determination. My chest swells, my shoulders go back, and then Santiago grabs my arm.

'The Golden Icon,' he says. 'Where is it?'

I am lost in my role as Tosca.

I think he is Scarpia so I push him angrily away. His eyes register shock and they harden quickly. His mouth is set firm.

'I don't have it,' I hiss. 'I buried it behind the Chiesa della Madonna dei miracoli last Tuesday and when I went back to get it yesterday morning, it was gone.' I turn to the stage but I speak quickly. 'Raffaelle is missing. I think Maximilian Strong or his nephew may have done something. They attacked me last night and have given me twenty-four hours to return the icon but I don't have it. They are sitting near you; an old man, and a young man with a shaved head. They are dangerous. They killed Dieter Guzman in Munich, and Seán in Ireland and...' I pause, a lump rises to my throat. 'And Michael.'

I turn from Santiago's suspicious gaze and I rush on stage.

It is Act Two. We are in the Farnese Palace and Scarpia the chief of police is anticipating the sadistic pleasure of bending Tosca to his will. My lover Mario Cavaradossi is being tortured as a punishment for hiding the rebel Angelotti and hearing his screams I reveal Angelotti's hiding place.

My voice fills the theatre. It is carried high up into the crystal dome, crowning the scene below encompassing the emotions. The timbre of my voice catches with passion and I am lost in the dramatic moment.

Cavaradossi must make his escape with me. I will do

anything to save him. I lie. I tell Scarpia that he can have his will with me if he gives us a safe conduct, and I wait for him to sign the papers for Cavaradossi's mock execution so that we will be free. But once I have the signed document in my hand I snatch up a knife and I plunge it into the chest of the man who threatens me and has taken my lover from me.

I am exhilarated, frightened, and emotionally spent, and as a parting gesture I place a crucifix on Scarpia's motionless chest and a candelabra at his head. As I leave the stage the audience roars with approval.

CHAPTER THIRTEEN

I gave jewels for the Madonna's mantle,
And songs for the stars, in heaven,
That shone forth with greater radiance.
In the hour of grief
Why, why, Lord,
Ah, why do you reward me thus?
Vissi d'arte, Tosca

At the beginning of Act Three, I am in the wings waiting for my cue, church bells toll the dawn and in the distance the sweet singing of a shepherd boy hangs in the air and whirls evocatively up toward the dome.

Cavaradossi is awaiting execution at the Castel Sant 'Angelo but he bribes the jailer to take a farewell note to Tosca. He is filled with memories of love and they give way to despair. His tone is rich and deep, filled with pain, love and loss.

E lucevan le stelle never fails to affect me, and Massimo's voice is filled with emotion and passion that awakens the nerves throughout my body making the tips of my fingers tingle and my body tremble.

I grip the stage curtain. My knuckles are white. My

stomach is taught. I am waiting to tell him that I have killed Scarpia and after the mock execution we will be free. We can escape.

Cesare's voice is so near to my ear that his breath tickles my lobe.

'Josephine?' he whispers. 'Are you feeling well? You are crying. Quickly, let me dry these.' He takes a tissue from his pocket. I hadn't noticed tears falling onto my cheeks. 'You are magnificent. Do not worry. Just feel the emotion coming from the audience. They are living your pain. They are experiencing your anguish.'

I take a deep breath but a sense of foreboding overcomes me, enveloping me with insecurity and doubt. I glance up at him. I want to tell him but I cannot speak.

Instead I take Glorietta's gift, the small Madonna from its security between my breasts. I marvel at the tranquility of her face. I understand her sacrifice. I kiss her and pray for strength to deal with whatever lays before me and return her safely to my cleavage beside my beating heart.

I sigh.

Michael had been lonely after Shona died. He had found refuge and comfort with me, just as I had found support and love from him. We both knew it was wrong. We both knew the hurt we would cause if we were discovered. The only truth was the one that existed between us and no-one else.

'They are loving it.' Cesare nods at the audience.

'We will escape together,' I whisper. 'I have committed murder for Michael.'

'Michael?' Cesare looks at me.

'Raffaelle,' I say.

Cesare frowns. There is concern and confusion in his

eyes.

'I mean, Cavaradossi,' I say. I take my cue and rush onto the stage, taking with me the bewilderment and disappointment in Cesare's eyes.

On stage Tosca instructs Cavaradossi how to fake his death. He caresses my hand. He is sad that I have murdered for him.

O dolci mani, he sings.

Then I hide, and watch soldiers fire a volley of gunfire, smoke fills the stage, and an expectant hush descends.

I wait until the soldiers leave and run to my lover, ecstatic with his performance at his mock execution. Cavaradossi has play-acted his death so I rush to his side but when he refuses to move I know that Scarpia's treachery has transcended the grave.

The mock execution wasn't a fake.

My lover, Cavaradossi, is dead.

The melodrama of my role transcends all else.

The soldiers have killed my love.

Now they come for me.

I hear them. I hear their soldiers' boots.

I have nothing to live for. I have been betrayed and deceived. I have lost.

God will judge me. 'O Scarpia, Avanti a Dio!' I cry.

I avoid my captures clutches and I throw myself from the ramparts and leap into the darkness to my death.

I lie still. My heart is thumping against the mattress placed behind the scenes to break my fall. Stage hands pull me quickly to my feet, whispering, *bravo*, and *eccellente*.

'Josephine, magnifico.' Cesare is shouting above the

applause. He hugs me. 'Can you hear them?'

Nico calls 'Stupendo!' He stands beside Dino. They are laughing and clapping.

'What has happened?' I ask.

'The audience love you. Listen to them. This is for you, you were magnificent,' Cesare laughs.

Through the closed curtains I hear thunderous applause, shouts of appreciation and feet stomping.

Nina is fussing by my side, she rearranges my dress, and hem line, another girl brushes my wig.

The girl with the red heart tattoo checks my makeup and applies powder to my cheek. Her peppermint chewing gum breath is in my face as she speaks. 'We can't have them seeing this bruise after that fantastic performance. My father is right. You are Tosca.' Her eyes glisten with tears.

Cesare passes me water to sip. They have attended to me so quickly I am disoriented.

Nico calls. 'Your curtain call. It's your first.'

'Hurry!' Cesare hugs me. 'They are waiting for you.'

At the side of the stage, Massimo hugs me and kisses my hand.

'We did it Josephine. We did it again. We still have our magic.'

We walk on stage. My senses are heightened. The lights are brighter, the smell of face paint assails my nostrils, and my heart is beating faster reverberating against my ribs.

The audience are on their feet, the sound is deafening. I curtsey and bow.

Massimo stands to one side and joins in the applause purely for me.

The orchestra are on their feet, and Andrei my

conductor, is also applauding my performance. He pushes his glasses onto his nose, perspiration glistens on his forehead, and under the stage lights he smiles at me as he once used to do.

We take another curtain call and then another, and another. Then they demand Andrei onto the stage. This time it is my turn to applaud a true maestro. He takes long strides and within seconds he is standing beside me. All the cast are applauding. His square glasses reflect the spotlights but I see tears in his eyes, and when he holds out his hand and pulls me toward him I am reminded of this scene. I have acted this many times with him, and fleetingly I think of the newspaper stories that will appear in the morning, and I know that after this performance I will weather the storm regardless of what is published.

'You are a true star. You are the only Tosca,' he shouts above the noise. Then he retires to my side insisting I take more credit for my performance but not before he kisses my hand and says.

'This is a night they will all remember. Thank you, Josephine.'

I stand alone.

I am in the spotlight. Applause fills my senses and its echo reverberates in the dome above me. I am smiling and when I turn my head to look for Cesare standing behind the stage curtain I see Raffaelle.

My heart leaps. I am relieved. I cannot believe he is here. He is dressed in his tuxedo and I wonder if he has seen all the performance.

He holds out something to me.

My smile freezes.

To the consternation of my fellow actors, I cross the

stage quickly.

'Raffaelle Where have you been? Where were you? I thought something had happened.'

He is smiling. 'I brought you this.' He pulls the bag open and I see a familiar dirty shoe box. I push the lid aside and pull the cloth apart. Staring up at me is the Golden Icon. It is exquisite.

Cesare grabs my hand.

'Josephine, they are calling for you, come on. You must go back this is your thirteenth call.' I nudge his hand away.

Nico is shouting at me. 'Come, Josephine, come. This is your moment. Don't waste it.'

He pushes Raffaelle and Cesare away, and grabs my arm propelling me toward the audience. 'You must go back out on stage. They are calling for you.'

I am carried along with Cavaradossi and Scarpia into the stage lights. A roar from the crowd greets us and I cannot help laughing.

This is my moment. One I never thought I would experience again.

I am Tosca.

Everything is perfect. The Golden Icon is here. Raffaelle is safe. Michael is with me.

Massimo shouts in my ear. 'The diva is back.' He holds my hand in the air and the crowd cheer and I laugh louder. I shake my head in disbelief and place my hand on my chest beside my heart and I feel Glorietta's gift to me, the lucky charm of the Madonna.

I am humbled.

The audience is mine, as I am theirs. I am once again their Tosca. Scarpia and Cavaradossi grab my hands and we bow together.

Then I am pushed into the spotlight as a young girl appears with a large bouquet of colourful flowers. I bow a low and deep curtsey, glancing toward the back of the stage. I frown. I think I glimpse Ian but that couldn't be possible.

'Where is Santiago?' I shout.

'Who?' Massimo replies above the noise. 'I think this is our record curtain call. Seventeen.'

I run from the stage. In the wings Ian is inching menacingly toward Raffaelle. I call out a warning and Raffaelle turns. I pull the bag from his grip and grab the Golden Icon roughly by the Madonna's neck.

Ian lunges at me but I swing the icon and smack it against his head. He stumbles and blood begins dripping from an open wound on his temple.

Instinctively I grab Raffaelle and push him in front of me onto the stage. We are greeted by a roar of approval and bright stage lights. I have a brief glance of Cesare, Nico and Santiago and I know that this is the right thing to do.

I will let the world see the Golden Icon and never will she be hidden or denied her rightful place. I hold the Madonna above my head like an Olympic torch.

'The Golden Icon,' I shout.

The crowd scream and thump their feet with delight, thinking it is part of the choreography. From the corner of my eye I see Ian, he reaches into his inside pocket and he takes out a gun.

I pull Raffaelle behind me, so I am standing between him and Ian. There is flash and a loud bang, I turn. Then another, and another and the sound echoes and ricochets around the dome above my head. I glance up thinking the glass is going to shatter and rain down on us all. I cover my head and drop the icon.

The applause is replaced by screams of fear, muddled noises roar in my head and Raffaelle's mouth opens wide. Although he speaks I can't hear his words; footsteps, running, pushing, and a searing pain seeps through my body. Perspiration runs between my breasts. My knees buckle. I am falling, falling, falling slowly until my head hits the floor.

There is chaos around me but all I see is Raffaelle lying beside me.

I gaze at him.

Then I reach out to trace my finger along his cheek, remembering where I slapped him, and although his eyes are open, I know he doesn't see me. A trickle of blood runs from the corner of his mouth. The bloody Golden Icon lies between us.

I fumble for Glorietta's gift and pull it from my bosom. My fingers are sticky and my body will not move. The lights dim. It gets darker and darker but calmness flows through me, voices recede, ebbing and flowing until it is Michael's face that is leaning over me. Smiling, loving and welcoming me into his arms.

'I've been waiting for you,' he says.

Then the lights go out.

CHAPTER FOURTEEN

Concealed harmony of contrasting beauties!
Floria, my ardent lover, is dark haired.
And you, unknown beauty, crowned with blond hair,
You have blue eyes,
Tosca has black eyes.
Recondita armonia, Tosca

I wake but my eyes remain closed. The sheets are cool on my skin. There is the sound of ragged breathing and I cough. It hurts. Something tight covers my nose and mouth. My throat is raw and I am reminded of another time and another place. It is easier to keep my eyes closed and my mind blank. I welcome the darkness and in it I search for Michael's face, his reassurance and calm confidence.

There are voices in the room beside my bed. 'She is awake? Josephine?'

I open my eyes. There are people in the room but it is only Cesare's face I see. He smiles at me. There are dark circles under his eyes. He lifts my hand to his lips and kisses my fingers. His voice is husky with exhaustion.

'You will be okay,' he says. 'You are going to be fine.' His hair flops forward into his eyes and then he disappears into darkness, and I succumb to an unconscious world.

When I open my eyes Santiago is sitting in a chair beside the window. Blinds are drawn and I don't know if it is night or day.

I don't care.

When he sees me move he leans forward resting his arm on the mattress. His normally inquisitive eyes are dark and sad. His voice is softer than I remember. 'Cesare needed to sleep. He has been with you for two days,' he says.

A nurse passes the foot of my bed. She is immaculate in a starched white and blue uniform. When she moves my arm her fingers are dry and cool against my skin. She concentrates on the monitors at my shoulder, readjusts my mask and writes on a clipboard before speaking to Santiago.

'The doctor says two minutes.' Her voice is deep. She ignores me and does not smile at him as she leaves the room.

Santiago pulls the chair closer to me. His face is at my level and my eyes do not leave his face. He is sombre and, like Cesare, there are dark circles around his blue eyes and I am reminded of Glorietta's vivaciousness, her full cheeks and her bright laughter.

'Do you remember what happened?' he asks.

I shake my head.

'You will recover he says. You will get better but I have some bad news.'

My eyes fill with tears. I swallow. My throat is dry.

'Water?'

I nod. Very tenderly he removes the mask, places his hand behind me to support my neck and I sip from a small glass. When I am finished I lean back against the pillow exhausted. I push the mask away from my face.

'Raffaelle is dead,' he says softly.

I pull the sheet to my mouth and bite down onto it, trying to ignore the memory pushing in my mind. I see his face lying on the stage beside mine.

Santiago takes my hand and I am surprised by his gentleness and grateful for his fingers and human contact.

'I am sorry.' He reaches for a tissue and dabs my cheek.

I do not speak and I struggle to sit up.

Seán is dead. Michael is dead. Raffaelle is dead.

He pushes my shoulders gently back against the pillow and I close my eyes.

'What you did was a very brave thing.'

I open my eyes but tears continue to fall. I have no idea what he is talking about.

'Do you remember?'

I move my head. No.

'You shielded Raffaelle with your body. I have watched it back on camera many times. It was a very protective and selfless act of love.'

He passes me another tissue.

'Will I tell you what happened?' His voice is soft.

I nod my head. It is easier to close my eyes than to see the pain reflected in Santiago's eyes as he speaks.

'When you warned me that Maximilian Strong was in the theatre I called for reinforcements. We were watching them from the monitors backstage on the screens.

'I suspected Maximilian had found Raffaelle and he was lying tied up somewhere or even dead. I had men at the lake searching for him. So, we were not prepared when Raffaelle arrived. We didn't know that he telephoned Cesare and he let him inside the theatre at the stage door.

'During the curtain calls Ian and Maximilian headed to your dressing room. We thought perhaps they intended to kidnap you but then they saw Raffaelle waiting in the wings. When you came off the stage Ian saw the Golden Icon and he made a grab for it but you hit him. Before we could do anything you had taken the Golden Icon onto the stage and Ian pulled out a gun.'

'I had to do it. It is what she deserved.' I am thinking of the Madonna.

'Panic broke out in the auditorium.'

'I thought the glass in the dome was shattering and falling down.' My voice is barely a whisper.

'After you hit Ian with the statue, my men arrived. They grabbed him but in the struggle the gun went off. You were hit and as you fell to the ground he fired again. Raffaelle died instantly.'

He looks into the middle distance before resuming his conversation. I am replaying the scene in my head, over and over. The curtain calls, the success and Raffaelle lying motionless beside me on the ground. I see his open eyes, his bloodied bushy moustache and his lifeless body.

'We arrested Ian and then we caught Maximilian Strong leaving with the rest of the theatre goers in the chaos that followed.'

I sink further into my pillow. 'Thank God you caught them both. They are evil murderers.'

'They are in prison. There are many crimes against them including the murders of Seán McGreevy and Dieter Guzman.'

'And what about the Golden Icon? Do you have it? Is it safe?'

'Yes.'

'Raffaelle stole it but he brought it back to me,' I say. 'He did the right thing in the end. He didn't deserve to die.' I am thinking of the curse that Dieter told me about.

'He didn't steal it,' Santiago whispers. 'He went and found it.'

I frown. It doesn't make sense.

'It was the shepherd boy, Alonso,' he says.

I shake my head but a memory stirs.

'Luigi's cousin has a son called Alonso who is a shepherd boy in the hills. He is a friend of my daughter, Sandra. He said that he met you and Raffaelle up near the Chiesa della Madonna dei miracoli last Tuesday morning, very early, and the next day the sheep were grazing nearby. There had been a storm and the rain had displaced the earth. That's how he found it. Raffaelle worked out that there was only one person who went up there, so he went to find Alonso, who admitted that he had found it. He told Raffaelle that he was going to tell Sandra about it and he was going to give it to me.'

'All those lost lives,' I say. 'If only I hadn't been so stupid to bury it up there.'

'Don't think like that, Signora Lavelle. We cannot keep blaming ourselves. I am guilty too. If I had acted quicker, I might have saved Raffaelle and you might still be an opera singer…' Santiago bows his head and doesn't return my stare.

We are silent for a few minutes.

'Who does the Golden Icon belong to?' I ask.

'The Italian art squad have it now,' he speaks slowly. 'They will make the right enquiries and it will be put on show in a museum somewhere, or perhaps it may go on tour or be displayed for a while in Ireland. It will certainly not belong to a secret art collector like Dieter Guzman or used by Ian and Maximilian to pay for drugs and brothels, nor will it be used to pay off a man's debts in Ireland.'

'You know Barbara?'

'I met her. After the shooting she was with David Mallory from the Irish Consul. Between them they told me the story of the Golden Icon and your trip to Munich. She still believes it belongs to her.'

'What will happen?'

He shrugs. 'It is out of my hands. I doubt anyone will feel sympathy for her, or for her husband.'

We sit in silence and I close my eyes. After a time when I think he is gone, I open my eyes but he is reading. The newspaper is turned toward the lamp beside my bed, his nose is sharp and his eyes are again inquisitive.

'You had excellent reviews for your performance. Eighteen curtain calls,' he says. 'It beats your own record and there would have been more.'

'And Glorietta? How is she?'

'They reopened the theatre on Tuesday. Dino Scrugli and Nico Vastano put a lot of pressure on the right people. They were afraid of losing money and going bankrupt with their first opera.'

'How was she?'

'She had a tremendous amount of support but after the drama of your performance her reviews were not so good.'

'That doesn't seem fair.'

'It isn't.'

'I appreciate your honesty.' My eye lids are heavy.

'She sang yesterday at Raffaelle's funeral.'

The pristine nurse with the starched uniform enters the room. 'No more,' she says. 'Time's up, Inspector.'

I am pleased when she saves me and injects my arm with clear liquid.

'Why did she do it?' I ask. 'Why did she insist that I replace her?' My eyes close and I am encompassed by warm welcoming fog that is soft and comfortable. I think he says, 'Get well soon, Signora Lavelle.'

A punctured lung. A punctured lung. She will never sing again. Never sing again. Never sing again.

These words go around in my head. 'I will,' I scream.

A hand reaches out and clasps my fingers. I open my eyes.

'You were dreaming.' Cesare's face is close to mine. He pushes curls from his eyes and smiles. 'The night-shift is back,' he says cheerfully.

I move my body to get comfortable and a searing pain stabs through my chest.

'How bad am I?'

His eyes have dark flecks of green that I have never noticed before. 'You are lucky to be alive, Josephine,' he says sadly, 'but you will not sing again. The bullet punctured your lung.'

I turn my head aside so he can't see the tears that fall from my eyes. They roll onto the pillow and tickle my sore cheek.

'I will call the nurse for pain killers.'

'Tablets or injections will never deaden the pain I feel.'

'Everything takes time.'

'Santiago was here,' I tell him. 'Raffaelle is dead.' I wipe my eyes on the sheet.

He takes my hands and leans his elbows on the bed. 'Sí.'

'He didn't deserve to die.'

'No.'

'And how is Glorietta?'

'Not good.'

I sigh aloud and there is discomfort in my chest.

'They loved each other. They should have stayed together. I should have taken the Golden Icon to Santiago. Raffaelle told me I was stubborn, but I wanted to do the right thing.'

'You did do the right thing.'

'I messed up.'

'You are alive, Josephine. You have your life ahead of you and you can hold your head up high. You protected Raffaelle with your body. And had the police been quicker neither of you would have been hurt. Santiago is filled with guilt, but none of us can lead a life saying, what if this had happened, or what if I had done that. What's done is done. The past cannot be changed.'

'And Raffaelle? His children? And Glorietta?' I am filled with despair.

'Think about yourself now Josephine, and concentrate on getting well. Everyone is speaking about you; Nico, Dino, Andrei, Massimo and Carlotta your agent wants to speak to you. The press have hailed you as a hero. There are reporters and television crews outside the hospital. Many fans are keeping vigils outside the window, lighting candles and praying for your recovery. They can't get enough of you.'

'Poor Barbara, what will she do now she doesn't have the Golden Icon?'

'She will manage,' he replies. 'You have returned the Golden Icon to Italy but the Italian Art Squad are playing it all down. Santiago insists no-one speaks to the press until you are well. You must focus on yourself. You have been recognised in the opera world again. You are an opera diva. Your talent is assured. Your place in history has been guaranteed along with the greatest.' He pats my hand. 'Nico and Dino are even speaking about a bronze statue of you in the foyer of the Teatro Il Domo. Dino is insisting that you go in the hall of fame and you will be with the greatest names of all time. You are reinstated as an icon.'

'It was my final performance.'

'Yes, but your career is not over. You can still be a mentor. Young sopranos will benefit from your advice and experience. You will be able to pick and choose your students and demand your own price. You are famous again. Even the critics say that you are the true Tosca.'

I turn my head, reach out to the bedside cabinet and pick up Glorietta's golden charm. I wonder who washed away my blood. Under the still, silent and watchful eyes of the Madonna I am filled with seething anger and frustration.

It is dark when I wake and I am alone. I am thinking

about the last and only time I was ever in hospital, in London, nearly thirty years ago.

My mind is lost in the past, and it takes me some time to realise that someone is standing at the half open door staring at me. The shadow looks huge on the wall and it begins to move toward my bed. Although I know Maximilian and Ian are in prison fear sends a shiver through me and I reach for the call button, but I pause at the sound of clicking high heels.

Glorietta is wrapped in a red pashmina over a simple silver dress, a single string of pearls hang at her neck, and sapphires glisten from her ears.

'Josephine?' she whispers.

My voice croaks. 'Sì, Glorietta.'

'May I sit with you?'

'Of course.'

'Are you comfortable? Some water?' From the bedside cabinet she pours fresh water into a glass and holds it to my lips. I sip gratefully, and lay my head back on the pillow, reminded of Santiago's gentleness.

'You look lovely,' I whisper.

'I wish I could say the same to you.' She pulls the shawl around her shoulders and sits on the chair beside my bed. Her face is covered in the half light. Her hair is swept up in a loose chignon and she smells of fresh air and sweet scent. We share a sad smile and her eyes pierce through the dim light and I believe she can see my soul.

'Tonight was the last night,' she says. 'It is all over now.'

'How was it?'

'Less eventful than the opening night.' There are small lines around her bright blue eyes.

'Thank you,' I say, 'for Tosca. I wish I had–'

'Shush, nothing can be changed. Do not torture yourself.'

'Raffaelle?' I say. 'I am so sorry. It was my fault.'

She passes me a tissue. 'He told me everything; that you had been blackmailed and you were forced to take possession of the Golden Icon. You had no choice.'

'He loved you.'

'After you left Comaso, he came to the villa. We were together again. You gave him back to me.'

'He was never really mine,' I reply truthfully.

'We were going to go to Florence,' she says. 'We were going to start a new life there. He always wanted to live amongst the artists. Did you know that?'

'No, I did not,' I lie.

She gives a small laugh. 'We were very excited. He believed that he could revive his career and have a prestigious art studio, and that he would become famous. He was a dreamer.'

'He was an artist. Like us.'

We sit in silence for a while, both of us lost in our thoughts, but comfortable with each other. Then Glorietta leans forward. 'You have the Madonna charm in your hand.'

'Thank you. It was a thoughtful gift. I feel she knows and understands me. She is giving me strength.'

'Cesare says you are getting stronger and that you will be able to leave here in a few days. Just because we were once rivals in the past doesn't mean that we cannot be friends in the future. Please come and stay at my villa to recuperate and get strong.'

'I will need to be strong for what lies ahead.'

'Your career is not over. You will become a world

famous opera coach.' She clasps my hand holding the Madonna. 'She will help you.'

'I hope so. For she knows the true meaning of loss. She understands pain and the sadness of giving up her son. Just as I do.'

'You have a son?' Her voice is barely a whisper.

'I have never told a living soul. It has been my secret.'

The letter I wrote to Michael thirty years ago and the details of my affair only underlined my concern that Karl Blakey would uncover the real truth. I had a deeper secret. One that I had kept hidden for all these years.

'I have an adopted son.' I speak slowly and deliberately. 'Michael was my husband's father, and the father of my son. He told me it was the right thing to do. He said that my career would never take off and I would never survive the scandal. He said my blossoming career would be ruined and that I could not expect adoration, fame and success from the public, once they realised the true parentage of my child.'

'When was this?'

'Twenty-eight years ago.'

She brings her hand to her mouth. 'And, you have kept this a secret all this time?'

'I had to. For Michael's sake. He said to me. *You can never return to Ireland with our son. You cannot keep the baby of your husband's father*. He told me it would ruin my reputation and my career, and I believed him.'

'Madre mio.'

'Michael was the only man I have ever loved,' I say.

'But he is the man who stole the Golden Icon in the war, no?'

'You know?'

'Cesare and Santiago have told me everything.'

'Michael always argued that lies and deceit were better than truth and honesty. He said that the truth would hurt more and that we must protect his family too; Seán my husband and his brother William.

'He believed that neither I, nor our son, would survive the scandal. I refused an abortion and insisted on having my baby even though I could not keep him.' I move my shoulder and I am filled with pain across my chest. 'He was wrapped in a beige blanket. I only saw black hair plastered to his head, his eyes were closed but I heard his defiant squeal as he was carried from me. I never even held my child nor looked into his eyes.'

'Oh Josephine, you poor girl,' she says, forgetting I am almost ten years her senior.

My leg has cramp and my ribs ache.

I pull the sheet around my chin and continue my story.

'Michael convinced me that I was doing the right thing. After doing the wrong thing for so long, he said, it was to make amends for our sin. My child would make others happy. Michael arranged the adoption. All I did was sign the papers. I didn't look at them. I didn't read them. I wasn't even aware what I was doing. I was too distraught. I was ill.'

I cough. My body is wracked with pain and my grief is tearing at my soul. Glorietta holds the glass and the water is cool against my lips. Her wrist smells faintly of a familiar scent. She places the glass back on the cabinet and I continue speaking.

'In my mind I have always called him Michael after his father. I think about him every day, what he looks like, where he is, what he does. And in all my darkest days I

have always known I sacrificed him for my career. It was
the price I paid for my wickedness. I always loved my child
but I never forgave his father. I betrayed my own son. It
was a high price to pay for Michael's love.'

'The ultimate price,' she says.

'I lost them both.'

'Then you must go and find him,' she whispers.

Our eyes meet in the glimmer of light that comes from
the corridor and the half open door.

'Get well, Josephine and go and find your son.'

'He will be a twenty-eight year old man.'

'It is time for you to make amends. You have lost too
much in your life, Josephine. You must go and find
forgiveness with the one man whom you think you
betrayed, neglected and abandoned, but, more
importantly, you must make peace with yourself.

'Do you not remember the note you sent to me with the
flowers to congratulate me when I won the role of Tosca?

Every man's life is a fairy-tale written by God's fingers.

'So, go and write your fairy-tale, and as Hans Cristian
Anderson said, Let God's fingers help you.' Her eyes are
bright, shining with tears and filled with optimism.

'You are right. I will never sing again, but I will find my
son. I will beg his forgiveness and if he will have me, I will
repay him with my love. It is all I have left.'

'It is all he will want.' She holds my hand as a mother
and daughter would do. We sit for a while with the
Madonna wrapped between our joint fingers and my eyes
close.

'Vai con dio,' she says, and she tiptoes quietly from the
room.

I am asleep. I think I hear footsteps and then breath on my cheeks, but I don't stir. I am thinking of my son and the man I once loved, and the life I may have had. When I wake I reach out for my water. There is an envelope propped against my glass.

It had not been there before I closed my eyes. I open it slowly tilting it toward the ray of light from the corridor.

The card is embossed with a red rose and the words *Get Well*. I open it and inside is a hand written message.

Looking forward to discussing our unfinished business. My Love as always

Karl Blakey x

THE END

All book are available on Amazon and Kindle

Culture Crime Series:

Golden Icon - The Prequel
Masterpiece
Book of Hours

Other Books By Janet Pywell:

Red Shoes and Other Short Stories
Ellie Bravo

For more information visit:
www.janetpywell.com
blog: janetpywellauthor.wordpress.com